Party Animal

PRICKLE ISLAND ZOO
BOOK THREE

ALI K. MULFORD

ISBN: 978-1-923184-11-4 (ebook)

ISBN: 978-1-923184-15-2 (Paperback)

ISBN: 978-1-923184-16-9 (Special edition)

Cover: Yummy Book Covers

Map: Holly Dunn Designs

Interior formatting: K. Elle Morrison

Party Animal

Ali K. Mulford

Dedicated to the flamingo who loved to motorboat people while having foot exams

PRICKLE ISLAND
ZOO
KEY
TOILETS
FOOD
SHOPPING
FREE WIFI
GIFT SHOP + ENTRY
ENTRY
CAFÉ
VET HOSPITAL
PLAYGROUND
REPTILE HOUSE
THE PECKISH PEACOCK
SAVANNAH
AVIARY
BABOONS

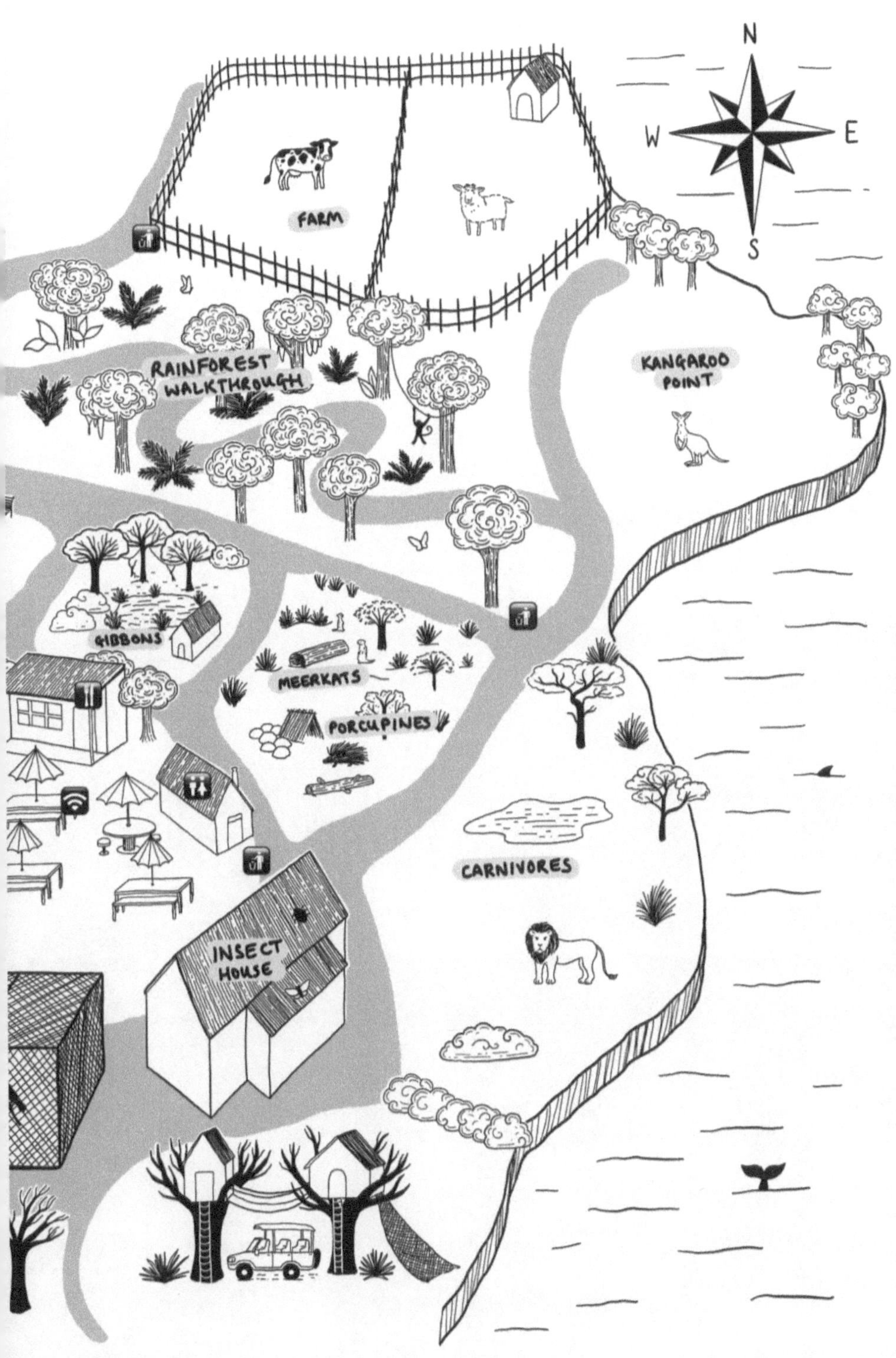

N
W
E
S
FARM
RAINFOREST
WALKTHROUGH
KANGAROO
POINT
GIBBONS
MEERKATS
PORCUPINES
CARNIVORES
INSECT
HOUSE

MEET THE ZOO TEAM

Evelyn Lachlan (she/her) CEO of Prickle Island Zoo

Hawk Lachlan (he/him) Carnivore Keeper

Lark Lachlan (she/her) (Moved to New Zealand)

Finch Lachlan (she/her) Head Veterinarian

Dove Lachlan (she/her) Birds and Primates

Heron Lachlan (they/them) Hoofstock Keeper

Crane Lachlan (he/him) Reptiles and Inverts

Wren Lachlan (she/they) Birds and Rainforest

Hannah Murphey (she/her) Farm animals

Aya (she/her) Food Prep Manager

Mateo (he/him) Gift Shop Manager

Daily Specials

kookaburra cucumber

sandwiches

$5.50

Macaw Macarons

6 for $12

Chapter One

Frankie

Was there anything more depressing than sitting alone at a romantic restaurant, looking out at the ocean? I took a loud sip of my too-sweet strawberry daiquiri and dropped my chin into my hand as I stared at my phone. He still hadn't called. He probably never would again.

The perky twentysomething waitress sidled over to me with the crisp white menu and I tried desperately not to start crying . . . again.

"Are you waiting for anyone?" she asked in her overly exuberant customer service voice.

I plucked the menu from her grip, my third drink making me more brazen than normal. "Nope. I am very, very, *very* alone," I grumbled. "I just had my fiancé tell me I'm *suffocating* him and that he needed his *freedom* so . . . it's just me tonight and every night forevermore, thanks."

Damn. That daiquiri had really loosened my tongue.

The mousy brunette flashed me a tight smile. "How about another drink on the house?"

"Thanks," I said, returning her half-hearted smile. I didn't want her pity, *but* when a free drink was on offer, I'd accept it . . . .

She gave me a sympathetic nod and disappeared while I buried my face in the giant pages of the menu. I really needed to get it together. I was in public for crying out loud! I was the sort of person who never caused a stir, always followed the rules, always waited in line, never rocked the boat, and *never* made a public scene. But maybe if I had been a little more of a shit stirrer every once in a while, I'd still be engaged! Nibbling on a breadstick, I glared around the room, defying any other guests to judge me in my pathetic state.

I was still reeling from Jake's sudden announcement that he was calling off our five-year engagement. *Five years!* And three more years of dating before that. Where had my twenties gone? I was almost thirty now and starting all over again as if Jake had just hit reset on nearly a whole decade of my life!

I'd given my best years to him and he just suddenly, out of the blue, said it's over? When he pulled the rug out from under me, not only did I have to move out of our apartment—that never officially had my name on—but I was also basically driven out of his hometown in Upstate New York. His family owned everything from the hardware store to the gas station, and there was no way I could stay in that town after he ended things.

And my café.

My sweet, beautiful café . . . The thought of it made me ache. I'd built my dream shop in someone else's hometown and now Frankie's Café was being turned into a pizza joint. They even kept the sign and just painted over the word "Café" with a poorly-drawn slice of pizza.

It had felt like someone had torn out a piece of my soul when I'd seen they'd repainted it, plastered the cheery floral interior with burgundy, green, and black. Now, the new "Frankie" was a little cartoon Italian man, and my whole life story was erased and covered over in cheap finishings. A part of me was missing now. A part I didn't think I'd ever get back.

But at least I had some place to go. I scrolled back through my new contract, reading it again and again while sipping the dregs of my daiquiri. This new job truly fell into my lap and still didn't feel real. I reread the welcome email to make sure the whole thing wasn't a hallucination.

Evelyn Lachlan, the CEO of Prickle Island Zoo, had thrown me a lifeline without even knowing who I was. I'd found a job as a chef on the swanky Prickle Island for the summer, room and board included in the position. I'd be far, far away from that little town upstate and all of those dusty blond-haired Dunn family members with their smug faces and their ridiculous "family values." They'd never been particularly welcoming of me, but I'd thought I'd managed to mostly win them over . . . that was before I'd come home to their son unceremoniously packing my suitcase.

Fucking Jake.

I frowned down at my phone—my only companion for this dinner. Maybe I should just get my food to go. I didn't want everyone wondering if I'd been stood up or if I was just naturally a very sulky loner.

I lifted my head up to look out the glass front doors of Neptune's Bounty restaurant when I caught sight of a familiar mop of dusty blond hair.

And when I saw his face . . .

My heart fell out of my asshole.

Jake motherfucking Dunn was *here*, at a random little waterfront restaurant in shoreline Connecticut?! Did I break a mirror or steal an ancient artifact from a volcano or something? What was happening?

I watched in rapt horror as Jake stepped back and held open the door.

Oh my fucking god.

A gorgeous, skinny blonde with a giant rack, who looked barely 21, waltzed in behind him. Soft waves of white-blonde hair cascaded over her shoulder, her dress a shimmering metallic, and sky-high stilettos that she walked in with a practiced ease. She tittered and beamed a too-whitened smile at my ex like he was a freaking movie star.

He was with someone. HE WAS WITH SOMEONE? We'd broken up two weeks ago and he'd already found another woman?

My stomach clenched as my thoughts spun out of control.

Oh god. What if they'd been together while we'd been together? What if *she'd* been was the reason he'd called it off? He'd found a younger, smaller, sexier version of me.

I shrunk down in my seat as Jake's hand dropped to the small of Tinkerbell's back and he guided her to the hostess. That hand used to guide me through a room like that. My eyes welled.

No. Fuck, fuck, fuck.

I desperately scoured the room. I needed to get out of here *immediately,* but there was no escape. Walking right past them was not an option.

Why did I wear my rumpled blouse with a fucking marinara stain on it? I hadn't even freshened my smudged makeup. I'd just checked into the waterfront hotel after I'd missed the last ferry to Prickle Island and stumbled my way over here from hunger alone. I could not be seen looking this pathetic after our breakup, especially not when he looked so damn good.

Jake's eyes swept over the room and my mind snapped in two. I darted to the bar before his floodlight gaze spotted me. I zeroed in on a man sitting alone at the bar—short black hair, tattoos peeking up the neck of his suit jacket and across the back of his hands that toyed with a whisky glass. I darted in his direction . . . except when I spied the back of his phone case, it had "She/Her" scrawled in silver words. *Huh.* I slid onto the stool and glimpsed the face of a ridiculously handsome woman.

My mouth fell open. She was truly stunning—an arresting mixture of masculine and feminine, strong jaw and deep, piercing brown eyes. She wore a business casual outfit of chinos, navy jacket, and a cream-colored T-shirt. My gaze trailed from her shortly cropped black hair to the eyebrow and snake bite piercings and down to the tattoos peeking from the collar of her shirt.

Well, she was certainly unexpected, but right then, I didn't care. I needed help STAT. Her eyes widened in surprise as I leaned into her. I probably looked like a rabid raccoon judging by the alarm on her face. She looked like I might bite her.

"I am so, *so* sorry to do this," I said, frantically searching the room behind her to see if Jake had seen us. "But my ex just walked in, my very, very recent ex, and can you please just pretend to be my date for like 30 seconds? I'll buy you a drink for your troubles, and I'll be eternally grateful."

The mystery woman's dark eyebrows shot up but a smile curved her lips. I shot a glance over to Jake and this time, he looked back.

"Fuck, he's seen me." I groaned, ducking my head behind the stranger's broad shoulders. "Oh god, oh god, oh god."

The woman took my hand and threaded her fingers through mine. She gave it a firm, reassuring squeeze.

"Frankie!" Jake called, trying to wave me down.

"Shit. Fuck. I'm going to cry." I gulped, my eyes misting again.

"No, you're not. I've got you," the stranger said, and before I could ask her what the fuck that meant, her other hand swept around to the back of my neck and she kissed me.

Chapter Two

Finch

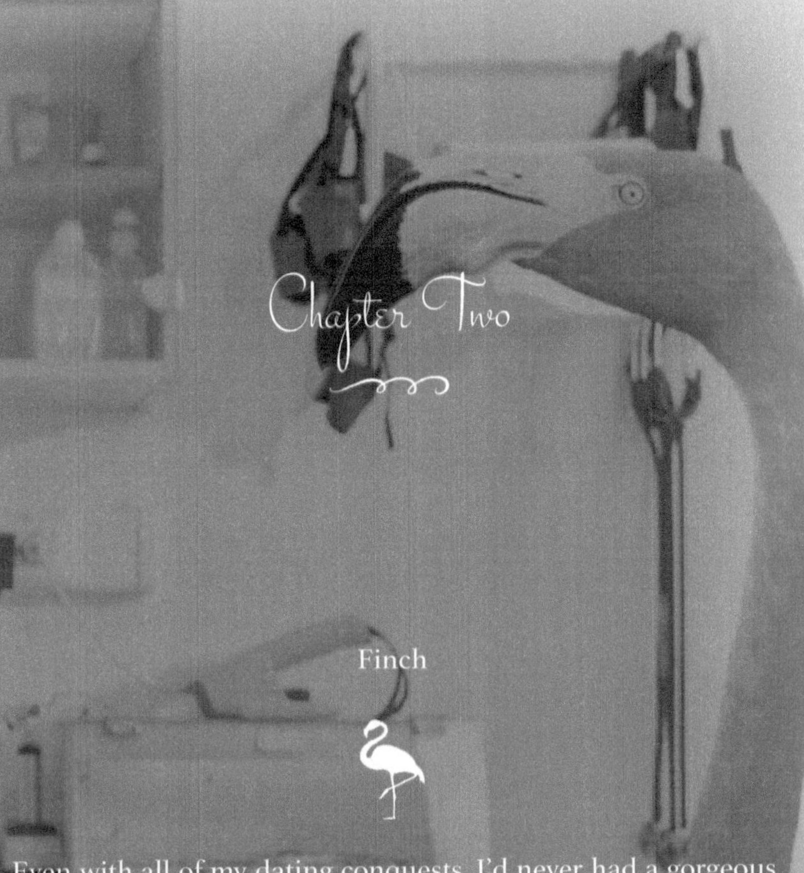

Even with all of my dating conquests, I'd never had a gorgeous woman saunter over and ask to pretend to be on a date before . . . but in this instance, I was certainly up for the challenge.

She tasted like strawberries and rum and, okay fine, *maybe* I got a little bit carried away tasting her before her meathead ex-boyfriend wandered over, clearing his throat. Damn could she kiss—soft, pillowy lips that enveloped mine with a kind of desperation. She kissed me frantically, passionately, like I was her only tether and she was drifting out to sea. But this wasn't the "I want you so bad" kind of frenzy I was used to. This was the "I'm about to have a panic attack because my ex is here" kind of frenzy, and I was having a really hard time remembering that, especially when she was practically climbing into my lap.

I wondered if she was queer. She was obviously single . . . *Not now, Finch! You're supposed to be helping her, not hitting on her, for fuck's sake.*

When we finally pulled apart, the stunning stranger looked at me with shocked eyes and swollen lips and I gave her a playful wink. It wasn't the first time a straight girl had used me to get revenge on an ex, and honestly, when they looked like her, I really didn't mind.

"Frankie, hey!" the weasel-looking man said.

I appraised him up and down with a tight smile—one that made men like him uneasy. I knew his type well, saw them every summer: rich, entitled, arrogant. He wore pristine white sneakers and a polo shirt, making him look like he'd stepped straight off the golf course. The girl who was with him seemed wildly age inappropriate even by my standards. She was barely wearing a napkin's worth of metallic fabric and heels that made her wobble like a newborn giraffe.

"Jake, hi!" my mystery woman—Frankie—said, way too enthusiastically.

She was like a spooked gazelle about to run headfirst into a fence. I'd seen that look many times before, albeit usually from a hoofed mammal and not a beautiful stranger. She needed to calm down before she bolted. I slung my arm around Frankie's waist and tugged her the rest of the way off her barstool to stand next to me as I rose and shook Jake's hand, squeezing it tight enough that he grimaced.

Frankie's voice was still tinged with panic as she said, "Jake, this is—"

"Goldfinch," I offered. "Yes, that's my birth name, unusual I know." I cut off the inevitable response. Men really thought they were so funny. "Nice to meet you, James. Is this your . . . daughter?"

Frankie spluttered out a cough beside me while Jake released an uncomfortable laugh.

"No, no," he said with a strained chuckle. "This is my fiancée, Olivia."

Oh, this motherfucker was a real piece of work. I could tell the word fiancée landed like a punch on Frankie's face. How long had they been split up before he'd gotten engaged to someone else?

I gave Frankie a reassuring squeeze as I said, "Congratulations!" I clapped Jake on the shoulder. Hard. I hoped it would leave a bruise. "Well, you two enjoy your dinner. This stunning woman and I have tickets to a show tonight." I kissed the back of Frankie's hand and was rewarded by her attention snagging on me instead of her shitbag ex. "Lovely to meet you, Olivia," I said, giving the girl my patented wink that made everyone blush. "John."

"It's Jake," the bastard said, trying to sound playful but clearly offended.

I looked at Frankie. "Babe," I said, running an adoring hand down her back. "I could've sworn you said John. Sorry, she's only mentioned you briefly. We've been a bit swept up in a whirlwind romance." I kissed the side of her head. "When you know, you know, eh, James?"

"Jake," he said, turning bright red while his fiancée crooned at how adorable Frankie and I were together.

Frankie could barely manage a smile. She was an absolute deer in the headlights, and I needed to get her out of there immediately.

"Ciao, you two," I said with another panty-dropping grin. "You take care of each other."

I steered Frankie away and heard Olivia lean into Jake and say, "They are so cute together, don't you think?"

Jake muttered a barely audible reply back. Good.

I walked Frankie around the corner and down an alleyway out of view of the large bay windows. She dropped her hands to her knees, taking in deep sips of air.

I definitely did not use that opportunity to look at her heaving breasts peeking from the neckline of her blouse. This Frankie person was an absolute goddess of curves. Those hips, those *thighs*. There was absolutely no way a toolbag like Jake knew what to do with a woman like her.

"I think I'm going to throw up." Frankie panted, and I quickly launched back into veterinarian mode.

I rubbed a soothing hand down her back. "Breathe. Breathe." I spoke in the same soft tone I used on all my animals. "You're okay."

She took a few more breaths before nodding and leaning her head back against the wall.

"No offense, but that guy seemed awful. I think you dodged a bullet there."

"He's the love of my life." She groaned.

"Oof." I grimaced. "Maybe you need to find a better love of your life, Goldilocks."

"Goldilocks?"

"You know, find someone who's just right."

"That's Jake," she said, shaking her head. "He's really a good person under all of that bravado. He just hides it."

He hides it really fucking well then, I thought, but I knew better than to reason with the newly heartbroken.

I continued my slow circles across her back. "How long ago did you guys break up?"

"Two weeks."

I let out a long whistle.

"Do you think they were—"

"Yep," I cut her off. "They were definitely together while you were together."

She sniffed. And I decided, fuck it. I spun her away from the wall and pulled her into a tight hug. She dropped her head into my shoulder and sobbed as I held her tighter. Sweeping one hand down her back, the other twined into her hair, holding her to me. She came apart in my arms, the dam of emotions she'd been battling to keep in finally broken.

"You're okay, you're okay," I assured her. "It's all going to be okay."

"You don't know that," she cried.

"I've only known you for a minute and somehow I really do," I said. Someone as beautiful and adorable as her would find another person in a heartbeat. But she didn't need to hear that right now so I simply said, "I promise."

I tried *really* hard not to think how good she felt pressed up against me. I was trying to reform my partying ways and this girl was in a whole heap of drama—and that's saying something coming from someone who worked with wild animals for a living.

"Thank you," she croaked, finally releasing me. "You saved me."

"Don't mention it. I have a thing for damsels in distress anyway," I joked, but she didn't laugh. "You going to be okay?" I asked. "Do you want me to walk you home or anything?"

She pointed straight up to the towering building above us.

"I'm staying in the hotel," she said. She wiped under her eyes, sweeping her dripping mascara up into a dramatic wing. She lifted on her tiptoes and kissed my cheek, making my skin tingle in the wake of her touch. "Thank you, Goldfinch, for rescuing me in there."

I liked the way she said my name, so reverent and appreciative. I smiled and gave her a salute. "It was an adventure knowing you, Frankie," I said. "Good luck with everything."

She offered me one last sad smile, and I had the overwhelming urge to turn around and kiss her until the expression morphed into a better one. Instead, I turned to the strip of restaurants and bars along the wharf and pulled out my phone to message my still-waiting Tinder date.

Chapter Three

Finch

"Another one?" I slapped a hand over my weary eyes. My sweaty skin still bore the faint waft of tequila even after a shower, three bracing cups of coffee, and a fresh pair of scrubs. I'd only gotten home a few hours before the start of my shift. Peeling my thirty-year-old ass out of bed after a big night out suddenly felt dramatically different than it did at twenty-nine.

Dove's voice sighed over the radio. "Yep."

I swigged back another giant gulp of coffee and vowed to myself I was instituting a midnight curfew from now on. I held the radio to my lips. "I thought you candled all the eggs?" I asked my little sister.

"I did!" Dove screeched. I'd bet she was stomping her foot indignantly judging by the parrot squawks in the background.

Obviously, she did not candle all the eggs. Or she missed

one. Or the macaws secretly laid another egg while she wasn't looking and hid one from the previous clutch—not an impossibility. Even after all her years of experience as a bird keeper, Dove wasn't infallible, none of us were, though she'd have my head for saying so. There was no point starting a fight over the radio, and our mom would blame me for it anyway.

Annoyed, I rubbed my eyebrow and stared up and the fluorescent lights above my desk. Without looking, I reached for my sunglasses and found them haphazardly placed among my disorganized stacks of paper. I put them on, darkening the too bright hospital lights.

"All right," I said, even though I wanted to say, "Fuck no! No more baby birds!" I skulled the rest of my coffee. This was a five-cup kind of morning. "I'll get the incubator set up and will meet you in Ward B."

"Roger," Dove replied.

I thought I'd made it to the other side of another baby bird season but *no!* We had four different breeding pairs of macaws at Prickle Island Zoo, and our military macaws had just decided to hatch their secret baby a week before the start of summer.

This breeding pair were the world's worst parents, though, and their chicks would need to be hand-reared. Their progeny was destined to go off to a breeding program in Costa Rica, and their offspring's offspring would one day be flying through national parks all throughout Central America. Our zoo was very proud to be a part of their numbers growing, but it meant at least another month of no sleep for me.

These chicks needed to be crop-fed every few of hours through the night for the first few weeks of their lives. They were worse than human babies, temperamental, needing just the right mixture of food and warmth and attention as they went from little pink blob to prickly teenager to fully-fledged parrot in a matter of months. I knew all of my zookeeper siblings would pitch in, each taking a shift, but since I now lived above the vet hospital, I always took the most ungodly hours so my siblings didn't have to wander through the zoo at 2 am.

Ugh. I stretched my arms above my head and then beelined to the break room to make another pot of coffee. Honestly, the zoo should've been sponsored by a coffee roastery for all the caffeine the Lachlan family drank.

Springtime was chaotic with all of the baby animals, but at least the zoo was closed to visitors so the workload wasn't as intense as in the summer. I scheduled a lot of my annual work to be done in the summertime because the visitors liked to observe all of the animal checkups from the other side of the floor-to-ceiling glass. But a baby macaw meant a full day *and* night schedule, and that was before I factored in the inevitable emergencies that always reared up when you worked with wild animals. It would be a lot, even for me.

I set the coffee brewing and swung my arms back and forth like I was hyping myself up to start a breakdance battle.

I loved my job. It was my entire life. My family, my legacy, my identity was wrapped up in: Goldfinch Lachlan, Head Veterinarian at Prickle Island Zoo.

But this summer would definitely put a damper on my abundant sex life. Say goodbye to all the summer parties I normally threw, all the zoo staff I normally wooed, all the summer island residents I normally hooked up with . . . I thought about that Portuguese yoga instructor from last year. Well, I could probably do a little bit of both.

That reminded me I still need to get my "work hard, play harder" tattoo. I was saving a spot on my ribcage for it.

My brain was still so foggy, I barely registered Mom walking in with an armful of fancy towels.

"Donations from the Johnson estate," she said, dumping the towering pile of monogramed towels into the washing basket.

There were three things a vet hospital could never have enough of: towels, bowls, and pens. Some of the island estates changed over their guest towels after practically every use and donated them to the wildlife hospital. It meant we had an odd mishmash of surprisingly high-quality linens and shit-stained, ripped, old ones. The hospital patients would certainly be sleeping in luxury tonight.

"You got home late last night," Mom said, folding her arms and leaning against the doorframe. "Or should I say early."

She gave me a side eye, that knowing Evelyn Lachlan look that made me groan. How did she do it? Seven kids and she managed to keep tabs on all of us. Even now that my sister, Lark, had moved with her boyfriend to New Zealand, Mom still knew everything that was going on in her life.

"It wasn't that late," I muttered, pulling out the shredded recycle paper from a bucket under the steel bench top.

Mom's eyebrows lifted into her hairline as I placed the shredded paper into a plastic bowl. "Oh really?"

Technically, I got a ride out with Petey. He'd taken up fishing in his semi-retirement and was up at crazy early hours even for us. I'd hoped I'd been stealthy enough that none of my family would've noticed I'd been gone all night . . . but when you lived in a place covered in security cameras, people were bound to find out.

"Okay, fine. I had a date," I finally relented, and Mom gave me a victorious nod.

I'd sort of had two dates if you counted that run-in with the blonde bombshell named Frankie. I'd spent the rest of the night with a British flight attendant, but we'd just ended up talking in the bar until closing time. I had lost all my mojo after the eventful start of the evening. It'd still been Frankie's face that had kept flashing through my mind as Petey and I had ridden across the choppy waves back to the zoo. I hoped she was doing okay. I hoped she'd find someone better than that loser, someone who cherished her.

But I wasn't about to tell my mother—and boss—any of that, especially not when she was giving me a knowing look.

"Finch . . ." She drew out my name in that warning tone of hers.

"I know, I know!" I threw my hands up.

I hated the way she worried about me. There was really nothing to worry about. Sure, I had a work-life balance that was skewed heavily toward work, but when I had free time, the last thing I wanted was a serious relationship. I wanted to have fun. I wanted to let off some steam. I wanted to unwind after a stressful day with people who didn't know me . . . .

Yeah, there was no way Mom would understand that.

It had been love at first sight for my mom and dad. Even thirteen years since his passing, Mom was still the ultimate romantic. She was the sort of person who felt completed by a relationship when I knew I would only feel trapped by one. What I needed even more, though, was to find a way to get her off my back. The second I'd turned 30, it was like all the alarm bells had started going off in Mom's brain.

Luckily, I was saved from whatever Mom was going to say by my older brother, Hawk, on the radio. "Carnivores to home base."

I lifted my radio before he even stopped talking. "She's with me," I answered, holding the radio between Mom and me for us both to listen. "Go ahead."

"Hey, boss," Hawk said. "You've got someone at the front office saying you've got a nine o'clock meeting?"

"Oh shoot," Mom said, looking at her watch. "The new chef is here. I gotta go."

Saved by the bell, thank God.

As Mom left, Dove entered holding a towel-swaddled chick the size of my thumb. She frowned at me when she realized I hadn't prepared much of anything yet.

"Sorry, I was being lectured by Mom," I muttered as I quickly started getting the heating pads out.

Dove's purple dipped hair spilled across her face as she bent down and retrieved a nesting basket. "About your date last night?"

"Ugh, not you too."

"Just guessing." Dove shrugged, adjusting her wire-rim glasses. "No judgement."

"You'd think having Hawk and Lars happily coupled up would make Mom ease off. Two siblings out of seven is plenty."

"Evelyn Lachlan doesn't know how to ease off," Dove countered, setting the chick into the plastic bowl filled with shredded paper to weigh it. "Ever since we signed that contract for the Deacon Harrow movie, she's been showing everyone photos of us when we were kids and saying, 'How cute, maybe they'll rekindle their romance.' Gag."

"Gag," I echoed mockingly. "To have dated a movie star. Sounds awful."

"We were ten years old!" Dove exclaimed. "We didn't *date*! We were just friends. Also, he's a literal movie star now. He dates models."

"Models are boring," I said, waving my hand. "Trust me, I know."

Dove fished out her phone. "Maybe I can bribe Hannah into having a baby just so Mom will leave us alone."

Hannah, the newest keeper at the zoo, was a chaotic ADHD tornado with zero impulse control who could probably be swayed into it by her best friend, Dove. Hawk and Hannah had been together for only a year, but it was already abundantly clear that they were endgame. Though, perhaps encouraging them to have children just so we could redirect our Mom's attention wasn't the best plan of attack.

I hastily plucked the phone from my little sister's grip. "I like the way you're thinking, but let's get this chick set up first."

Daily Specials

kookaburra cucumber
sandwiches
$5.50

Macaw Macarons
6 for $12

Chapter Four

Frankie

The zoo café was certainly grander than my little one upstate. It had a floor-to-ceiling aquarium against one wall and a tube slide for one thing. Plus, dozens of tables and booths that currently all had the chairs flipped up apart from the one where I sat across from a silver-haired woman with warm brown eyes that crinkled as she spoke.

Evelyn Lachlan. The CEO of Prickle Island Zoo had an undeniable warmth. She had a tanned face and sinewy body that looked like she'd been working outdoors her entire life. She was an odd juxtaposition, wearing a blazer, work slacks, and hiking boots as if she couldn't decide if she wanted to dress like a corporate executive or a park ranger. It was her calm sort of confidence that drew me to her the most. She was the sort of person that everyone would look to in an emergency, the kind who knew a little bit about everything. She made me feel like everything was going to be alright.

"You can contact Aya about all the food ordering," Evelyn said, ticking off her onboarding check sheet. "She handles all of the suppliers for both human and animal alike."

I chuckled. "Okay."

"Only the best for our animals." Evelyn gave me a smile. "You'll have a few days to get settled in, get to know the waitstaff and line cooks. You'll be working closely with the front of house manager, Mateo. He's lovely, so if you need anything, feel free to reach out to him. The gift shop staff and volunteers will be arriving today so plenty of helping hands. Take this week to learn your way around, practice any new recipes." She leaned in conspiratorially. "I am sure my kids would all love to be culinary guinea pigs if you need any opinions on baked goods."

We both laughed. "Excellent. How old are your kids?"

Evelyn waved a hand. "Oh, they're all grown," she said wistfully. "I can't believe it. Seven kids and my youngest just turned eighteen. Where did the time go?" She shook her head. "They all work here at the zoo except for one who moved to New Zealand."

"Aw, wow, that's lovely. I didn't realize this was a family business." I looked around the space, taking it all in. The place didn't have the vibes of a little mom-and-pop business. It seemed run like any other state-of-the-art zoo. It was wild to me that it was all run by one single family.

Evelyn jotted something down in her notebook as she said, "I am very fortunate that they all *mostly* get along. There were a few dicey teenage years with some of them, let me tell you, but they still back each other up. Even more than running a zoo, raising my family has been an adventure."

"With seven kids, I can only imagine."

She leaned across the table and patted my forearm. "I have a feeling you're about to be everyone's favorite person," she said. "The last chef, Savannah, was before she retired at the end of last summer. She knew what all keepers know: you can get anything you want with a good food bribe."

"She left some great recipes. I'll be sure to include the favorites in the cabinet and menu selections." I looked around the space again, romanticizing what it would be like filled with eager patrons. "This will be a bigger gig than I'm used to," I admitted. "We didn't have this number of customers at my café and I only had one employee, but I really appreciate you giving me a chance. Especially so last minute."

Evelyn's smile lines deepened. "I'll be honest, I don't think I was ready to fill the position until you applied and I realized we only had a few weeks until summer!" Even her laughter was warm and welcoming. She was like bottled sunshine, motherly and warm but confident and astute too. I didn't think I'd ever worked for someone who genuinely seemed nice. "Besides, you're selling yourself short. Your food has won many awards. I've done my research, Francesca Benedetti. If anything, this seems like a step down for you."

"A sidestep into something new," I amended, matching her infectious smile. My new boss was instantly buoying my low spirits. This job would be great, things would get better, and I'd have a whole summer on a beautiful island far from Jake to figure out my next move. "I really appreciate this opportunity, more than you know. My world kind of got upended a couple weeks ago and I really needed a change."

"This is a surprisingly wonderful place to reinvent yourself," Evelyn confessed. "And our menu. It hasn't changed in over two decades. I have children younger than this menu." She chuckled and looked down at the dated, laminated paper between us. "But business is growing, especially in the last year, and I think it's time for an upgrade—new blood. I want you to work your magic over this place."

I brandished my leather-bound notebook. "I was writing

down some animal-themed ideas on the ferry ride over. Some things that'll work more for kids and things to appeal to the adults. I'll draft up a proposal—"

"Free rein," Evelyn cut in, waving her hands with a majestic little swirl. "I trust you."

I blinked at her, my brain taking a second to catch up. Unless you owned your own place, having free rein to redesign a menu was pretty much unheard of—let alone a café and a restaurant like the zoo had. My thoughts doubled pace: we could do different themes, seasonal foods, sampler plates, different specials each day of the week . . . This was a great opportunity for me. I had a bunch of recipes I had been testing out when Frankie's Café had closed.

I bobbed my head, feeling for the first time in weeks like maybe my luck might be changing. This would be good. A fresh start. Evelyn seemed to understand how much I needed that judging by her perceptive smile.

"We've set you up with an apartment at the Salty Dog," Evelyn said. "I think you'll like it there. It's a rustic, nautical bar less than a ten-minute walk along the waterfront from here." She checked her watch. "But Kirby probably won't be up for another hour—bartenders," she said with a playful roll of her eyes. "So I'll let you have a poke around the café and get settled in. Feel free to go explore the zoo and say hi to the animals too. Now's the best time, before we're swarmed with summertime visitors."

Talk about a job with benefits. Not many people got to go hang out with giraffes and meerkats on their lunch break.

I stood in unison with her and shook her outstretched hand. "Thank you again, Mrs. Lachlan—"

"Call me Evie," she said. "Welcome to the team, Frankie. I'm looking forward to working with you."

I watched her leave and then wandered aimlessly around the café for a few minutes, staring at the aquarium fish and seriously debating testing out the tube slide. Technically, I had two locations to supervise now: the front of house café *and* the restaurant in the middle of the zoo called the Peckish Peacock. Evie had mentioned in her correspondence that I'd also have the opportunity to do some catering for zoo events. The excitement of everything I could achieve in this place eased some of my nerves. I felt a little more justified in taking this job.

I could do what I did best: feed people. And I wouldn't have to worry about all the admin of running a business. All the nightmarish paperwork would disappear, and I could do the actual hands in the flour work that I loved.

I shook out my hands and rolled my shoulders. "Okay, good," I encouraged myself aloud.

Navigating through the chairs and around the cabinet, I went to inspect the kitchen. The room was humid and stuffy, so much so that I could barely take it in. I flicked the overhead fan on and went straight to the back door to prop it open with one of the rubbish bins. When I turned back round, my belt loop caught on the door handle. I jerked forward, almost toppling over.

I glared down at my belt loop. "Seriously?" I reprimanded the inanimate object.

"Need some help there, Goldilocks?" a familiar voice called.

I extracted myself from my entrapment and whirled to the sound. "Goldfinch?"

Chapter Five

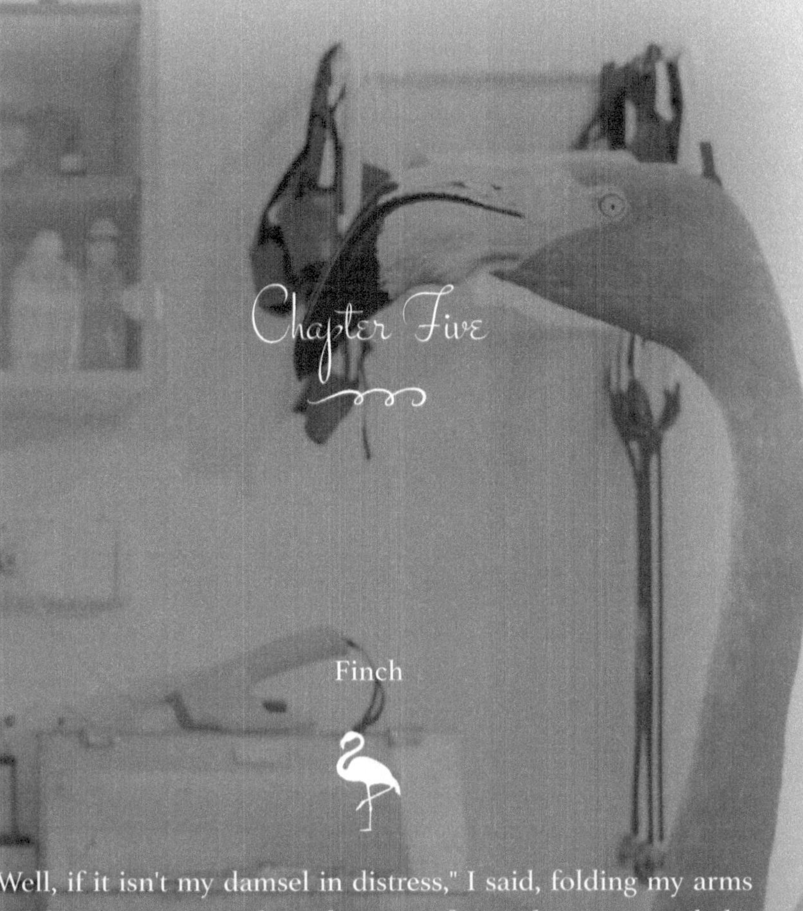

Finch

"Well, if it isn't my damsel in distress," I said, folding my arms and leaning against the splintering fence that separated the main path from the back of the café.

Of all the things I'd expected to see on my way back from the petting zoo . . .

I'd just been checking our miniature cow's, Colin's, abscess, mind still foggy from a late night, when the girl I'd kissed in town appeared at my family's zoo—my family's currently closed for the season zoo. She looked equally baffled to see me, as if *I* were the one out of place, not her.

Frankie yanked herself free from the door handle, her cheeks flushing a shade of scarlet as she looked me up and down. Her eyes lingered on my lab coat, her slender brows pinching as her gaze drifted to the stethoscope around my neck. I could see the wheels turning as she started putting together the missing pieces.

"You . . . work here?"

I laughed down at the Prickle Island Zoo logo across my lab coat. "What gave me away?" I cocked my head. "The real question is, what are *you* doing here, Frankie?"

Frankie's lips curved like she was seemingly impressed I remembered her name. She hooked her thumb to the door held ajar by a trash can behind her. "I just, uh, got a job here. I was meeting with Evie, Evelyn, well, your mom, I guess? That's so weird."

"Wait, *you're* the new chef?" I asked incredulously, my mind racing to catch up. "You're Francesca Benedetti?"

She folded her arms, making her chest stick out more and the buttons of her sweater stretch in a way that made me swallow and pick a point directly above her head to look at.

"Yes, why?"

"You just . . . don't look like I imagined." I waved a hand at her statuesque height, only a couple inches shorter than me, and her shining waves of blonde hair that made her look more like a Nordic ice princess than an Italian chef.

"Not all Italians have dark hair," she chided, rolling her ocean blue eyes. "I'm Italian on my dad's side, hence the last name. My mom is Dutch."

"Ah," I said. Hence the hair, height, and thighs that I wouldn't mind choking me. I cleared my throat. This was *not* what I should be thinking about. Especially now that I knew she'd be working here all summer. I absolutely *could not*, under any circumstances, hit on her. She was officially off limits. "I hoped I'd run into you again."

Way to not hit on her, Finch!

"Oh," she said, tucking a strand of golden hair behind her ear. I couldn't help but study the way her cheeks pinked up, trailing out to her ears and down her neck like a rosy haze.

I laughed awkwardly and shifted my weight side to side. Something about her . . . it put me off balance. Normally, I was smooth and suave and knew exactly what to say, but this girl made me nervous.

I knew she shouldn't make me feel anything. She'd been engaged to a slimy guy like two weeks ago!

I rolled my shoulders as if I could stretch away the thought. "Well, welcome to Prickle Island Zoo," I said, flourishing a hand like a court herald.

"Thank you," she replied, checking her watch. "I'm just about to head out to the place I'm staying. Your mom organized the accommodation for me. Do you know where the Salty Dog is?"

"My home away from home," I said with a chuckle. "You'll like it there. Kirby and Aya are good people. Aya's our food prep manager so you could probably get a ride over with her in the mornings. Or walk. It's only like ten minutes." Great, I was rambling now. I was starting to sound like Hawk's girlfriend, Hannah. "But . . ."

"But what?"

"You know the Salty Dog is a bar, right? I hope you brought ear plugs."

"I might need to go to the store and grab some. Thanks for the tip," she said, fumbling to cross her arms over her chest. Was she nervous too? God, I was calmer bumping into women I'd done all sorts of wicked things with than this. I'd just kissed Frankie once and she had me bouncing on the balls on my feet like an anxious bobblehead.

"Popping to the store *might* be a problem." I pinched two fingers together. "The general store doesn't have them, and the other shops don't open until the first day of summer when all of the tourists start coming over on the ferry."

"Right," she said tightly. "Well, I guess I'll just make do."

"I have some!" I volunteered. *Seriously. What the fuck was wrong with me?*

"Oh, that's okay. I shouldn't—"

"No, no, please, I have a million packets," I said, waving a hand. "We had a flock of cockatoos in the hospital a few weeks ago for their annual deworming and beak trims. Earplugs are an essential."

She blinked at me. "I never thought I would hear that sentence."

"Welcome to life at a zoo." I waggled my eyebrows. "Prepare for much stranger things, I can guarantee you will encounter them over the summer." I grabbed out my swipe card. "Come on. The hospital's just over there."

She tentatively followed me through the winding bamboo-lined paths and through the staff shortcut to the back gate of the hospital. We walked in stilted silence that I'd normally fill with my witty repartee, but I had no idea what to say. Something about Frankie had me tongue-tied. I wanted to ask about her ex, about the job, about her life. She was the sort of intriguing person who made me want to peel back all the layers and figure her out. I wanted to ask all sorts of things, but instead I just silently wandered up to the glass doors of the hospital, waved my keycard over the door, and ushered Frankie in.

As we walked into the brightly lit hallway, the waft of chemicals and cleaning solutions filled the air. It was a unique scent, like acid and urine mixed with perfumed soap and iodine and the sharp tang of metal. The lights buzzed overhead, my eyes sharpening as we walked down the echoey, tiled hallway.

As we passed the surgery room, Frankie whispered, "Am I allowed to be back here?"

I arched my brow at her. "Why are you whispering?"

"I don't know," she said a little louder. "It just all seems very important and official, like a real hospital."

"It is a real hospital," I countered. "Our patients just aren't humans."

"Well, it feels like the sort of place random new employees aren't allowed to go. I don't want to get in trouble on my first day."

"Trouble? I'm the veterinarian," I pointed out, tapping on my name embroidered on my coat. "You're allowed wherever I say as long as you're with me, okay?"

"Right, okay." Why was she so adorable? I felt like we were two kids sneaking around in here instead of me showing her my very boring and sterile office.

"Hey, Finch," Dove called as she turned the corner. "Where did you put the restock of syringes for—oh!" She pulled up short, staring at Frankie and then glowering at me. "I thought you were going to cool it on boning girls at the vet hospital."

"Dove—"

"If Mom sees you've brought another random girl—"

"Dovey—"

"I mean, she's stunning." She waved Frankie up and down. "I don't blame you, but—"

"Dove!"

"What?"

"Dove, meet Frankie Benedetti, the new head chef of Prickle Island Zoo." Like a kid displaying an art project, I held up my hands to display Frankie, who was trying very hard to contain her laughter.

"Oh." Dove looked between us. "Oh!" She launched forward to shake Frankie's hand as Frankie bit her lips together. "Dove Lachlan, rainforest walkthrough and bird keeper. Sorry about that. I'm one of Finch's annoying little sisters."

"You're the only annoying," I muttered.

The twins, Crane and Heron, seized that opportune moment to waltz into the vet hospital carrying Matilda, the boa constrictor.

"Finch, are you—"

Dove jumped in between us and loudly proclaimed, "This is the new chef, Frankie!" before my other siblings could make more snide comments about my dating habits.

I rolled my eyes.

"Wow," Frankie said, looking between all of us. "There's a lot of you."

I gestured to the twins. "Meet Crane and Heron. They are both easily bribed with baked goods should you ever need to."

"Ah, right," Frankie said with a chuckle. "Evie warned me about you two." She put a hand to the side of her mouth and whispered, "I make a mean banana bread."

Heron shoved Crane to the side and rushed up to her. "Have you ever wanted to pet a giraffe?"

"Whoa there, team," I said, hooking a finger into Heron's khaki collar and yanking them backward. "Let's let Frankie settle in here before we start trading food for animal encounters, okay?" I pointed at Crane. "And no surprise tarantulas."

Frankie's eyes bugged as my little brother rolled his eyes. "You're no fun."

"You're twenty-one now, wrecking ball," I said to him. "No more pranks."

"Especially if you want to enjoy my baking," Frankie added. "And I promise you it's the best you've ever had."

Crane's expression tightened at that threat. "Okay, fine, no tarantulas."

I flashed Frankie a grin. She already knew how to wrangle the twins, it seemed.

Taking her gently by the elbow, I steered her through the labyrinth of my prying siblings. The Lachlans could be a lot when we bombarded people all at once. I fished in my desk drawer and pulled out a sealed packet of foam earplugs. "Here," I said, passing them to Frankie. "These should get you started."

"Thanks," she replied. "Uh." She looked around at all my

siblings, who were now all lingering in the doorway to my office like circling lemurs waiting for grapes. "It was nice meeting you all!"

They all said their pleasantries over the top of each other and waved her off as she headed, bemused, back out of the vet hospital. She stole one last look my way as she went, giving me a quick wave. I waved back a little too enthusiastically and felt all of my siblings' eyes land on me at once. Curse them, they missed nothing.

"Ten bucks says Finch hooks up with her by the end of the week," Crane murmured to Heron.

"No more bets," I said, pointing between them. "I'm not like that anymore." They both erupted into laughter, and I scowled at them. "I am *this* close to swapping Bart's castration for yours. Now tell me why you're here or get out of my office."

Their reply was cut off by my phone beeping. Lark's message popped up: *Describe her please!*

My eyes found Dove, who was smiling down at her phone. "You already messaged the family group chat about this?" I raked my hair off my face. "The devil works fast, but Lachlans work faster," I muttered.

By now, all of my siblings had been informed of Frankie's presence in my office. I didn't know why, but I didn't like the idea of all of them talking about her, even if it would inevitably be complimentary.

"What do you two want?" I sighed, pointing at the boa constrictor still happily draped across Crane's neck.

Dove grinned at me and started dancing down the hall. "I think I'm going to name the new chick Frankie!"

Daily Specials
kookaburra cucumber
sandwiches
$5.50
Macaw Macarons
6 for $12

Chapter Six

Frankie

Aya perched on the stool beside me as her wife, Kirby, leaned across the bar at the Salty Dog. The two of them were British, though they'd both lived on Prickle Island as a couple for the last thirty years. It would've been sweet to see this loving middle-aged couple if I hadn't just had my heart stomped all over. Instead, the little, secret looks they gave each other across the bar made me sad.

"She gave you earplugs?" Kirby asked incredulously with a shake of her head. She had shortly cropped coils of obsidian hair and an easy-going smile that many bartenders used to listening to people's woes had—part bartender, part therapist. "The summer hasn't even started yet," she added with a tsk, pretending to be offended. "This place is quiet as a graveyard until the first day of summer vacation. And even then, we close up at 1 am, nothing crazy."

"Besides." Aya nudged me with her elbow. "We'll be long asleep before it gets rowdy anyway."

"How does it work, you two having such different schedules?" I wondered aloud. "You'd be like two ships passing in the night."

"We actually are both pretty nocturnal." Aya gave her wife another adoring look, pouring more salt in my wounds.

I hated how bitter it made me feel, seeing the two of them. It would've been easier to pretend love didn't exist at all than that it just didn't exist for me. This was supposed to be Jake and me. We were supposed to be a happily married couple, giving each other these secret looks, building a life together. He'd ripped my whole future from me.

"I do a split shift," Aya said. "Most of the time I'm done by 8 am and Kirby and I sleep most of the day and get to spend the afternoons together before work." She looked at me. "As a chef and an avid baker, I'd imagine you're used to keeping all sorts of hours too."

I chuckled at the "avid baker" line. I *might* have nervously chatted their ears off about different methods for making sourdough before I'd finally calmed down enough to settle into actual conversation.

"Yeah, my mornings are so early, some consider them late nights too," I said. "I used to wake up at 3 am to get the dough out of the curing baskets." I pursed my lips, considering. "But I think I won't get up until 5 for this job."

"What a rogue," Kirby said, throwing a bar rag over her shoulder and scooping ice into a tall glass.

I sighed, thinking of my kitchen back at Frankie's Café. I'd never have one of those sacred early mornings baking in that kitchen ever again.

"That was one hell of a sigh," Kirby said, sliding a fruity wine spritzer across the bar to me. "Spill."

I told the two of them about Jake, about the sudden breakup, about the run-in with his new fiancée, though I carefully left out the part about Finch rescuing me. These two seemed to be like honorary aunties of the Lachlan family, and I didn't want to be dragging someone they'd known from infancy into my own drama. Aya and Kirby gasped and groaned at all the appropriate times, validating the whole story.

"You know the hot, young thing won't last," Aya said with a wave of her hand. "How old is he?"

"Forty-one," I said, "Twelve years older than me." They both grimaced at that. "When I was twenty-one, I'd thought it was a charming age gap, that I was just so mature that the only man I was interested in was someone serious." I could tell they were wearily disappointed in that statement. I wondered how many similar stories they'd heard from across this bar. "I thought he was responsible and mature. I thought I was making a smart decision for my future in picking him . . ."

"Oh, honey." Aya groaned.

"Yeah, there's no way that rebound fiancée is going to last," Kirby said. "Talk about a midlife crisis. He will be crawling back to you before you know it."

"Do you think so?" I hated how hopeful I sounded. Did I even want that?

"Not that you should take a sleazeball like that back," Aya added.

"Either way, you need to win the breakup." Kirby pointed at me. "There is no sweeter victory than when someone breaks up with you and you just start *thriving*—even if it's pretend." She tipped her chin to my phone of the bar. "You need to find someone to make him jealous. Eye candy you can post all over your socials of a hot guy—"

"Or girl or person," Aya interjected, and the two of them

studied me for a second as if trying to discern who would be my perfect match.

"You need to find a nice, sexy, ten levels up of a person and plaster them all over like a freaking 'I'm winning at life' billboard."

"I am so far from winning at life," I grumbled.

"Pff," Kirby balked, waving her hand. "Post all the photos of you living on a luxury island, feeding tigers and monkeys, *and* making award-winning food to the adoration of thousands per day, with some sexy French bartender."

"Sexy French bartender?" I asked.

"We know people," Aya said with a shrug. "I bet Chloe would pretend to be her girlfriend, or . . . what about Francois?"

"Ooh Francois, he's working at the Holloways' this year. I'll ask him."

"No, no." I waved my arms into an X. "Listen, you two paint a very nice picture, and I really appreciate all of your support," I said, looking between the two of them. "But let me just lick my wounds for a little before you pair me up with Francois or Chloe or whoever."

"Good to know that both are an option," Kirby said with a wink.

I'd always known I'd liked women, but I'd never dated one before so it'd never really felt like something worth advertising. I'd paired up with Jake right after college, and it'd just seemed like, decisions had been made. I'd been sorted. I hadn't needed to pick apart my sexuality anymore even if when I dreamed about being with someone, I only ever dreamed about women. Yep, best not to scrutinize that revelation too closely.

"Take as much time as you need," Aya said, rubbing a hand across my back. "A lot of broken hearts have sat on these bar stools. We're very good listeners, okay?"

I almost wanted to cry as I sipped on my drink and nodded. "Thank you."

"If we're coming on too strong, just tell us to back off," Kirby added. "We have a tendency to adopt all of the zoo staff, but we're nosy bitches at the best of times so just tell us to leave you alone if we're prying."

"No, it's really nice actually," I said. "Thanks."

These two felt more maternal toward me than my own mom ever had. I loved my parents, they were good people and they always supported me and my siblings in theory, but they were never really interested in our lives. They didn't think parents should be friends with their children. They were good caregivers, but not particularly loving, and that had left all of us kind of adrift when we'd left home. Now they lived in the Caribbean and hardly ever called except for holidays. I kept slightly closer tabs on my siblings, but no more than any other social media friend from high school.

I thought I'd make my own family ... with Jake.

Maybe Kirby was right. Maybe I still could have Jake. Maybe I just needed someone to make him jealous enough to come crawling back. I'd seen the way he'd looked at Finch when she'd put her arm around my waist—he'd been angry, jealous, possessive. Maybe I just needed to push him a little further and he'd remember the life we'd built together. I could start a new Frankie's 2.0, and we could get married and have kids and stick to all the plans I'd been grabbing onto for the last eight years . . . *or* maybe I should put Nair in his shampoo, rotten fish in his ventilation systems, and destroy him piece by piece like the asshole he was. I still hadn't decided.

I raised my glass to Aya and Kirby. "Thank you for letting me stay here this summer. I'm looking forward to getting to know you two better."

They clinked their glasses with mine. "We only let serious staff members stay here. Evie must really like you to even suggest it." Kirby took a swig of her beer. "With all of your accolades, I can see why."

"I'm excited to have a fellow staff member that doesn't have Lachlan as a surname," Aya said. "You, me, Kirby, and Mateo are seriously outnumbered by the Lachlan clan."

"Also, technically Hawk's girlfriend, Hannah, isn't a Lachlan," Kirby cut in.

"Yet," Aya said. "I give it less than two years."

"There's too many names to remember." I groaned, rubbing my temples.

"I'll draw you a diagram," Aya said, and I gave her a grateful look.

"I need to go do inventory before bed." Kirby leaned over the bar and kissed Aya and then looked at me. "And if you have any leftover muffins at the end of your workdays, I'm quite partial to raspberry white chocolate," she added with a grin.

Aya shouldered me. "You're about to become everyone's favorite person."

"You're the second person today to tell me that." I offered her a half-smile. My first thought was too pathetic to say aloud: I only wanted to be one man's favorite person, and right now he was engaged to someone else.

Finch

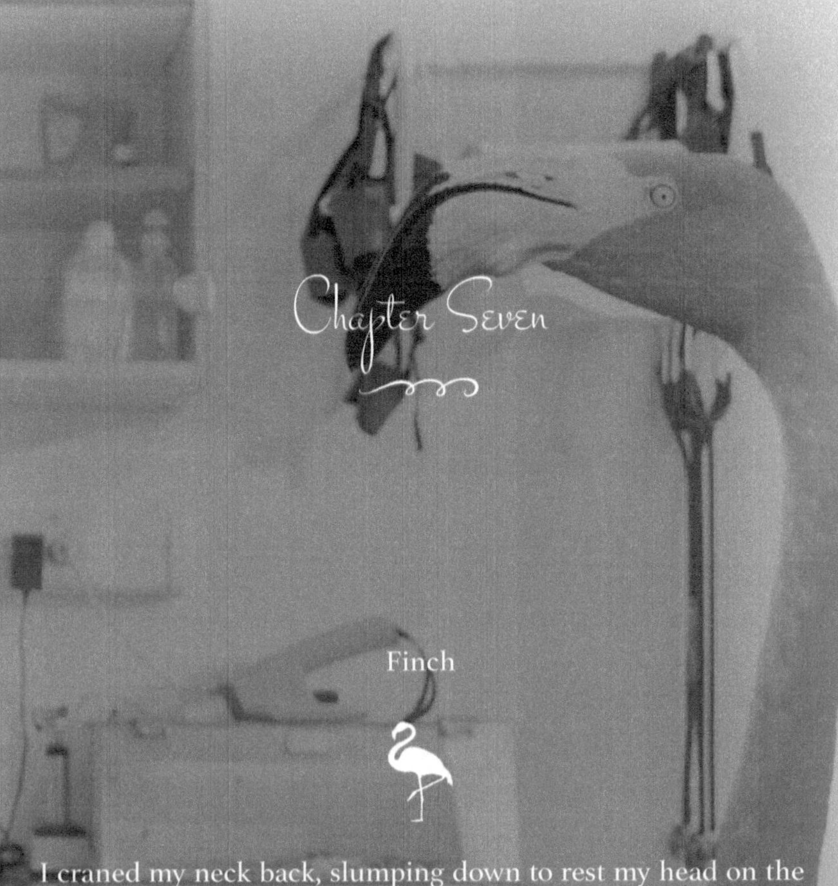

I craned my neck back, slumping down to rest my head on the bench and look up at the stars. The squeaks of curious marmosets sounded behind me, like they were wondering who was sitting at the lookout bench at this time of night. An unopened bottle of tequila sat beside me along with a stack of red Solo cups. I pulled my leather jacket tighter around me, the June nights still brisk.

I saw the flicker of a flashlight long before I heard Dove's voice say, "Well, if this isn't the most depressing sight I've ever seen."

"Don't tell Lark," I said without lifting my head. "I can feel her eyes judging me all the way from New Zealand."

I heard the scuffle of Dove's boots as she wandered over and sat on the bench beside me. "I won't."

"What are you doing wandering the zoo at night?"

"Getting away from the circus back at the monkey house," she muttered with a little harrumph.

Hawk had converted the old monkey house into a makeshift apartment for us years ago, and the three eldest—Hawk, me, and Lark—had moved in to get out of our overly stuffed house. There'd been a time when we'd all lived in the family home at the top of the zoo. Four of us in one room, three in another.

I lifted my head to look at her. "The twins giving you grief?"

"I was so excited when Lark moved out!" She threw up her hands in frustration. "I would get to move into the monkey house with you and Hawk and get away from those two. And then you had to go and refurbish the vet hospital attic and Hawk built his cottage—"

"You wouldn't want to be sharing a place with Hawk and Hannah though," I cut in. "Those two fuck like bunnies. You'd hate that."

"Yep. It's the same reason I haven't asked to move in with you," Dove muttered. "I don't really feel like introducing myself to a new girl every night when I get up to pee." I frowned at her, but she ignored me. We both knew I didn't have a leg to stand on. "I'm thinking of moving back into Mom's house now that the twins' bedroom is free."

"Wow, it's really that bad then?"

"Heron is fine, but Crane . . ." She shook her head as I laughed knowingly. "He never outgrew the 'wrecking ball' nickname. He's like a thirteen-year-old living in a twenty-one-year-old's body. For all his pedantic cleanliness with the reptiles and invertebrates, you'd think he'd have the good sense to clean up after himself."

"Yeah, maybe just let the twins run rabid for a while," I said. "They'll outgrow their bachelorhood eventually."

Dove tipped her head to the bottle and cups beside me. "So why are you sitting here like the ghost of frat boys past?"

"Ugh," I grumbled, sweeping my short hair off my face. "I went down to the volunteer house like I do every year for the first week parties, and you know what they were doing?"

"What?"

"Sleeping!"

"How dare they?"

"Only like four of them were even up," I said. "It's not even midnight. They all wanted to get an early night for their shifts the next day . . . like, seriously? They're college students for fuck's sake!"

"We do have a lot of serious volunteers this year," Dove said. "I actually even like the ones that have been paired up with me. They're both studying wildlife biology and actually want to know all of my bird fun facts. It's great!" Dove quickly reined in her enthusiasm. "But yeah, not a lot of college kids just looking for a crazy summer this year. Times are changing, I guess."

"What happened?" I groaned, waving a hand over me. "I used to be fun! People looked up to me. I was the life of the party. Now I'm the creepy old guy who hangs out with college kids."

"You're not the creepy old guy." Dove shifted to face me. "You just need to find some people your own age to go out for drinks with. Go to the Salty Dog to party, not the volunteer house."

She was right. My years of being the cool older sister of the zoo had quickly faded away.

"If it's any consolation," Dove added. "Both my volunteers wanted to know if you're single."

"Thanks." That used to make me proud, and now it just felt disquieting. I was too young for a midlife crisis like this!

"Frankie's doing good," I offered.

"The human or the bird?" Dove quipped.

"You really made our lives complicated by naming the bird after her. I'm talking about Frankie, the chick. Francesca? Benedetti? Benny, maybe?" I brainstormed new nicknames for the bird.

"I'm glad she's doing good." Dove nodded. We didn't really know if the bird was a he or she. They were notoriously hard to sex and it didn't really matter so I wasn't going to send her bloods off for testing. She was a de facto "she" until adulthood because most zoos often defaulted to "he" and Dove and I wanted to even the score. "You want me to take over some of the night shifts for a while? You could go out on a few dates. You seem . . . burnt out."

"I'm not burnt out. I'm just having a mellow evening," I countered even though we both knew I was normally not so melancholy.

"Okay." She held up her hands defensively. We spotted another flashlight moving through the trees two paths over. "Now who is *that*?"

"Wren," I said. "She's taking Chicken Wing to say goodnight to Jackie."

"What?"

I chuckled. "It's sweet."

Ever since we'd found out about the star-crossed love between our one-winged penguin, Chicken Wing, and our spider monkey, Jackie, the youngest Lachlan had been taking them to say goodnight to each other. I didn't think the rest of the family knew, but I'd spotted Wren doing it a few times on my late nights sneaking back into the zoo.

I looked at Dove and gave her a half-hearted smile. "You want to stay in my guest bedroom tonight? I promise there will be no random girls to bump into when you get up to pee."

"That would be really nice, thanks," she said. She grabbed the bottle of tequila. "You could've left this down at the volunteer house."

"They didn't even want it!" I erupted, making my sister cackle with laughter. I couldn't help but laugh as well. "What twenty-year-old doesn't want a free bottle of tequila!"

"Okay, okay," Dove said, ushering me up the path back to the vet hospital. "Let's get you to bed, Grandma."

I whirled, pointing a scolding finger at her, but that just made her laugh even harder as we wandered back through the nighttime zoo.

Daily Specials

kookaburra cucumber sandwiches
$5.50

Macaw Macarons
6 for $12

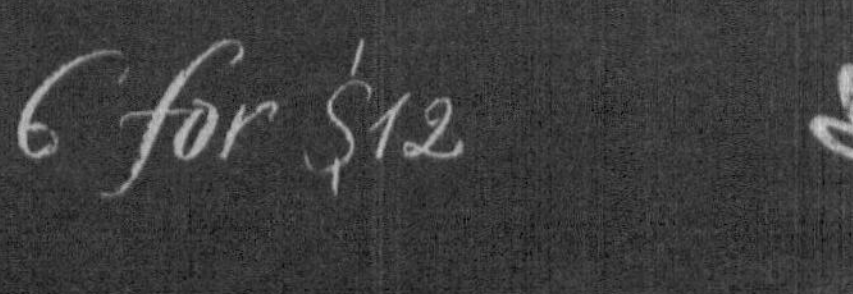

Chapter Eight

Frankie

"Knock, knock."

I stood up too quickly and banged my head on the angled beam above me. Finch cringed.

"Oh, Finch, hey," I said a little too quickly, trying to play it off like I hadn't just smashed my freaking skull into the ceiling. "Must remember there's a beam there."

Finch's cheeks dimpled as she walked to the freezer. "You'll get the hang of it after a few more knocks, I'm sure." Her laugh was deep and rasping and made my stomach do all sorts of strange flippy things. She fished out a packet of frozen corn and wrapped it in a dish towel. "Ice. Animal doctor's orders."

"Thanks," I said, taking the cold bundle and putting it on my head. It would probably hurt once the adrenaline wore off, but my heart was jackhammering so fast that I couldn't feel the egg forming. "What's up?"

"Something smells delicious," Finch said, ignoring my question and strolling to the kitchen island in the center of the room. She lifted the tea cloths covering my cinnamon rolls. "Wow."

"They're not good." I held out my hands like she was about to pick up a grenade. "They're just practice ones. I'm working out the oven settings with a few test batches. I've got to account for the salt air and humidity. It's different than upstate. Obviously."

"You better not tell the twins about these test batches or they'll all be gone by lunchtime," Finch quipped, putting her hands in her scrub pockets and leaning against the brick wall of the Peckish Peacock. She looked like some sort of sexy, androgynous *Grey's Anatomy* character with the way she leaned like that. She seemed like the sort of person who would be calm in an emergency, that catlike cunning, shrewd mind that could go from playful to razor sharp in a second. I wondered what she'd look like in action during a code red . . .

Finch reached for a roll, and I darted forward.

"Oh no." I waved my arms like a referee over the rolls. "These aren't up to scratch. I'm throwing these out."

"What?" Finch scoffed. "They look perfectly fine. Delicious, even."

"I don't want my first impression to the world to be *these* rolls." I huffed, dusting my flour-covered hands down my emerald-green apron.

"First, the *world* may be a little extreme." Her lips curved up, making her piercings glint with the movement. "Second, the warthogs have a more refined palette than I or any of my siblings do and they routinely eat bugs so . . ."

"You're exaggerating."

Finch guffawed. "Have you *met* my siblings? Honestly,

zookeepers are just as feral as their animals when it comes to free food."

I couldn't help but smile at that. It was really sweet the way this family teased and joked about their siblings. They were constantly poking fun but in a loving way, as if they actually liked each other as people and not just out of familial obligation. How many families could actually say that?

The Lachlans were the most welcoming group I'd ever met. I didn't know grown siblings could actually be friends. It was beautiful, but it also made me ache for something, the same ache that had kept me glued to Jake even when we'd fought, even when we hadn't made any sense, even when I'd questioned if I was making a big mistake. I wanted that feeling of place, of rightness, one I'd never really had with my own family, one that existed so readily here with this rowdy bunch of zookeepers.

"May I?" Finch asked, lifting a sticky roll. She laughed at my pinched lips and tight expression. "You're a bit of a perfectionist, aren't you?"

"I don't—"

"I'm a literal garbage disposal," she pushed. "I promise I won't judge you."

I craned my neck to look up at the ceiling so I didn't have to meet her eyes as I said, "Fine. On your head be it."

I could still see from the periphery as she took a bite. Maybe she'd spit it out. Maybe she'd try to make a funny remark to cover for how truly horrendous they were . . . . But then an indecent moan escaped her lips and she said, "Sweet baby boa constrictors, this is seriously fucking delicious."

"You don't have to say that—"

"I wouldn't lie to you," she said with a warm laugh. "You can look at me now." She waved a powdered sugar-covered hand in front of my face. "Frankie, look at me." I finally lowered my gaze to find her standing a hair's breadth from me, licking frosting off her full lips. I cleared my throat as she said, "Really. These are like orgasmically good."

First the lip licking and the smell of sweet cinnamon on her breath, now the mention of orgasms. I felt the tingling across my cheeks and knew I was definitely turning bright red. It didn't help that Finch looked like a tatted, masc Xena Warrior Princess. God, I got all giggly and weird around hot people. I had no chill.

I bet she had really sexy orgasms too, deep, groaning, throaty ones, not cringy, embarrassing ones like me. And now I was thinking about her sex face. *Great*, that was really intrusive.

"I can do better," I said, sounding just as flustered as I was.

"Well, if this is your version of bad," Finch said through another mouthful, "I am certainly not prepared for your best."

I opened the window, trying to act like I was wafting the smell outside and not stealing some fresh air to cool my flushed cheeks. "Did you smell the baking? Is that why you've come for this unexpected visit?"

"The twins are like hounds for this stuff," Finch said as she finished the last bite. "I give it ten minutes before they get here with that window open."

"They can have as much as they like, except for two. I told Aya and Kirby I'd bring some home."

Finch arched a pierced brow. "Oh, so they are good enough for Aya and Kirby, but not for me?"

"Yes."

"Why?"

I shrugged. "I don't know. I care what you think, I guess," I muttered, sweeping my hair nervously behind my ear. *Ugh, god, Frankie, pull your shit together.* "So, Goldfinch—"

"Finch," she corrected.

"Finch. Right," I said, cocking my hip, and I noticed the way her eyes dipped to my waist. "To what do I owe the pleasure?" I tried to suck in my gut. This shirt was too tight and she was probably staring at my rolls, and not the cinnamon kind. *Wonderful.*

Finch swept a hand through her short hair. "I, uh, just wanted to say hi and, uh, clear the air between us."

"Clear the air?"

"Just that we kissed at that restaurant and now we're working together, and I just wanted to make sure that wasn't weird and that you're okay after everything that happened with Sgt. Douchebag."

"I'm okay, well, mostly," I said with a laugh as I put the frozen corn on the stainless steel countertop. "You rescued me. It was like knight in shining armor worthy, so thank you." I wanted to thank her for that hug in the alleyway too. The way she'd held me like she could fuse my broken heart back together with her arms alone . . . That hug still echoed through my body. Never had it felt so good to be held in someone's arms. But I couldn't say that aloud, so instead I simply said, "No weirdness, I promise."

"Well, I never knew I wanted to be called a knight in shining armor until now," she teased. "So we're all good?"

"All good," I said, sticking my hand out. She quirked her brow at it but shook it anyway.

Jesus, Frankie. A handshake? Really? What the fuck is wrong with you?

I needed a quick getaway. I hooked my thumb behind me. "Well, I was just heading back to the Salty Dog. Needed to grab something, so, uh, I'll see you around."

I turned too quickly and almost ran smack dab into that fucking beam again, but Finch was faster, reaching out and grabbing me by the wrist. She yanked me backward so that her chest fused with my front, and I sucked in a sharp breath. We stood there frozen for a beat as her thumb swept over my pulse, and I swallowed at her calloused hands on my skin.

"You keep on saving me there," I joked a little breathlessly.

"All the knight talk got to my head," she joked, finally releasing my arm and stepping back. "I've got to get to surgery."

I turned to look at her. "Oh my god, I hope you're okay."

Her brow furrowed. "Not my surgery . . . I'm doing a removal on a partial tail drop on a leopard gecko. Vet, remember?"

"Right." I let out a loud, uncomfortable laugh. "Of course. I knew that."

I needed to go crawl into a hole and never emerge. I whirled, ducking under the beam this time and bolting out the café door.

"See ya!" I called over my shoulder as I fled that embarrassing situation.

I walked double pace down the path out of the zoo to the main strip of shops. What the hell was wrong with me? This wasn't 7th grade. I could kiss another adult person and then just move on like it wasn't a really great kiss. It was all just for pretend anyway. It wasn't like I wanted to repeat it again and again and again.

I let out a shaky breath. "I hope you're okay?" I groaned, embarrassment burning through me as I stormed down the path. "God, Frankie. Good job."

Chapter Nine

Finch

I stuffed another cheese-covered piece of crusty bread in my mouth, my stomach gurgling with my weekly overindulgence in dairy.

"Finch?"

"Huh?"

I looked up to realize Crane was holding out a photo on his phone. I must've zoned out. All the late-night chick feedings were starting to make me loopy.

"Owl, easy," I said, correctly identifying the mystery poop in his photo. I skewered another piece of bread and swirled it in the fondue pot in the center of the table, mindlessly eating while my siblings nattered away.

It was Sunday, which in the Lachlan household meant

Sunday Funday Fondue Day. It was yet another one of our zany family traditions along with our family's own dinner party game called "It's feces but what species?"

Probably only zookeepers thought it was good fun to quiz each other on animal shit while we were eating. I was the reigning champion, but my heart wasn't really in it tonight.

"Another late night?" Mom asked, and I knew she was implying I'd been on a date.

I shot her a look. "Yeah, I was with a chick and not the fun kind." I pointed an accusatory finger at Dove. "You need to have a talk with the macaws about breeding season because this shit is ridiculous. Also—" I turned on Mom. "Will you *please* just lay off? It's like I turned thirty and all of a sudden, you're constantly on me about the girls I'm seeing. Aren't these two all disgustingly shacked up enough?" I waved to either end of the table. On one end, Hawk and Hannah sat canoodling and playing footsie under the table, on the other, a laptop sat with Lark and Logan sipping their morning coffees on a Zoom call from New Zealand.

"I'm not doing anything," Mom said with a guilt-inducing shrug. "It used to never bother you when we'd point out your trysts."

"You've been pointing them out a lot lately."

Mom grabbed the salad bowl and started mounding leafy greens onto her plate. "I'm just wondering if you're ever going to have a relationship that lasts more than two dates."

"What about Dove?" I waved dramatically at my little sister. "She's only a few years younger than me."

"Traitor," Dove hissed. Wren chuckled from where she sat next to Mom, working on her embroidery instead of eating. Dove leaned in and whispered to her, "Just you wait. You'll be joining us in this hellscape soon enough."

Wren shrugged in a very similar way to Mom. Wren was

truly Mom's carbon copy—a cozy, little homebody who'd rather be knitting than out partying. I'd waited all her teen years for a rebellious phase, but now at eighteen, I knew we were never going to get one.

"There are four of you ahead of me to pair off first," Wren said. "With any luck, there will be a dozen nieces and nephews to draw her attention and Mom will skip right over worrying about me. I think I'll be just fine."

Mom did her "time out" gesture and looked back at me. "I'm not saying you need to *pair off*," she said dramatically. "Not ever, if you really don't want to," she added, even though her face was pinched. "But maybe a companion who's known you for more than twenty-four hours might be nice some time. I can't help but worry about you—"

"I'm seeing someone," I exclaimed, and the whole table went silent. Cutlery froze midair, mouths stopped chewing, and all side conversations abruptly halted.

Only the thudding tail of mom's dog, Phoebe, could be heard as all of my siblings and my mother stared at me in unison.

I couldn't take it anymore. I was exhausted and frustrated and I couldn't deal with my entire family's disapproval and judgement. I used to be admired by them. It was like one day I blinked and their opinions of me 180-ed. I was the youngest person in US history to complete my veterinary degree. I used to be called a savant. I was routinely asked to keynote at conferences and had co-authored several scientific papers. I was held in high esteem in my community, and moreover my younger siblings used to envy me and my accolades, but now that Lark and Hawk had both found their people, it was like they all pitied me, and I hated it.

I needed to put an end to it, even if it was all lies.

Mom held a scandalized hand to her chest. "You're . . . seeing someone?"

"Yes," I said. "This isn't how I wanted to tell you, but seeing as you won't just leave it alone, yes, I'm seeing someone." I gave Mom a look sharper than a surgical blade. "And we've been on more than three dates."

"Exclusively?" Heron asked, leaning into the table until their sleeve dipped into the salad bowl and Wren had to yank it backward.

"Yes," I said, trying to sound happy, but it came out more like a defensive growl.

The table erupted into utter chaos, everyone talking over each other. Even Lark and Logan started shouting over the Zoom call, waving dramatically to get my attention. Hawk and Hannah had managed to disentangle themselves and were barking a chorus of "Who? When? How?" at me.

"It's Frankie," I blurted out before I could take it back. I panicked and picked the first person I could think of, and she seemed to be bouncing around my mind a lot lately.

Shit.

Crane slapped the table so loud, all the silverware clattered. "I knew it!" He pointed at Heron. "You owe me twenty bucks!"

"Frankie?" Dove asked incredulously. "As in the chef, Frankie? I didn't know she was gay?"

"She's bi," Wren cut in.

Dove and I gaped at our unassuming little sister. "And *how* do you know that?"

Wren answered without looking up from the embroidery hoop she concealed in her lap. "Gaydar," she murmured. "And she told me when she saw my sapphic flag pin on my jacket."

"Aha," Crane said, holding up a victorious finger.

Frankie was bi? She hadn't told me that. I didn't know how she could've casually dropped that into conversation, but for some reason, I wished I'd known. Unless I was incredibly mistaken, she *had* seemed to really enjoy that kiss we'd shared so . . . that tracked, but still, that information made my whole brain light up like a Las Vegas casino.

"I wanted to wait to tell you until we'd been going out for a little while," I continued, digging that hole even deeper for myself. "Especially since it's complicated with her working here. We just wanted to keep it low-key for now."

Mom removed her reading glasses and rubbed her eyes. "You *had* to pick an employee to finally have a relationship with?" I opened my mouth to speak, but she held up a hand. "No, no, I'm excited for you both, don't get me wrong. Frankie is really lovely. I like her a lot."

"She's funny and nice *and* great at cooking," Heron said, dropping their chin into their hand. "You're shooting way above your pay grade, sis."

Boy, did I know it. Especially considering that the person I was "dating" didn't even know yet. *Crap*. How was I going to ask her? This wasn't like a "give me a ride to the airport" kind of favor. What was I supposed to say? *Hey, for the rest of the summer, can you pretend to be my girlfriend all day, every day so my family leaves me alone?* Yikes, she'd probably quit on the spot. I was well and truly fucked.

"If you two break up, I'm team Frankie by the way," Crane proclaimed, placing his chameleon, Stella, on his shoulder.

"Thanks, bro," I muttered. "So much for Lachlan family loyalty."

Heron pointed at me. "Just don't break her heart."

My eye started twitching. "Why do you assume it would be *me* doing the heart breaking?" The twins raised their eyebrows at me in mirror to each other and gave me a judgmental once-over. "Fair point." I scrubbed a hand down my face. "Look, this is all very new, and I'd appreciate it if you all could butt out and let me enjoy my relationship without your input."

Hawk shook his head at me. "Did I just have a stroke, or did Finch say the word *relationship*?"

I glared at my older brother. "E tu Brute?"

I'd really done it now. Why couldn't I make up a fake online girlfriend who lived in Canada like a normal person? I needed to find Frankie immediately and tell her about this ruse before all my lies caught up to me.

Daily Specials

kookaburra cucumber
sandwiches
$5.50

Macaw Macarons
6 for $12

Chapter Ten

Frankie

When I turned the corner from the Salty Dog, I stopped so suddenly that gravel flew out from under my feet. I managed to windmill my arms and catch my balance on a picket fence before the reason for my abrupt stop spotted me.

"Mother fucker." I glared to the sky. "Why do you hate me?" I groaned at the clouds.

Strolling arm in arm down the sidewalk ahead of me were Jake and Olivia. You'd think moving to a small island off the coast of Connecticut would grant me a reprieve from running into my ex, but no! Why did the universe want to ruin my life?

Olivia spotted me first. "Oh, hey! Frankie!" She gave me a warm wave, too naive to realize we shouldn't be so freaking pleasant to each other. She was the other woman. We should hate each other.

I smiled at her through tightly clenched teeth. *Keep smiling, bitch*, I thought.

"Frankie." Jake had the appropriate level of discomfort in his voice at least. "I didn't know you'd be here."

"I didn't know you'd be here either," I said with an awkward laugh. I should've put on makeup. I should've worn that bra that pushed my boobs up to my chin. I should be wearing a revenge dress. *Someone call Shonda Rhimes because I need a glow-up immediately.*

"What brings you two to Prickle Island?" I asked coyly. *Stay calm, stay calm, stay calm.*

"We're staying at our friend's beach house," Jake said, tipping his perfectly gelled head to the right.

"My dad is good friends with the Waltmans," Olivia offered, as if I should know what that meant.

I deserved an Oscar for the way my smile didn't waver. Not a freaking inch. Great. Not only was Olivia stunning, with boobs so perky I bet those nipples looked you straight in the eye without a bra on, but also, she was rich. Well, that certainly would seal the deal for good ol' Jake.

"Oh, wonderful," I cheered as if I knew who the fuck the Waltmans were.

"And you?" Jake asked, looking around like he might find the answer behind me. "Why are you on Prickle Island?"

"I'm the new head chef at the zoo." Jake's eyebrows raised in surprise, and I kept going, just making the situation even worse for myself with my lies. But I *needed* to win this breakup, so help me God. "That's how Finch and I met. She's the zoo veterinarian."

"Omg, that's so sweet!" Olivia cheered as Jake's frown deepened. I really enjoyed how much he hated the mention of Finch.

"I'm sure we could get you two a behind the scenes tour to

meet the animals sometime," I suggested. "Zoo dates are really romantic."

What a weird fucking flex. What the hell was I talking about? How many muffins would I have to bribe the twins with for overpromising animal encounters to my ex and his new fiancée?

Olivia's pink sundress swished as she bounced with excitement. "Oh, that would be so awesome!"

I really wanted to suggest that Jake could buy Olivia a balloon and take her to get her face painted along with the other parents, but I bit my tongue. I wanted him to rue the day he left me, but this wasn't Olivia's fault. My mind flew back to my mission to make Jake jealous that I'd been dreaming up since that run-in at the restaurant. This was a good start— dating a hot veterinarian.

"A zoo chef can't be all that interesting," Jake said in that needling way he always did. "Burgers and fries, I'm guessing?"

I shot him a hateful look as my smile widened. "Oh no, it's awesome. I have both a café and a restaurant that I oversee and carte blanche to play with the menus. *Plus*, I'm doing catering for special events. Even one for Ethel Holloway herself." Recognition lit up Olivia's face. Everyone knew the Holloways. They were right under the Vanderbilts of old-money families. "We have an annual gala coming up in July that I'm catering for. You should ask the Waltmans if they can get you tickets."

Ooh, did I like the way Jake's frown lines deepened at that jab. He was jealous all right, and it made me delighted.

"That sounds amazing!" Olivia said, clueless to the verbal sparring match that was currently taking place.

"We'll have to check our schedules," Jake countered. "We'll probably be back in New York by then."

I shrugged as if it didn't matter one whit to me. This breezy Frankie act was fun, even if my heart was punching through my chest. But if I was going to get revenge on this asshole, I needed to play dirty.

"Oh!" Olivia exclaimed as if just remembering. She jittered with excitement as she spoke like a manic Chihuahua. "My dad is having a yacht party next Friday. You and Finch should come!"

My mind quickly grabbed for an excuse, but Jake beat me to it.

"That would be way past Frankie's bedtime," he said to his fiancée. "She's always in bed by eight."

It had been a point of contention between us. Jake wanted to go out, and I was much happier at home in sweatpants with a good book. Especially since I had to wake up so early and he didn't. But that had never seemed like a good enough reason for him.

"It works out great with Finch," I said pointedly. "Since she has to get up early for her job too. You know, since she's a doctor."

"Veterinarian," Jake corrected.

I shrugged. "The only difference is doctors only know how to treat one species and she knows how to treat hundreds."

Olivia snort laughed at that. Damn, she was cute. I almost couldn't hate her for stealing my man. She'd have to forgive me, though, when I stomped all over his heart for what he did to me though. Maybe she'd realize he was a walking red flag and save herself too.

"And we'd love to come to the party," I added to Olivia, turning a carefree smile back to Jake. "We're still in the honeymoon phase so we're always looking for a fun, new adventure. Thanks for the invite."

"No problem," he gritted out even though he wasn't the one to offer.

"Anyway, I should get going. I'm making Finch salmon risotto," I said, name-dropping Jake's favorite meal. I swore I saw a flash of puppy eyes on his face before he schooled his expression. "I'll see you two at the party! Text me the details, Jake should still have my number."

I debated for a second if I should do it and then decided fuck it, since we're being brave. I shot forward and gave Olivia a big hug. She squeezed me back with a surprised giggle. Then I turned to Jake and hugged him, my breasts and hips pressing into him in the sort of hug I knew would turn him on. His arm circled my waist, landing low on the small of my back, mere inches from acceptable, and I knew he wanted to drop his fingers lower and squeeze. I pulled back, flashing a megawatt smile at that confused look on his face, waving and sweeping my long blonde hair over my shoulder before sauntering off with an extra swish to my hips.

God, I hoped he was watching this expert hip swish.

I felt on top of the world. I was going to come out victorious and Jake would be a sniveling, jealous puddle when I was done with him. But then I turned the corner and remembered one minor flaw in my perfect plan: I needed to convince Finch to pretend to be my girlfriend . . . again.

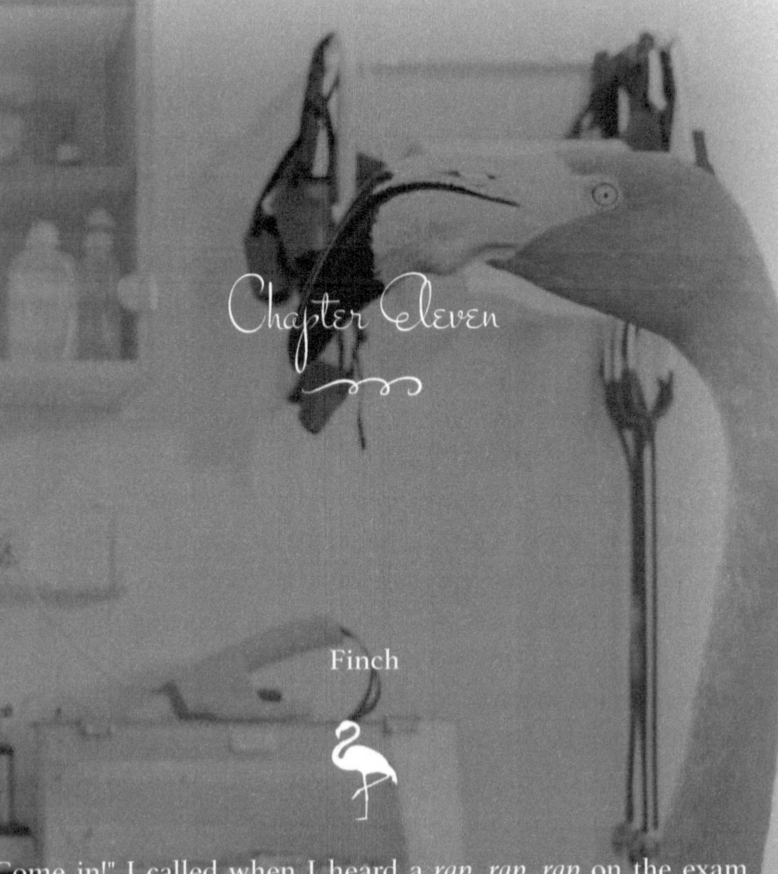

Chapter Eleven

Finch

"Come in!" I called when I heard a *rap, rap, rap* on the exam room door.

I lifted my head to see Frankie peek her head in, her long ponytail falling over her shoulder as she looked into the room and spied my patient: a flamingo with an injured foot.

"Hey!" she said a little too cheerily, and I knew she was putting on the voice.

"Hey," I called back, snipping the sticky bandage around the flamingo's foot. I'd give it less than 24 hours before he managed to work it off and I'd have to replace it.

I was going to find Frankie before my family had a chance to interrogate her about our supposed relationship. But then I'd gotten a radio call from Heron saying there was a flamingo with his foot stuck in the zebra's watering trough. *How*, I had no idea, but the bird was successfully rescued from his blundering ways, and after an X-ray concluded there was no break, all that was left to do was wrap up his foot to protect the three stitches. Then I was planning on going straight to the café to find Frankie before one of my siblings spilled the beans.

"Just the person I was looking for," I said, grateful Frankie had summoned herself to my office instead of having to hunt her down. "What's up?"

"Can I, uh, talk to you for a sec? I need to ask you for a favor."

"Small world," I murmured more to myself than her. I needed a favor too. "Yeah, come on in. He won't bite. Flamingos have pretty flimsy bite pressure anyway, even if he did." I tilted my head to beckon her in. "Here," I said, directing the flamingo's feathered body toward her. "Hold this."

Frankie's eyes flared as she knelt beside me, careful to fold her shin-length linen skirt under her knees. "This?" she squeaked but she took the bird's body, gently holding his wings in place.

"Ron, meet Frankie. Frankie, meet Ron," I said.

"You named your flamingo Ron?"

"Technically, his full name is Ronald Ulysses Swanson," I said. "Dove named him."

"Oh, so this is who that emergency radio call was about?" she asked, looking up at Ron's long neck.

"Yeah, not my favorite way to start the day, but such is the life of a zoo vet."

"I'll bet," she said, chuckling as Ron started chittering his beak, making little clicking sounds up Frankie's arm like he was trying to groom her. He was such a love bug, even more of a Casanova than I was.

"That means he likes you," I assured Frankie as I got the last layer of tape out to finish bandaging his wounded webbed foot.

"Oh good. I really couldn't handle any more rejection right

now," she joked and then grimaced. "Speaking of, you'll never guess who I just bumped into at the shops."

"No!" I cursed, almost dropping my scissors. "Sgt. Douchebag?"

She gritted her teeth, seemingly unhappy about her ex's new nickname, but if the shoe fit. "Yep," she said, popping her P. "I pretended we were still together. I hope that's okay?"

"Perfect actually—"

"Good because they invited us to a yacht party next Friday and I need you to come with me and pretend to be my girl-friend?" She took a deep, gasping breath after the confession flew out of her. Her brows pinched together, her face going pale, as if she were afraid I was going to say no. "Please, please. I really, really need this. I'll find a way to make it up to you. Anything you want."

Ron chose that opportune moment to slip his beak into the neckline of Frankie's blouse and extend his long neck all the way down her shirt.

"Whoa!" Frankie yelped.

I shot forward. "Ronald!" I scolded the bird, dipping my hands into Frankie's shirt without thinking and fishing around for the flamingo's beak.

It wasn't until my fingers grazed across Frankie's breasts that I realized I was digging around her shirt and touching all over her smooth, warm skin.

"Sorry!" I bit out, finally grabbing Ron by the beak and feeding his long neck back out the top of her shirt.

Frankie's cheeks were flushed a gorgeous pink that matched the shade of the bird in front of her.

"I'll forgive you if you promise to come to the yacht party with me?" she asked hopefully, determined despite her nerves.

"Very subtle." I rolled my eyes. "Agreed, on one condition."

"Anything."

The way she said it, all breathy and eager, made me clench my jaw, pushing down on the heat rising in my gut.

Anything. She'd give me anything, and fuck if I couldn't think of quite a few things I'd like her to do for me. God, I needed to get laid. It had been nearly four weeks, which in my world was practically a dry spell. After the night I'd kissed her . . . Nope, I wasn't going to read too much into that, especially after I'd just inadvertently touched her boobs.

"My family has been all up my grill about my dating life," I confessed, releasing Ron to let him wander around the room. He immediately tried to attack his bandage, but it would take him a while. "I guess you might say I've developed a reputation."

"Even *I* have heard about this reputation in my time here," Frankie teased.

"You've been talking to my siblings, haven't you?" I didn't know why, but I didn't like the idea of Frankie knowing about my playboy lifestyle. "What have you heard?"

"That you've slept with every woman over 21 on this island apart from your family, Aya, and Kirby."

"I'm guessing Kirby told you that." I should get Frankie out of the Salty Dog before they tell her any more misguided stories from my life. Having her stay with those two gossips was a mistake.

"Yep." Her ponytail swished as she laughed. "I'm a little offended you haven't tried to hit on me yet."

"I literally grabbed you by the back of the neck and kissed you a few weeks ago," I deadpanned.

"Only after I asked you to pretend to be my girlfriend in the bar," she replied.

"Yeah, well." My words faded off. She had a point. Normally, pursuing a stunning woman like Frankie would be right up my alley. "I don't normally chase after the recently heartbroken," I said, even though that wasn't even remotely true. Everyone had been fair game to me before. Sex was great for getting over a breakup. I was the perfect revenge lay in the sapphic world. It was honestly a public service for all those heartbroken lesbians.

"Okay," Frankie said, and I swore she sounded a little disappointed.

"Did you *want* me to be hitting on you?" I asked skeptically. When her flush deepened, I laughed and leaned in. "Maybe just a little?"

"Just wanted to be included," she joked breathily. "What was this favor you wanted to ask me?"

"Oh, right." I remembered and leaned back. "I need you to pretend we're seeing each other exclusively." I added hastily, "To my family at least."

"What?"

Now it was my turn to go red. My ears burned with embarrassment. "I *may* have told them at our last family dinner that we were dating to get them off my back about my sex life." When she just gaped at me, I continued, "You told the same lie! Don't look at me like that."

"My lie was a one-off—well, two-off—the bar and then this yacht party and then we're done. Your lie is something I'm going to have to pretend every single day for the entire summer!"

Ugh, she had a point. I really, really didn't want to tell my family we'd broken up already or worse—that it was all a lie. I'd never hear the end of it.

"You said Jake is staying on the island for the summer?"

"Yes," she said carefully.

"Then you're going to want us to pretend more than once too," I pointed out.

This was a mess. I was doing a really poor job of explaining it too. Normally, I was smooth as glass, but this made me feel like all rough edges. I knew how to do one-night stands, not relationships. This was all too complicated. "Look, this arrangement would be good for both of us. I get my family off my back for the summer, and in return you make your ex so jealous that he dumps that girl and comes crawling back to you, begging your forgiveness. Win-win."

"I do like the sound of Jake begging . . ." Frankie pursed her lips, considering. Finally, she sighed and shrugged. "Okay, I guess it's actually a smart idea," she lamented. "It lends credibility to the lie. But we need to be convincing." She pointed an accusatory finger at me.

I blew her a kiss. "You don't think I can be convincing, babe?" She blanched at the endearment. "See, it's *you* that needs to be convincing."

"We have to get our story straight, uh . . ." She looked all around the room. "When's your lunch break?"

"What?"

"Your lunch break? I'll bring up sandwiches and we can hash out all the details."

"Um, yes to sandwiches—always—but what details?"

"How we met, our first kiss, our goals, our hobbies, all that stuff. We need to act like we know each other if this is going to convince anyone."

"No, yeah, that's a good point," I said. "Okay, 12 o'clock. Meet in my office and we'll figure out all the smoke and mirrors."

"Okay." She sounded so relieved. "This is going to be the best fake relationship ever." She said it like she was trying to convince herself.

As she stood, Ron waddled over and started grooming up her legs again. But this time, when his head dipped under Frankie's mid-length skirt, I held my hands up like I had a gun pointing at me.

"You're on your own," I said as Frankie shot me a look. "Unless." I took a teasing step closer. "You want me to help?"

"Don't you dare!" She laughed as she moved Ron's long neck

out from under her skirt, flashing a long strip of creamy, soft thigh as she did.

I swallowed the lump in my throat at the sight, thinking of how good it would feel to trail my lips up that stretch of skin. My stomach dropped. What was I getting myself into?

Daily Specials
kookaburra cucumber
sandwiches
$5.50
Macaw Macarons
6 for $12

Chapter Twelve

Frankie

The way Finch moaned as she bit into the sandwich made my mouth go dry. I swallowed thickly, watching her enjoy the lunch I'd made for us. We sat in squeaky old office chairs. Her desk was mounded in papers and files, not a single inch of bare desktop to set the food, so we just ate over napkins on our laps.

"So . . . ," I said, trying to recover from her audible enjoyment. "You like the food I take it?"

"You are an absolute goddess," Finch said through another giant mouthful, and I chuckled. "Seriously, forget the wild animals, people will be taking the ferry over just for these sandwiches. What is this pesto stuff?"

"Homemade," I said with a grin. "Naturally."

Finch looked up from her food orgasm and grinned at me. "Look at you, all confident. I like it."

I smiled back, sitting a little straighter. It was the one thing I felt certain about. Cooking was the one time I had control in this chaotic life of mine. I knew I made good food that people enjoyed, and I was proud of it.

"Feeding people is the best job in the world," I said. But I particularly appreciated it when ridiculously attractive people enjoyed it. "Probably not as important as saving animals' lives, but it makes me feel like I have some value."

Finch stopped chewing. "You have inherent value. Always." She pinned me with a look. "We're going to unpack that comment later, Goldilocks."

"See, you sound like my girlfriend already," I teased.

"One day, we need to do this properly," Finch said, tucking back into her sandwich like she was making out with it.

"Do what?"

"Have a proper picnic on the beach instead of in my cluttered office," she said, looking around the space that was one step away from being an episode of *Hoarders*. "Especially now that you and I are pretending to be together. My mom would die if she heard I went on a beach date with you."

"I'd like that," I said, taking a nibble of sandwich to give my hands something to do. "Not your mom dying," I amended quickly, "the beach date part."

Finch laughed through her mouthful of food. "I assumed."

I tried to steer the conversation back on course. "When are your days off?"

Finch's laugh was so loud that food sprayed out of her mouth, and she hastily blotted it up off her desk. "Sorry. I don't just work with animals. I am one," she quipped. "The wombats have more table manners than me."

I chuckled. "I didn't realize asking about your days off was such a funny topic."

"I don't really take days off," Finch admitted. "I mean, technically I do. Legally, I do," she said, pointing two fingers at me as if I were a spy. I held up my hands in defense. "But I almost always have some patients that need checking on. There's always more to be done."

"Sounds like you need a break."

"Probably," she confessed. "Maybe taking one won't be so hard now that I've got a girlfriend who needs my attention."

When she winked at me, I immediately broke our gaze, rattled like a schoolgirl as I stabbed at my fruit salad with a fork. What in the world was wrong with me? I'd met really attractive men before, but they'd never put me so off kilter. There was just something about women . . .

"So how did we meet?" I asked, wishing I could subtly turn on the overhead fan.

"We met at a restaurant in town," Finch said. "I feel like the more truth we have in there, the easier it'll be."

"Okay," I agreed. "I sat beside you at the bar and was immediately taken by you."

"Ah, I believe it was *I* who was taken with *you*," she cut in.

"It was a mutual taking," I amended.

"And I knew from the moment I met you, you weren't just another hookup." Finch licked her lips and took another bite. "You were special."

"Are you talking to me or the sandwich?"

"Both," Finch said, and we both laughed. "I knew I wasn't letting you go. A gorgeous woman who makes the world's best cinnamon rolls and doesn't judge me for being a workaholic or when I spit-laugh and keep my office dirtier than a pig sty. Whatever could you possibly see in me?"

"Besides the fact that you're the most handsome woman I've ever met?" I asked before I could stop myself. Finch grinned. "And a doctor. Caring for wounded baby animals is surely the world's best panty dropper."

"I can confirm," Finch said, licking pesto from her thumb.

"And then we found out we were working together," I continued.

"But it was too late," Finch countered. "You'd already ensnared my heart."

"Perfect." I gave a nod.

"This is going to be great," Finch said with a winning smile. "Jake is going to be so jealous, he will regret all his life choices in no time."

My smile faltered even as I said, "Good."

For a split second, I'd forgotten about Jake, caught up in this daydream of us being each other's dream girls.

Finch's radio beeped and she leaned across her stacks of papers, turning the dial up. "Was that for me?"

"Yeah, where are you?" Heron asked. I was getting better at identifying all of the zoo staff from their voices alone. They all had radio names too, but that was a lot to keep track of.

"Having lunch in my office with Frankie, why?"

"Oooh," Crane interrupted, making kissing sounds. "Make sure to turn your radios off before you start banging, okay?"

Hannah immediately jumped on. "Too soon."

Finch guffawed. "What do you want, Heron?"

Heron let out a long sigh, which I'd already learned meant more work for Finch was about to be relayed to her. "Jailbreak has managed to tear down one of the flags from the savannah seating area and has it stuck in his mouth."

"Jailbreak?" I mouthed to Finch.

"Zebra," she replied.

"Of course."

"Could you come give me a hand? He's probably fine, but worth a check. I'm recalling the herd now," Heron said.

Finch sighed down at the food in front of her, looking like a kid whose ice cream just got knocked out of their hand. Still, she said, "Yeah. On my way."

"Anything I can help with?" I offered.

"You're already doing me a giant favor, Goldilocks. That's more than enough." Finch shoved the rest of her sandwich into her cheeks until they were puffed out like a squirrel. She said something mostly unintelligible, but judging by the way she hooked her finger at the door, I guessed it was "got to go."

I blinked at the radio. "You're going to have to tell me what that whole turn your radio off before banging thing is about."

Finch's cheeks dimpled and she swallowed a hunk of sandwich like a snake swallowing its prey whole.

"Oh, it's a good one," she said with a wink. "I'll walk you home tonight and tell you."

"You'll walk me home?"

"You're my girlfriend," she reminded me. "And Kirby owes me a drink and you happen to live above her bar. Meet you back here at 5?"

I barely had time to nod before Finch was racing out the door, leaving me a flustered mess in her wake.

Daily Specials
kookaburra cucumber
sandwiches
$5.50
Macaw Macarons
6 for $12

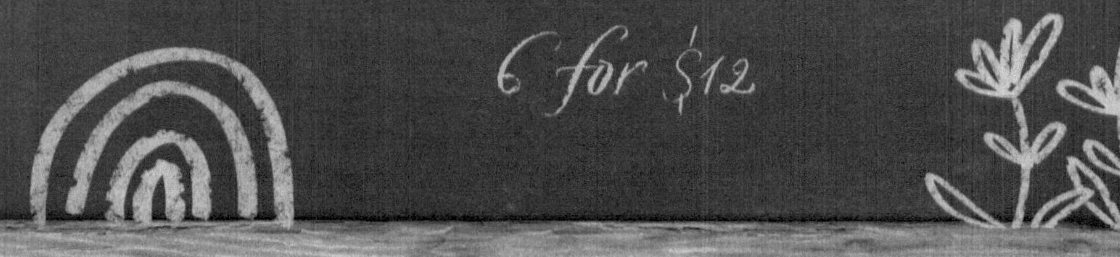

Chapter Thirteen

Frankie

I wandered the quiet paths after closing hours, needing some time to cool off after the full-on adrenaline of the day. The zoo had been teeming with visitors flocking to the island for the first weeks of summer break. Cabinet food had been demolished, the soft serve machine had broken, and there'd been a long line out the door of the restaurant that wound around the aviaries. At least those waiting had the comedic stylings of our two rowdy cockatoos to keep them entertained.

With an outstretched hand, I trailed my fingers through the tall grasses that lined the lion viewing platform. I needed to rethink the menu. We needed more food that could be turned over quickly to keep the lines down. Luckily, the cooks and waitstaff working at the Peckish Peacock were truly rockstars who managed to keep up with my frantic demands.

My brain was still whirling, trying to come up with a game plan for the next day. I wasn't ready to return to the Salty Dog and the boisterous sound. Even with the earplugs Finch had graciously donated to me, it was like I could feel the presence of so many people around me. I didn't know how Aya slept through all of it . . . probably with a lot of practice.

I headed in the direction of the savannah. It was always a calming place at the far end of the zoo. The giraffes lazily roamed their paddock, grazing the last of the leaves hanging from their feeders.

I passed the playground and the Jeep with the adorable "Hawk and Hannah" bumper sticker. They had the sweetest love story. Hannah had been more than happy to regale me with it while I'd been rolling out the dough for the miniature pizzas this morning. When I'd asked how she and Hawk had met, she'd been practically vibrating with eagerness to tell me.

A thought hit me all at once: I'd never leapt with excitement to tell someone the story of how Jake and I'd met. Had we really been so doomed from the start? Or was Hannah's love just exceptional? Jake's reticence to marry me should've been a giant red flag, but he'd said he wanted to save up first and his reasons had been understandable and . . . it was only now in retrospect that I saw it all so clearly.

Maybe I had been unconsciously dragging my feet too. Maybe I'd found justification in his poor reasoning because I hadn't been sure either. It was just what people did. They paired off. They got married. That kind of sparkly, incandescent love was a fairy tale. Or maybe that kind of love was real. Maybe it just wasn't meant for all of us.

The sound of a clicking fence jarred me from my thoughts.

I turned to find a zebra standing between the fence of his enclosure and the visitor lookout railing.

It took me a second to comprehend what I was seeing. "*How did you manage to get in there?*"

I wandered over to him, trying to spy a break in his enclosure fence but unable to spot one.

"What did you do, Houdini?" I asked as the zebra reached his head over the fence and opened his lips out like I was a keeper with a bushy branch of food.

"Uh . . ." I turned around, looking for the escape route, and finally spied a missing post from the enclosure that a cheeky little zebra might be able to squeak through. At least the visitor railing ringing the savannah was enough to keep him contained.

"This way," I said, beckoning the zebra back with my hand. "This is the way home."

He didn't seem the slightest bit interested in following me. Still, he reached over the fence like I might feed him, and I wondered if he was responding to the fruit embroidered on my apron.

"Is this what you're looking at?" I took the apron off and held it higher, and the zebra's head followed. "Aha!" I moved the apron along the fence line, clicking my tongue. "Come on then, let's go."

To my great relief, he began to follow, trotting along with the promise of a fruity treat. But, because I couldn't have nice things, he zoomed forward a little too fast and snatched the apron from my grip.

"Shit!" I lurched forward, reaching for it as he shook the fabric side to side. "Shit! Shit! Shit!"

Oh god, why did I think this was a good idea? Now everyone would see *my* apron in the savannah enclosure and then I'd need to explain to my new boss why I didn't just call a keeper for help. Here I was, thinking I could be so slick, but what if something happened to the zebra? What if he choked on my apron and I accidentally ended up killing him? What would Finch say?

Fuck, I was going to have to tell Finch and then she'd hate

me and want to stop fake dating me and then I'd be publicly shamed by Jake and my life would fall apart even more than it already had . . .

"No," I shouted, scolding my own panicking thoughts. "Give that apron back to me, you stripey bastard!"

I climbed up on the log beside the fence and leaned my whole upper half over, reaching, reaching, yes!

With the very tips of my fingers, I snagged the apron. Yanking it forcefully from the giddy zebra's mouth, I tossed it back over the fence, but when I tried to climb back down, the belt loop of my jeans hooked over the back of the fencepost. I was jerked upwards, my jeans giving me an instant wedgie. I scrambled to climb back up but the log beneath my foot broke, and then I was just dangling from the impressively fucking sturdy loop of my jeans.

"Fuck!"

I flailed, looking like a small-town production of *Peter Pan* flapping about on a wire. What if I was stuck here all night? I reached for my phone in my back pocket and then was faced with the impossible question of: Who the fuck do I call? Who would be the least embarrassing person to discover me like this? No one. No one could see this. I'd never live it down.

I let out a growl of frustration. Aya maybe? I figured I'd face the least amount of ridicule from her, but it would still be mortifying.

"Need some help there, Goldilocks?" a smug voice called from behind me.

No! Fuck my life. I immediately knew who it was—the voice of the person I least wanted to witness this humiliating display.

This situation had dramatically swung from bad to worse. Maybe if I didn't move, she'd think I'd died and just leave me impaled on the zebra fence like a wedgie-touting scarecrow.

"I'm fine," I gritted out, arms still flailing as I hung by my ass crack.

"You look fine," Finch said, and I already knew that self-satisfied look would be on her face. "You normally wear your jeans so far up your ass you can taste the denim?"

My hands immediately flew to cover my ass, and Finch chuckled.

"Here," she said, and before I could protest, I heard her hasty boots approaching. Her arms banded around the top of my thighs and she lifted me up, finally relieving my rope-burned nether region.

Holy shit, she was strong.

She lifted me like it was nothing, unhooking my belt loop and slowly lowering me to the ground. I turned in her grip and her hands stayed on my waist for a split second as she smiled down at me before she yanked her hands away like they were on fire.

"Thank you," I said sheepishly. "I promise I'm not trying to make a habit of needing rescuing."

"You were just giving me the opportunity to be gallant," Finch said with a wink. "So, were you trying to lure Jailbreak back to his enclosure with your apron? Foolproof plan."

"How long have you been watching me?"

Finch tipped her head up to the lamppost set in the middle of the lookout and I spied the camera mounted on it.

"Great," I muttered.

"I was passing through the prep kitchens and saw you on the monitor," she added with a chuckle. "It was even funnier without the sound. I was going to leave you to it, but then you got yourself stuck and I thought I shouldn't leave you here hanging by your pants all night."

"There's a hole in the fence line." I pointed behind me, hoping it would redirect the conversation away from my clumsiness.

"We know." Finch crossed her arms and grinned down at me.

"You know?"

"Why do you think we call him Jailbreak?" she asked.

"Because he's striped like an old-timey prison outfit?"

"Ah." She nodded. "That makes sense too. But no, he comes out here and grazes in the afternoons."

"And you just let him?"

She shrugged. "Saves us from having to mow." We both laughed at that. "He only does it after hours and he's a friendly old man regardless. Besides, who would be foolish enough to climb over a railing to get to him?"

"Yep," I said, my blush burning across my cheeks. "What kind of crazy person would do that?"

Finch's smile widened. "You ready to walk home?"

I swept my hair off my sweat-beaded face. "You don't have to—"

"You better get used to this, Goldilocks," Finch said. "We're being watched now." We both looked back up to the security camera above us. "It's time to put on a show."

"I know, but we can put on a show during work hours. You really don't need to—"

"Let me walk you home," Finch pushed. "It's good for me to get beyond the fence line every once in a while. Who doesn't like an evening stroll along the ocean? Besides,"—she leaned in, her breath smelling of cinnamon-spiced coffee—"the company's not so bad either."

"Okay," I said, unable to hide my smile, feeling ridiculously giddy at this preposterous arrangement we'd made. "I like the company too."

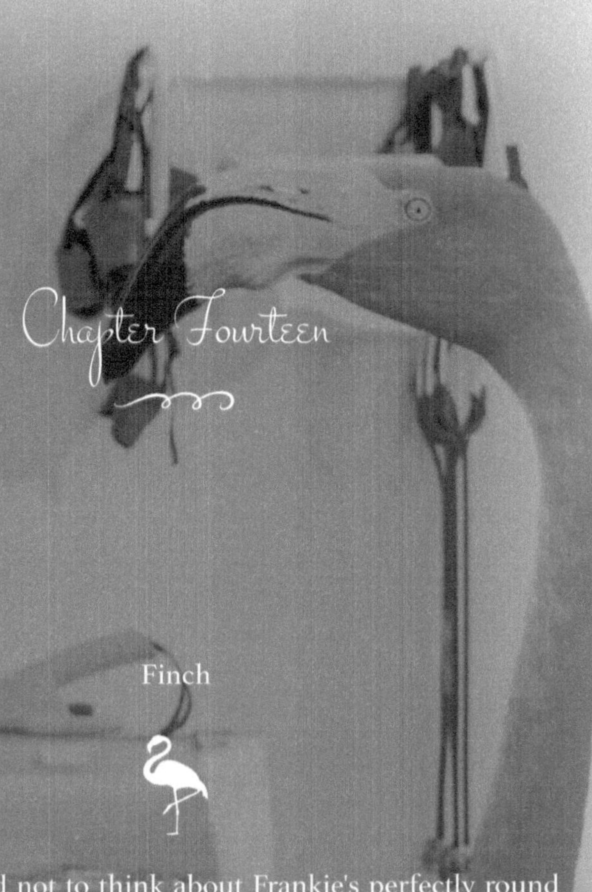

Chapter Fourteen

Finch

I was determined not to think about Frankie's perfectly round ass all day, nor her thick thighs that I would blissfully love to swallow me whole as I buried my face between them.

Fuck. I *really* needed to get laid.

The last thing my fake girlfriend needed was me wanting to sleep with her.

Frankie wasn't what I should have on my mind. Especially not as I weighed Cranky Frankie aka Francesca aka Chessie B aka Benny Benedetti—I was still workshopping the nicknames.

The pink, little macaw chick made a groaning sound that would one day hopefully turn into a proper squawk. I stared at the chick's weight with a frown. She hadn't gained anything. Not even 0.001 ounces. She should be practically doubling in size every day at this stage in her development. Her eyes should be opening soon, and her feather sheaths should start emerging, making her look like an ugly, little porcupine. The ugly porcupine phase was my favorite. The chicks' personalities really started to shine through and they turned into little escape artists. They were the cheekiest of all the animals that came into the wildlife hospital, but I kind of loved that about them too.

Maybe this little one would never make it to that spiky feather phase. I hated to even think it. But these first few weeks were the most precarious. I planned to change up her diet, sometimes that helped, but not gaining any weight was undeniably bad, and all of my vet Spidey-Senses started tingling.

But despite my struggling patient, my mind was still turning over the walk home with Frankie. I couldn't stop thinking about every moment we'd spent together. Something about her was intoxicating.

Even as I went about syringing up the chick's formula, a smile was still plastered on my face. It would probably be inappropriate to request a copy of that camera footage of her dangling from the fence, wouldn't it? I had definitely not just watched it to stare at Frankie's ass. I had been keeping an eye on the situation for safety purposes. *Yeah, right.*

For some reason, I wanted to replay the way she looked up at me too. I was probably misreading her expression, projecting onto her what I wanted to see. But I loved the way she craned her neck up, and then those deep blue eyes met mine. Dammit, I knew I was veering into an unhealthy fixation with her. This was what happened to my brain when I abstained from sex apparently.

If I'd actually cared about Frankie's zebra predicament, I should've radioed Heron to go help her. They had been already working up at the giraffes and were closer. But I didn't radio anyone. Not just because I'd known Frankie would be embarrassed, but also because I'd wanted to be the one to lift her up and feel her soft body pressed against mine and have an excuse to breathe in her intoxicating bakery scent like powdered sugar and honey. I bet I could taste it all over her skin . . .

Fuck me, I must be ovulating or something because my hormones were being ridiculous. Luckily, I had a trunk full of sex toys upstairs that would help me fix that. My mind instantly conjured the image of Frankie in my bed while I took her with my strap.

Jesus.

This was bad. This was really, really bad.

"Listen to me," I said to Benny.

I pointed at the little pink blob, who flapped her tiny wings, eager for her next feed. I liked the flapping. It meant she still had some vigor at least, despite her lack of weight gain. "You are going to metabolize all of this and not just shit everything out, and you're going to get big and plump and strong, and I'm going to build you the coolest little aviary, you got that?"

Cranky just flapped at me, ignoring my pep talk.

"I will not have all these sleepless nights be in vain, Francesca," I said as I touched her tiny beak, and she started bobbing up and down for food. "So help me God, you will thrive, you tiny pink cockblocker."

"Well, it'll be easy to find your truck in the lineup of limos and BMWs," Kirby taunted as she walked out from the front entrance of the Salty Dog.

I stepped out of the truck and leaned against the door. Kirby let out a whistle as she took in my navy-blue suit and pressed white shirt unbuttoned down to mid-chest. Her eyes trailed down to my feet.

"Loafers? Seriously?"

"It's a yacht party," I said with a shrug. "They were a gift from the Westworths last Christmas and I've never had a reason to wear them."

"Well, you look good." Kirby gave an approving nod.

"Any sightings of my date?"

"She'll be down in a minute." Kirby crossed her arms and narrowed her eyes at me like she always did when she was trying to sniff out one of my lies.

"Is there anything I can help you with, Detective Amadou?"

Kirby rolled her eyes. "I'm just trying to figure out what games you're playing with my new friend."

"Games?" I scoffed. "Is taking a pretty girl to a party a game?"

"It is if you don't have real feelings for her," she countered. "When Frankie told me that the two of you were *dating,* I had to seriously consider if I knew any other lesbians named Goldfinch."

"Kirby."

"Don't Kirby me, Goldfinch Lachlan," she said, pointing an accusatory finger at me. "I've known you your entire life. You've never wanted a real relationship. How convenient that you suddenly want one when your mother has turned her sights on you, hm?" I forced myself to maintain eye contact. I knew looking away would reveal too much. "How fortuitous that you found a co-worker who is desperately seeking revenge on her ex at the exact same time."

"You think I'm using her?" I growled, offended. Maybe I was, but Frankie was fully aware of it. Besides, she was using me too. It was a mutually beneficial arrangement. "Can't two friends help each other out?"

"So you're friends now?" Kirby cocked her head and my gut plummeted. She had a unique ability to catch me in my lies. "I thought you two were dating?"

"You are the last person I expected this inquisition from." I folded my arms in mirror to her and glared at her. "You've never had anything to say about every other girl I've dated."

"That's because you've never dated. Every other girl has been a casual fling," she shot back. "And I know Frankie and I like her and she's in a very vulnerable place right now. I know how you get women twisted in knots. Hell, I've poured many a free drink for all the one-night stands you ghosted."

"I'm not taking advantage of her," I gritted out. "Nice to see where your loyalties lie. You've known Frankie all of one month, and yet you've never been this protective over me."

"Because you don't need protecting," Kirby said. "Look, I don't want either of you to hurt the other. And don't think for a second I haven't had this exact same conversation with Frankie either."

I straightened at that. "What did she say?"

"She said she's aware that you haven't done long-term relationships in the past, but this is still new and she's willing to see where it goes anyway." Kirby seemed less than enthused about that response.

I gave her a smug look, impressed Frankie didn't crack under Kirby's relentless scrutiny. "Well, I am willing to see where this goes as well," I said, puffing up my chest.

Kirby threw her hands up and looked up to the cloudless summer sky. "It's like watching a slow-motion train wreck but fine." She waved to me. "I will save a few extra bottles of whisky for you. I have a feeling you're going to need them by the end of the summer."

"Love you too, Kirby," I said with a mock kiss.

The screen door to the Salty Dog opened and out stepped Frankie in a teal summer dress that made her eyes sparkle like sapphires. Her hair was elegantly pulled half-back with curls cascading over her shoulders. I studied her from her espadrilles to the sparkly teardrop earrings to her shiny, painted pink lips. She was like a nymph of summer, sweet, smiling, voluptuous, and it made my insides melt like candle wax.

I roughly shoved my hands into my trouser pockets to keep from reaching out to her as she approached my truck. "You clean up nice, Goldilocks," I said.

"You do too," she echoed, her eyes lingering on the unbuttoned collar of my shirt, studying the tattoos that crawled across my skin. I wished I could bottle up that look. She studied me with hungry, appreciative eyes, but there was more than just heat in her gaze, unlike most of my conquests. She looked at me with some kind of admiration too, one that made me want to stand a little straighter.

I pushed off the truck door and opened the passenger side for her, giving one final wave to Kirby, who stood scowling in the doorway.

"You didn't think I'd show up in scrubs, did you?" I asked with a laugh.

I went around to the driver's side and climbed in.

"I didn't know what to expect," Frankie confessed. "Here." She passed me a little box from her purse. "A thank you for doing this for me."

"I don't need a gift . . ." My words died off as I opened the box to a little pocket square patterned in navy, white, and teal. It perfectly tied our two outfits together. "How did you know I would be wearing this?"

"I asked Dove. She texted me a photo of your suit."

"And that would explain why she wanted to "hang out" while I was getting ready. Very smooth that one."

Frankie shrugged. "I thought it would make us look more couple-y."

"It does. Ten points for the attention to detail, Goldilocks." I tucked the pocket square in my lapel pocket and grinned.

"So dapper," she said, adjusting the fabric with a smile, and I had to fight the urge to lean in and kiss her wrist, her flesh so close to my mouth. Never in my life had I felt so untethered, so desperate to run my lips across someone's skin.

"Well, I think this will make Jake suitably jealous," I said, turning the key. The engine rumbled to life.

"You think?"

"With you in that dress?" I gave her another appraising look. "He will curse the day he ever broke your heart."

"Especially with a hot date on my arm." She smiled ruefully at me. "You know, we're going to have to be more couple-y than we are at the zoo," she warned.

"I figured as much," I replied. "It's a party after all."

"I hope that's okay."

"Goldilocks, believe me, it's no hardship to pretend to fall head over heels for you," I said with a laugh. "Especially in that dress." I pulled out of the parking lot and turned onto the road to the north side of the island. "Now let's go make a whole yacht of rich assholes jealous."

Daily Specials
kookaburra cucumber
sandwiches
$5.50
Macaw Macarons
6 for $12

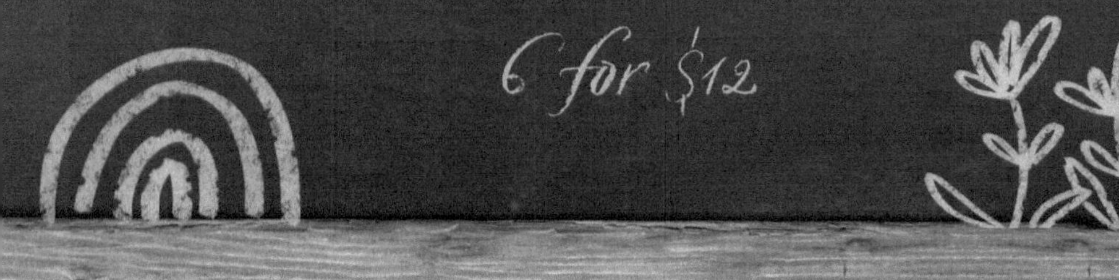

Chapter Fifteen

Frankie

I really had thought men looked attractive in suits until I saw Finch in one. *That* was how a suit was meant to be worn. Holy moly. Thank all the butch gods for this gift to all womankind. I was starting to wonder if these heart palpitations weren't from the nerves of seeing Jake and were due to the fact I'd have to pretend to be dating someone as ridiculously sexy as Finch Lachlan. I found myself not-so-subtly stealing glances at her the entire ride over to the docks.

The sun was still high in the sky, glinting off the water. Another glorious summer day on Prickle Island. We passed the tall hedgerows of island estates, gated gravel driveways to one side and rustic seawall to the other. The road grew quieter with fewer and fewer cars, and I imagined taking lazy Sunday drives around the shoreline with Finch, imagined what it would be like to live on an island and be able to do this whenever we wanted. The daydream was cut short when we hit the busy intersection to the marina, where it seemed half the island was invited to climb aboard one of the giant yachts moored there. This place looked like the Fort Knox of marinas: guard towers, barbed wire fences, security cameras everywhere.

When Finch parked the vet truck between two cars that probably cost more than most people's houses, she turned to me and asked, "Ready?"

Taking a deep breath, I said, "Not really, but let's go."

I reached for the car door. "Wait!" Finch interrupted, hustling to unbuckle her seat belt. "Let me get your door for you."

I followed her line of sight to the crowd waiting to be checked off the guest list and realized this cute gesture was because people might be watching. *Time to put on a show,* I reminded myself.

I let Finch open my door and took her hand to help me out of the truck. The crowd looked like they were all attending a black-tie event in gowns and tuxes, and I suddenly felt very underdressed. I thought the event would be more summery than glamorous. My footsteps faltered as we approached the line, but Finch's arm slid across my back and curved around my waist, pulling me into her as she kissed my temple. My brain short-circuited at the brush of her soft lips.

"Have I told you you look amazing yet?" she murmured into my ear, sending tingles down my neck. "Or was I just thinking that to myself the entire car ride over?"

"I feel underdressed," I whispered back.

"You are perfectly dressed," she corrected. "Trust me. I grew up around these people. The ones that are trying the hardest are the ones they look down upon the most. The real money doesn't even think about it. See that guy?" She pointed to a man who looked like he'd walked straight off the tennis courts, still in sneakers and a sweat-stained polo shirt. The line parted for him, and he walked straight past the bouncer checking the guest list like he was the King of England.

Finch's lips found the shell of my ear as she whispered, "You look like a modern Venus. To think any differently makes me wonder if you looked in a fun house mirror on the way out the door."

My blush burned my cheeks as I leaned into her. "Thank you," I whispered. "And you look—"

"Incredibly handsome?" she asked. "I know."

"So humble."

"I'm just demonstrating how to be confident," she said with a roguish smile. "I'm hoping I'll rub off on you."

I tried very hard not to snort giggle at that, liking the idea of her rubbing off on me . . . probably a little too much.

But then I heard Jake call my name. Finch folded me tighter to her side, as if in protection from a stampeding bear.

I turned to see Jake in his usual charcoal-gray suit that he wore to all his family's semiformal occasions. He wove through the line, his eyes hooked on me.

"They're with me, Tom," he called to the security guy checking the guest list, and the giant in dark sunglasses and an earpiece nodded to him, waving us through.

Was there actually royalty on the boat tonight? What was with all the security?

"Welcome to the *Seafarer's Wife*," Jake said as we skirted through the crowd and onto the ramp leading to the yacht.

"What a weird name for a boat," Finch whispered in my ear, and I chuckled.

"He acts like it's *his* yacht," I whispered back.

I bet Jake loved that, pretending he was this man, maybe even thinking he'd become him someday. Finch and I exchanged glances, and I had a feeling she was thinking the same thing.

"Thanks for inviting us," I said louder, trying to sound nonchalant.

"Impressive yacht," Finch added mildly as we boarded the gangplank.

I didn't know the first thing about yachts, but this thing was massive and packed with people. Waiters in black shirts and white bow ties milled through the crowd with trays of Champagne while a DJ was playing golden oldies at the front of the bow. Bow? Was that right? I had no idea. I didn't grow up by the ocean and all this nautical stuff was a mystery to me.

"Jake!" Olivia called, flagging him down from the second floor.

"Excuse me, ladies," Jake said with an entitled smile. "Go explore, enjoy, we set sail in the next half hour to cruise the islands."

"Splendid," Finch said in a mocking British accent, but Jake didn't seem to notice.

I elbowed her as he walked away.

"What?"

"We're meant to be smugly above all of this," I whisper hissed. "We're supposed to be so blissed out in love that we don't care that he's an arrogant asshole."

Finch turned to me, snaking her arms around my waist and pulling me flush against her. She was the perfect height for me to fit in the nook of her arms, her athletic build complimenting my curves, the perfect juxtaposition of hard and soft.

Relaxing into her hold, I suddenly realized the way I relished it was too real. I quickly stepped away and asked, "What are you doing?"

"Pretending to be blissed out in love? Obviously," Finch said, rocking us side to side like we were loved-up teenagers waiting in line at a theme park. "Am I doing a good job?"

"Yeah." I groaned. "I need a drink."

Finch didn't miss a beat, taking my hand and leading me as if she already had sniffed out where the bar was. "Let's go."

She confidently guided me through the crowd. People hastily parted to make way for her, eyeing her piercings and tattoos like she might be a mob boss's daughter. We beelined to the nearest waiter and Finch snagged two flutes of Champagne, holding them in one hand with impressive deftness without releasing my hand with the other. We wove through the party until we found a slightly quieter deck at the back of the boat.

I let out a sigh as the salty air rolled in off the ocean, the lights dimmer and the music softer. There was an overwhelming amount of people on this boat, and even though I couldn't see him, I felt like Jake was watching me from every angle.

Finch passed me a flute, clinked our glasses together, and drank. "Better?"

"Yeah, thanks." Bubbles burned down my throat as I searched the unfamiliar faces milling about. "This feels like a mistake. I should've said we were busy."

"Don't worry, Goldilocks," Finch said. "You've already proven you're a million times better than him. This appearance will definitely seal your victory."

"I don't feel particularly victorious," I grumbled. "I feel like the girl he dumped who's so pathetic that she's still trying to impress him."

Finch skulled the rest of her Champagne and set her empty glass on a nearby hightop. She leaned back against the railing with a sigh. "I still can't believe you were ever with a guy like him."

"He wasn't always that bad," I said, pursing my lips. "I don't think . . . I mean maybe he was and I just didn't want to see it."

"Why didn't you want to see it?"

"I don't know." I took another sip of Champagne, hoping the tingling bubbles would give me some liquid courage. "We met after college, and he was older and interested. He seemed like a good guy, and it just was like the logical next step in my life."

"Logical," Finch echoed.

"Yeah. It just felt like time to partner off with someone."

Finch studied me. "So not because of some burning, undying love for him?"

"People don't really feel that way about other people."

"You know, I used to agree with you," she added wistfully. "Until my siblings started finding their partners. Now I don't know what to think." She sighed, snagging another glass from a passing waiter. "But what I *do* know is I've heard a very similar story to yours from a *lot* of the women I've slept with when it comes to dating men."

"Oh really?"

"Yep."

"Great," I muttered. "I really don't want to dissect if my decision to pick Jake was just me being unaware I was gay."

Finch laughed around the rim of her glass. "You said it, not me, Goldilocks."

"Do you think that's what this was?" I cringed. "Maybe I . . . Oh god—"

"Whoa, don't spiral out," Finch jumped in. "I meant that to comfort you, not freak you out. Sorry."

"It's fine. I just—"

"Bi people exist," Finch reminded me. "I should know, half of my siblings are."

"Yeah. They exist," I hedged. *I just wasn't sure if I was one of them*, I thought silently to myself.

Men were transactional; women were magical. It had been one of those thoughts that had popped up every few years, one I'd shove far, *far* down because it wasn't worth scrutinizing. I'd picked Jake and he made sense and I'd started my life in his hometown, and I hadn't wanted to give that up just because I dreamt of women in a way I'd never dreamt of men . . .

But now. Here. With Finch. Maybe I could admit to myself that there were some signs I wasn't ready to fully see before.

"I should've become a nun," I muttered.

Finch snorted. "Yeah, for some reason I really don't see that happening for you. You're too good a chef for one thing."

"Nuns eat," I countered.

Her dimpled smile made my stomach somersault. "They do."

"I don't want to have to start dating again after all this." I moaned, the past few weeks catching up to me all at once. "Maybe I'll just get a bunch of cats. I'd found a person, even if he wasn't *my* person, and I don't want to have to rebuild a whole life with someone new. Especially now."

"Now?"

"I was so much more attractive ten years ago. And like sixty pounds lighter too." I waved myself up and down. "Now I've got to find someone who likes my personality well enough to tolerate all this."

Finch spluttered, Champagne spraying everywhere. She leaned overboard to spit the rest of her drink into the dark water below. A few people paused to look as Finch blotted her shirt with a cocktail napkin, but she didn't care as she turned to look at me, shielding me from the rest of the prying partiers. "Sorry, please tell me you didn't just say *tolerate*?"

"Um? I did?"

"Goldilocks."

"What?"

Finch pinched the bridge of her nose. "Oh god, how do I say this respectfully?" she murmured to herself before squaring her shoulders to pin me with a look. "There are a *lot* of people who see you—all of you—as an absolute asset, so incredibly desirable. Every dip and curve and . . ." She coughed loudly, her face getting flushed. I bit my lip, trying to contain my smile. She couldn't really mean that. "Believe me when I tell you, there are people who would want to take all day getting lost in your softness. Don't accept anything less." She cleared her throat. "That's all."

Now it was my turn to get all flushed. Fuck if I didn't want Finch to get lost in all my softness. Never had someone made that sound so appealing.

I looked out to the ocean, my nerves making me jittery. It was only then I realized we'd set sail. My hand instinctively shot out and gripped the railing. I gulped as I took in the swirling dark water all around the boat. "How long until we get back to shore?"

"Why do you look a trapped ostrich who's about to run straight into a fencepost?" Finch asked with a chuckle.

"Because we are *trapped* on this boat." I anxiously shifted my weight back and forth. "It's not like we can just get off whenever we want."

"So let's just enjoy our time then."

"I bet there's not enough life jackets for all of us," I snapped, knowing I sounded like a maniac. "What if the boat sinks? Oh god, they're going to use the shipwreck as a douchy scuba diver site."

"Shipwreck?"

My eyes flared, and I knew I was being ridiculous but couldn't rein in my panic. "What if we hit an iceberg?"

"You think there's icebergs in shoreline Connecticut?"

"It's a safety hazard."

"We'll just swim back to shore. We're not going out to sea. We're touring the islands . . . . Wait." Finch held me at arm's length and studied me, realization dawning on her face all at once. "Do you know how to swim?" I frowned and folded my arms. "You don't, do you?"

"I can swim fine," I muttered. "If doggy paddle counts."

"Okay, well, first, I am proud of how spiteful you are to agree to come to this party when you're scared of the water,"

Finch said, those damned cheeks dimpling again. "And second, I'm going to teach you how to swim."

"What?" I glared down at my hand as she tried to peel my fingers off the railing.

She linked our fingers together, and I gripped her hand just as hard. "You live on an island now. You need to learn."

"With what time are *you* going to teach me how to swim?"

She shrugged. "I'll make time. We can use the Holloways' pool. Hannah has a key."

I liked the sound of her making time for me. I knew what a big deal that was in her chaotic schedule.

"As long as you don't make me wear those ridiculous floaties," I relented.

"Wouldn't dream of it," she replied with a grin. "And as for tonight." She leaned in and dropped her mouth to my ear. "If for some reason the boat sinks, I'll swim you to shore. Okay?"

"You'll be too drunk by then," I said, nodding to her second drink.

Finch set her flute down with stubborn determination. "I promise," she said. "I'd never let anything bad happen to my girlfriend, fake or not." She threaded her fingers through mine and tugged me away from the railing. "Now come dance with me."

"I'm not a very good dancer—"

"It's a slow song," Finch cut in. "You basically just have to hug me while I rock you side to side. Stop overthinking everything just for tonight, Goldilocks."

The sun was swiftly setting, casting the sky in a beautiful burnt orange glow as Finch dragged me to the dance floor.

I chuckled as her hands enfolded me again and she pulled my arms up to hold around her neck. I couldn't help but think about how well she and I fit together, the way we moved. Maybe it was just Finch working her magic, but I swore I was working a little bit of magic on her too.

"Thank you for doing this with me," I said, gazing up into her dark eyes.

Her warm breath tickled my face as she laughed. "This is what blissed out in love people do, don't they?" Finch asked.

"I have no idea what they do," I whispered, getting caught in her gaze.

But for the first time in my entire life, I really wished I did.

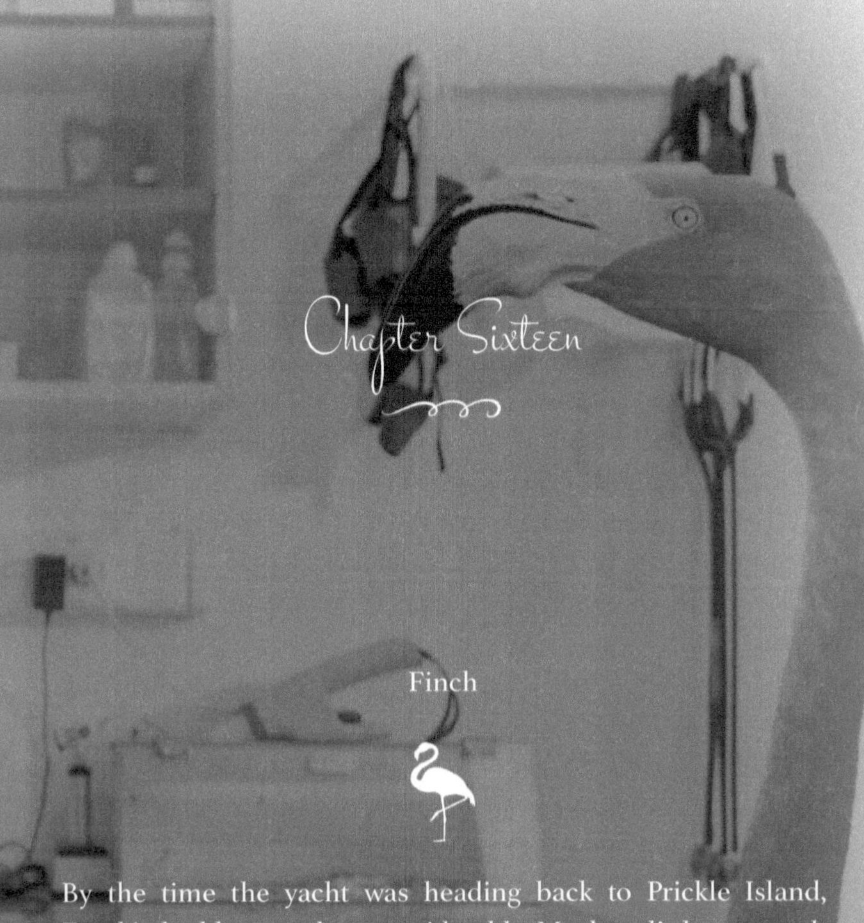

Chapter Sixteen

Finch

By the time the yacht was heading back to Prickle Island, Frankie had loosened up considerably. Maybe a little too much after five glasses of Champagne, but it was my mission to help her forget she was sailing on a boat. I couldn't believe she didn't know how to swim. I was determined she would by the end of the summer.

We leaned against the back railing away from the crowds, looking out to sea. Most of the other partiers had congregated inside to hide from the cool evening wind.

"Here," I said, taking off my jacket and wrapping it around Frankie's shoulders.

"I'm okay—"

I ran my hand down her goose bump-covered arm and pointedly raised my eyebrow. "Just take the jacket, Frankie."

She stuck out her bottom lip but did as I commanded, folding it around herself and sighing.

"This smells amazing," she said. "What cologne do you wear?"

I huffed. "Does soap count?"

"You do not just naturally smell this good. There's no way," she said with a drunken chuckle. She rose up from where she leaned to stick her nose against my neck and take a big inhale. I laughed at the feeling of her nose pressed against my skin. "Curse you. You really do just smell that good."

"I think we might have lost track of how many glasses of Champagne you've had there, Goldilocks," I said. "You don't strike me as the sniff attack type of miscreant when you're sober."

I'd been abnormally restrained when it came to drinking that evening. I was originally thinking I'd have to call Hawk to drive us home after a big night of partying. It was what I was known for—drinking people twice my size under the table. But after promising Frankie I would save her in the event of a catastrophe, I'd decided one and a half glasses of Champagne were enough. It had been a surprisingly easy decision.

Frankie hiccuped, pointing her face into the wind. "Why do you always call me Goldilocks?"

I shrugged and lifted a soft lock of her golden hair.

"Right, I should've thought of that."

"That's not the only reason," I confessed. "You know my full name?"

"Goldfinch," she said. "It's a beautiful name." Her hand lingered on my lapel.

"I guess I just liked the idea of our names matching, Finch and Frankie, Goldilocks and Goldfinch," I confessed. "My other siblings ended up with someone with the same first letter of their name. I don't know, it just felt kind of lucky." I swept a hand through my hair. "I'm going to shut up now."

"No," Frankie said, leaning further into me. "I think that's really sweet."

I hoped she was too drunk to remember that the first time I'd called her Goldilocks had also been the first time we'd met. To give a stranger a nickname that I hoped would compliment my own . . . It had been a spur of the moment decision, just a weird off the cuff fantasy. The idea of someone like her ending up with someone like me had just been a fun delusion. I hadn't planned on ever telling her the truth. But when she looked up at me with those big blue-green eyes, the truth had a way of just tumbling out of my mouth.

Those stunning eyes drifted over my shoulder and snagged on something. "What? Is Jake watching?" I leaned down, trying to shield her from view of the deck above. "Do you want me to kiss—"

Frankie bridged the distance between us before I could even finish the question. Her mouth collided with mine and I moved instantly, pulling her into me. God, her body was so blissfully soft, those gorgeous, cushioned curves that pressed into me, and just . . . it was everything. *She* was everything. Her taste, her smell. I kissed her as if my lips could convey how much she deserved someone to adore her, someone to worship every inch of her, someone so very different than Jake.

I knew that creeping self-doubt in her was his fault, knew that someone like him relished in chipping away at someone like her. It enraged me. The fact she didn't realize how much she electrified every single nerve ending in my body. My hands fisted in her dress, pulling her closer as her hands lifted into my hair and her mouth grew more insistent.

This was so much more than a kiss to make someone jealous. This was like a frenzy, something that had been building in me for weeks, like we couldn't stop even if we wanted to.

I wanted to devour her.

The boat horn blared, making us jolt apart and snap out of the haze.

"Sorry," she said with an awkward giggle. "I got a bit carried away in this act."

"Believe me, I don't mind," I said, swiping my thumb under her swollen bottom lip to fix her smudged lipstick.

She lifted her hand to my mouth and did the same. I didn't know if she was aware that she licked her lips as her eyes fixated on my mouth, but my satisfied smile grew wider at the action.

I looked over the side to see we'd arrived back at the dock. When? The night seemed to have just disappeared. I wished we were still out in the harbor, still dancing, still kissing, still connected. Now that this party was over, would we ever even have a chance to do this again? I didn't care that it was all just a game of pretend. Frankie made me want to pretend a little bit longer.

Daily Specials
kookaburra cucumber
sandwiches
$5·50
Macaw Macarons
6 for $12

Chapter Seventeen

Frankie

There was a tempo to zoo life, a dance, and I was starting to finally get the rhythm of it. The café and restaurant were a well-choreographed production now, working in tandem to keep the hungry patrons happy. We'd had record numbers of visitors during the first few weeks of summer, thanks to the streak of good weather.

I didn't want to admit it aloud, but I had a sneaking suspicion that the staff was hoping for a rain day soon. We had so much to catch up on, and we needed a stormy, quiet day to do everything that had been put on hold during the frantic days. Mateo, the front of house manager, had been a big support system to me, supplying me with staff to run the café and basically supervising it for me while I was up working at the Peckish Peacock.

I spent my early mornings before the zoo opened baking everything for both the café and restaurant, and then, once the zoo opened, I headed up to the restaurant for the rest of the day. They were long days, leaving me exhausted, but the exhaustion was kind of nice too. For one thing, it meant I didn't have to overanalyze that kiss on the yacht. The things that Finch had said to me . . . the way it had felt to dance with her, to be her singular focus, the buzzing spotlight of her attention solely on me. Everything I thought I knew was being turned upside down. My life, my sense of self, my sexuality were all at once going through great upheavals.

Hannah interrupted my swirling thoughts when she poked her head in the back door of the Peckish Peacock. Her pastel pink hair spilled over her shoulder as she surveyed the kitchen chaos. Her locks were dipped a rose blush in the same style that Dove's tresses were, and I wondered if the two of them did each other's hair in matching pink and purple. Especially considering there were no hairdressers on the island in the off season. The two keepers almost looked like twins, but it was easy to remember Hannah—the pink-haired one—was not a Lachlan sibling because she didn't have a bird name.

"How's it going?" she asked as she surveyed the kitchen chaos. "Need a hand?"

This was one of the many things I loved about working at Prickle Island Zoo. There was an incredible generosity of spirit amongst the whole staff. No one was done until we all were done. People stayed late and woke up early to give each other a hand. It had the clear energy of a family, and not in that hollow, corporate speak sort of way. At the heart of the zoo really was an actual family that cared deeply for each other and for the work.

"Things are winding down now, thanks," I said, wiping the sweat off my forehead with my hair band. It was like a hot box in there today, the July temperatures soaring.

"Oh good," Hannah said but still lingered in the doorway.

"You done with your shift already?" I asked, eyeing the stack of empty buckets set beside her mud-splattered boots.

"Almost," she said.

"Okay . . ." I was certain I was missing something. "Do you want something to eat? We have—"

"Oh no, that's okay," she said too quickly. "I mean, your food is amazing. I just—" She flailed a little too quickly and almost fell backward, which was truly an incredible feat considering she hadn't moved her legs at all. She recovered with a laugh. "And *that's* why they call me Hazard Report Hannah," she said with a chuckle. "I would like to say I'm not always this awkward, but we both know that's a lie."

"You don't need to be nervous around me," I said. "I'm nobody."

"Well, that's not true." Still, she didn't get to the point, and I had a feeling there was one.

"What can I do you for, Hannah?" I finally asked.

"Okay, fine." She threw her hands up and accidentally knocked her knuckles on the windowsill. I winced in unison with her. "Everyone wants to know how the yacht party went, and I drew the short straw and I was going to subtly weave it into conversation, but as you can see, there is nothing subtle about me."

"Everyone wants to know how the yacht party went?"

"Well, mostly Evelyn, and Hawk, and Dove, and the twins, and Mateo, and Aya . . . . Oh, and Wren."

"That's literally everyone."

"It's just, Finch has been walking around with this hazy lovesick smile all day and we all need to know. Did you guys say the "L" word yesterday? That's the working theory at least."

My face fell. I liked the idea that Finch was walking around in as much of a daydream as I was. The party had been wonderful, and even if it was all pretend, the companionship of it had been real at least. The connection between us might be strictly platonic, but I could say for certain we were at least friends by now and that felt really good.

Although, friends didn't pretend to spot their ex watching to get the girl they were fake dating to kiss them again. I'd never be able to admit that to Finch. I'd had too many glasses of Champagne and just really wanted to make out with a woman . . . something I realized had always been a desire of mine whenever I got drunk, but *that* was something I'd need to unpack at another time.

I realized Hannah was still waiting to hear my answer.

"I don't know if I should really be sharing all the details of our relationship," I hedged. "I feel like that's more Finch's place since you all are her family."

Hannah pouted. "Fair enough, and I respect your boundaries, but please give me one tiny detail to tell Evelyn. I really want her to like me."

"She definitely already likes you," I said with surprised huff.

"I know, but like, she might be my mother-in-law some day and I need her to really, *really* like me and think I'm worthy of her son."

I chuckled. "Honestly, I think you've won the mother-in-law jackpot with someone like Evelyn Lachlan. She's like, a cool eco-warrior Mary Poppins."

Hannah had an infectious laugh. She was like a golden retriever personified. "Maybe one day you'll hit that jackpot too." She immediately held out her hands. "I shouldn't have said that. It's too soon to be suggesting you and Finch are going to get married. Strike that from the record, sorry. I just get really excited about the idea of another person dating one of the Lachlan siblings. We need to form an alliance."

"Is this an episode of *Survivor* now?" I gave her a sideways look. "Do we need an alliance?"

"I mean, not really, but just in case."

I shook my head. "I don't think Finch and I are in the same place as you and Hawk. I've seen that bumper sticker of you two on the Jeep. Finch and I aren't bumper sticker official yet."

Hannah nodded like a caffeinated Muppet. "Well, if ever you need anything, I'm here for you."

"Thanks, that really means a lot to me," I said as she stooped and picked up the buckets. "And Hannah?" She looked at me over her shoulder. "You can tell Evie that we slow-danced half the night and it was very romantic."

"Eee! Thank you! You're the best!" Hannah cheered and went tearing off through the zoo to wash her buckets.

I wondered how many minutes it would be before the Lachlan family group chat was being flooded with the latest sibling gossip. As I turned back to the towering pile of dishes, my stomach soured. It was going to be awful when this agreement between Finch and I ended. I hadn't realized how invested everyone would be. What we were doing might end up breaking a few hearts even if it wasn't either of ours, and the guilt started to gnaw at me. But it was too late. We'd already jumped off that relationship cliff and now all we could do was brace for our collision back to earth.

Chapter Eighteen

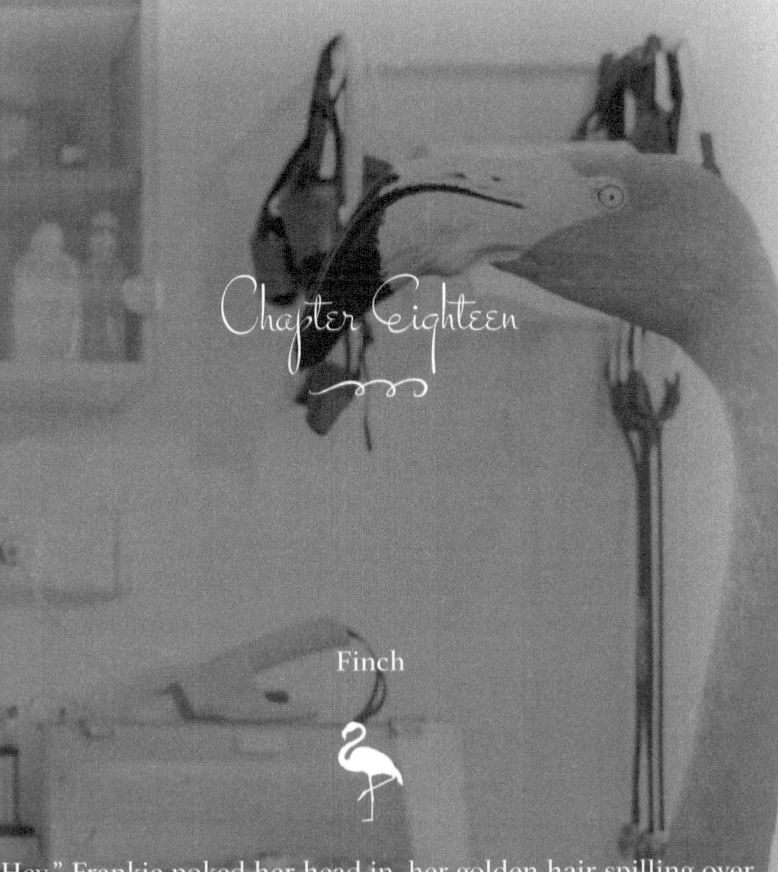

Finch

"Hey." Frankie poked her head in, her golden hair spilling over her shoulder. "You got a sec?"

I cleared my throat, the sight of her giving me vivid flash-backs from the yacht party. The things she'd unlocked in me . . . The things I was hoping to unlock in her . . .

I cleared my throat and grabbed my radio, clipping it onto my baggy pants pocket. "You ready to walk home?"

Walking her back to the Salty Dog had become my favorite part of the day. I didn't take time to go for wandering walks by the water of my own volition, let alone find them fun. But with Frankie, we never seemed to run out of things to talk about. She knew a little bit about everything, from the history of sour-dough to the filming of *Bridgerton* and everything in between. It was the best twenty minutes of my day.

"Actually, there are some teenagers who've locked themselves in the toilets by the Peacock," she said, hooking her thumb over her shoulder. "I think they're trying to pull an all-nighter at the zoo."

"Of course they are," I said with a sigh.

"Is that a regular thing?"

"Happens at least once a year." I headed out the door, giving Frankie's hand a tug as I went. "Come on."

These fuckers were eating into my walking Frankie home time and I didn't appreciate it.

Frankie trailed after me as I stormed back through the zoo. "Is there protocol for kids hiding in bathrooms?"

"Yes," I muttered, walking faster. "It's called the Finch has been up all night with a baby macaw and has zero fucks left to give protocol."

Frankie chuckled as she hustled after me toward the Peckish Peacock. "I could just radio one of the keepers if you—"

"Nah, we've got this, Goldilocks," I said, reaching the bathroom door and pounding on it. "Hey, dickwads!" I shouted and heard the ridiculous laughter of two teenage boys. "Get the fuck out of there."

No one replied, but I could clearly hear them. I balled up my fists, ready to pummel down the door. I had to be back here to feed Frankie, Cranky, Benny in an hour and I didn't want to miss my walk with human Frankie because two teenagers were playing *Night at the Museum.*

I was about to punch my fist through the door when Frankie put a hand on my shoulder. "Give me your radio."

I arched a brow at her but did as she requested. She took the radio and switched it over to another frequency so my siblings wouldn't hear. She pushed in the button, the loud beep echoing through the brick and tiled space. "Peacock to Security."

She passed me the radio, the scratching crackle really

selling our ruse. I took a few steps away, bemused as she egged me on to speak.

"Security, go ahead."

She snatched the radio back. "Hey, the restaurant is all closed up for the night," she said. "I thought I heard something in the bathroom, but it was nothing." A wave of victorious whispers swept out the bathroom window.

I lifted my hands up in a "What are you doing?" gesture, but Frankie ignored my confusion. She wandered over to the power box outside the restaurant window and opened it. She winked at me, and my heart jumped into my throat as she lifted the radio back to her mouth. "I'm going to go ahead and cut the power so you can go in and fumigate for those spiders."

My smile widened as she flipped the power switch and the teens inside gasped.

I took the radio back and said, "Roger. Yeah, those wolf spiders have taken over that toilet block. Can't see the tiles the way they carpet the floor by sunset."

Frankie bit her lips together to keep from laughing. I wandered over to the back wall of the toilet block as Frankie skittered her fingernails over the paneling.

"Shit."

"Fuck."

The teens inside chorused. We heard one of the stalls opening, and I grabbed Frankie by the crook of her arm to pull her into the bushes with me, holding a finger to my lips. Within a few heartbeats, the delinquents had fled toward the front entrance.

"That was brilliant, Goldilocks," I said, looking down at Frankie, who beamed up at me.

It was only then I realized the position we were in. She leaned against the back wall, my hands placed against the paneling on either side of her head. I caged her in with my arms as Frankie's eyes dipped to my mouth, and I could tell she was thinking of that drunken kiss. Did she want me to kiss her? All it would take is for me to lean down . . .

"Finch!"

I scrunched my face. "What, Mom?"

"Why were there two boys fleeing for their lives through the zoo?" She raced around the corner. "And why are you using the other frequency for radio—oh!"

Mom stopped short when she saw the compromising position Frankie and I were in. But this wasn't just some random girl I was caught in the bushes with. This was meant to be my girlfriend. I decided not to ricochet away from Frankie and instead slung my arm around her shoulders and guided her toward Mom.

"I was about to walk Frankie home, and we were just shooing away some last-minute stragglers," I said.

Mom put her hands on her hips. "You mean terrorizing them?"

I shrugged. "I wanted to punch my way in." I dropped a kiss to Frankie's head. "But Frankie's idea had more finesse."

Frankie's cheeks reddened in response to my chaste kiss. I loved the way I could fluster her. Even more, I loved the way she flustered me. I didn't think it was even possible anymore, but here she was, making me feel like I'd never kissed a girl before, giddy and uninhibited.

"You two are just so cute," Mom said, her anger quickly morphing into something sweeter.

"And on that note," I said, dropping my hand to the small of Frankie's back. "We'll be on our way." I passed Mom my radio. "I'll be back in an hour to feed Frankie, the bird."

"I can do it," Mom cut in, practically bounding after us. "Why don't you two go have dinner or something? There's a new seafood place on the western wharf?"

"It's fine, Mom—"

"How many years have I been doing this, Goldfinch?" Mom reprimanded.

I rolled my eyes, already knowing I was in a losing battle. "A century?"

She frowned and folded her arms tightly. "I know how to crop feed a macaw. I was the one who taught you how to do it. The diets are all written on the whiteboard. I'm sure I can manage."

"She's just not been gaining weight like I want her to and—"

"And you'll be back to feed her again in five hours anyway," Mom said pointedly. "I've got this one. Go have dinner." I opened my mouth to protest again, and Mom looked at Frankie, switching tact. "Frankie, would you give me one minute to speak with my daughter? Thank you."

"Oof," Frankie murmured from the corner of her mouth. "Good luck."

I chuckled as she stepped out of my hold and wandered halfway down the path toward the front entrance.

"Mom," I started.

"No." Mom pointed a scolding finger at me. "A girl like her doesn't come around every day, Finch." She waved at Frankie, who was very pointedly inspecting the trees instead of watching us. "She deserves your attention. If you're too addicted to your job, you're going to miss out on something exceptional. Don't screw this up."

"First you want me to have a relationship, now you want me to be better at it," I growled. "When will it be enough for you?"

Mom stood her ground, channeling her patented CEO boss bitch energy. "You know I'm right."

"Will you just leave this alone?"

Mom narrowed her eyes, clearly unwilling to leave it alone. "You're going to work yourself to death."

"I am very happy with my workload, thanks, boss, baby macaws aside. Maybe talk to Dove about that one."

"I don't want to see you lose her just because—"

"Whether I lose her or not is none of your business," I insisted. "And believe me, I know how special she is."

Mom's eyes softened at that. "Good."

I scrubbed my hand down my face, instantly regretting saying that. I was making all of this worse for myself. The lies would eventually catch up with us. But instead of admitting the truth to my overbearing mother, I just said, "Can I go walk my girlfriend home now?"

"And have dinner with her, yes," Mom said with a winning smile. She cupped my cheek. "I like how happy you are with her. The way you look at her . . . it's beautiful, honey."

"Gross," I muttered, and Mom laughed as I walked away. "Oh, and Finch—"

I looked over my shoulder. "Yeah?"

"Bring Frankie to Sunday dinner," she said.

I clenched my jaw through a smile. My mother was the most meddlesome person I knew. But if Frankie and I were really dating, why wouldn't I want to bring her to family dinner?

"Of course," I gritted out.

I charged off toward Frankie, thinking about how screwed I was. But the second I caught up to her and we headed off on our evening walk, I instantly felt better. Frankie was like a soothing balm to my anxieties. She always made me feel better just by existing. At some point, I'd have to tell my mom the truth, but right then I just wanted to enjoy walking by Frankie's side.

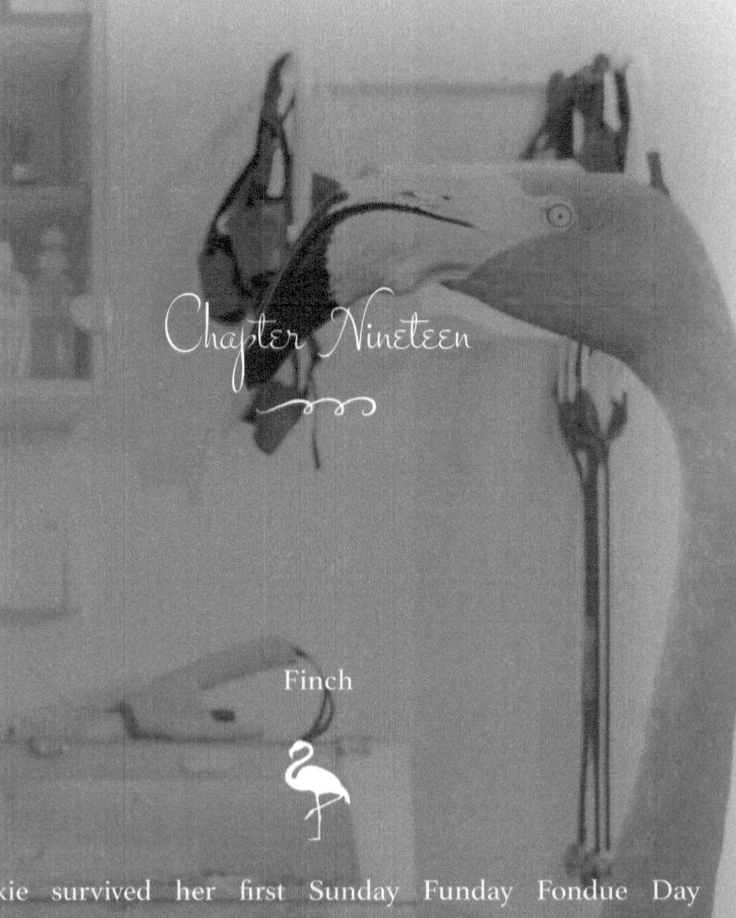

Chapter Nineteen

Finch

Frankie survived her first Sunday Funday Fondue Day surprisingly admirably. She threw in jokes at just the right time, knew how to prod the twins in just the right way, and expertly identified the giraffe poop on Wren's phone during a rousing game of "It's feces but what species."

As evening died down, Frankie said, "I should probably be going." She patted her napkin to her lips one last time and gracefully stood. "Thank you so much for this delicious dinner."

"It was your garlic knots that really made it special," Mom said with a smile. A rowdy chorus of siblings agreed from all corners of the house. "Otherwise the meal would've been abundantly cheesy."

"I can walk you home," I offered, hastily rising to a stand beside Frankie.

The twins had already disappeared somewhere in the house, probably playing video games, Hawk and Hannah were tackling the dishes, and Wren had gone for her post family dinner walk, which we all knew was to escape the post-dinner sibling chaos, the adorable introvert.

"You're coming back next time, right?" Hannah asked eagerly as she passed a plate into Hawk's outstretched dish towel.

"I hope so," Dove called from where she lounged on the couch, texting on her phone.

"Why wouldn't she?" Mom asked, looking at me for confirmation. "You're Finch's girlfriend. You're always welcome here."

"Of course," I said, snaking my arm around Frankie's side. "But sometimes I just want to keep her to myself and not throw her back in this lion's den."

Mom rolled her eyes. "Well, we'd love to see you at the next family dinner, Frankie, if you'd like to join us."

"Thanks," Frankie said. "I'd love that."

I looked at her like she'd grown a second head. I was trying to give her an out, but clearly she didn't want to take it.

"I'll walk you back to the Salty Dog," I offered, and Frankie held up a hand.

"No, no, really, it's fine." She checked her watch. "It's almost time for another bird feeding anyway."

"I can do it!" Dove chimed in without looking up from her phone.

"Really, it's a short walk," Frankie said, patting my arm. "Get some rest."

"Rest? Finch?" Hawk guffawed. "She invented burning the candle at both ends."

I snickered at my brother as Frankie stepped away toward

the door. Mom leaned in and whispered to me, "Aren't you going to kiss her good night?"

Frankie let out a surprised cough, clearly overhearing.

"Yes, but not in front of all of you leering hyenas," I muttered. I turned to Frankie and put my hand on the small of her back. "I'll walk you to the door at least."

She smiled and farewelled the raucous bunch one more time before we stepped out into the cool breeze. The days had been hot and humid, but the evening was still pleasantly cool. And the sky was so bright with glittering stars, not a single wisp of cloud blowing past.

"Well," I said when we got out of earshot of the others. "I tried to spare you from more of the fondue insanity, but you walked right into that one."

"I really did have a good time," Frankie said, her smile pulling wide. "And I don't think any group has ever appreciated my garlic knots so much."

"Yeah, I think they're about ready to start a cult and make you their leader." I chuckled. "You know you're going to be expected to bring those every time now, don't you?"

"I know," she said smugly. "I don't mind. Those reactions are exactly why I became a chef. I love the way people can connect over food."

I had the sudden image of connecting her with some strawberries and chocolate sauce. I balled my hands into fists to force the vision away. That was not what she meant.

Frankie's eye caught something over my shoulder and her cheeks dimpled. "What?" I whirled just in time to see three heads ducking from Mom's kitchen window. "Didn't realize the most watched animal in the zoo would be me."

I rocked back and forth awkwardly on my feet.

"I suppose they'll be expecting us to kiss," Frankie said, tucking a stand of her hair behind her ear. "We could just angle our heads for a second and no one would know."

"Or I could just kiss you," I suggested. "If that's okay? Just a quick peck."

She nervously bit her lip. "Nothing we haven't done before," she added with an awkward chuckle.

I put my hand on her waist, heat radiating off her soft side. Something about this felt far more intimate than the other times we'd kissed in a crowded restaurant or yacht. I leaned a little closer and whispered, "You sure?"

"Uh-huh," she rasped.

I smiled and leaned down, brushing a gentle kiss to her lips. She lifted up on her toes and kissed me back, deepening the connection. My skin tingled with the contact. She tasted like the chocolate-covered macadamias Mom had passed around after dinner. I desperately wanted to taste her even more. My tongue swept out, licking her bottom lip, when a loud laugh sounded from the window and Frankie immediately dropped back to flat feet.

"Wild animals, the lot of them," I muttered, glancing over my shoulder to the once again suspiciously vacant window.

"We are very convincing at this little ploy, I think," Frankie said, brushing her windswept hair off her face.

Too convincing, I thought.

"Uh, see you tomorrow then," Frankie said as she spun and dashed toward the back entrance of the zoo.

I laughed, folding my arms across my chest and watching her skitter off into the evening. I thought about staying there, trailing her figure with my eyes until she disappeared beyond the dip of the hill, the blonde hair like a beacon in the street-light's glow. I let out a long, wistful sigh. Maybe I needed to pretend I was in a relationship more often . . .

I turned back to Mom's house and saw the twins were now crammed in the window alongside Mom, Dove, and Hannah.

I threw up my arms. "Seriously, you guys?"

"I wouldn't have believed it if I didn't see it with my own

eyes," Hawk teased from the doorway, holding a hand to his chest. "Finch is in love."

"We haven't gotten to the love stage yet," I corrected. Did I have to start telling her I loved her in front of people? Kissing was one thing, but that felt like crossing some strange emotional line.

Hawk shook his head at me like I was clueless. "I see the way she looks at you and, more importantly, I see the way you look at her," he said.

"I look at her with my eyes like a normal person."

"Uh-huh." He flashed another self-satisfied smile. "You're screwed, sis, sorry to break it to you."

Shoving him out of the doorway, I heaved a dramatic sigh. "I expected this from Mom, but you, Hawky Puck?"

Hawk shrugged. "It's cute."

"I am not *cute*. I am devilishly handsome," I corrected.

"And I'm sure Frankie would agree," he said with a mocking thumbs-up.

I wandered back inside to steal some clean socks from Mom's dryer before heading back to my apartment for the night. Hawk was wrong. I didn't look at Frankie like anything. He just had his love goggles on ever since he'd met Hannah. This was all just a very elaborate act and Frankie and I had successfully fooled him. She and I both were simply excellent actors.

Daily Specials
kookaburra cucumber
sandwiches
$5.50
Macaw Macarons
6 for $12

Chapter Twenty

Frankie

I emerged from the Holloways' pool house—that was bigger than any house I'd ever lived in—and took in the swimming pool. Swimming pool was a misnomer. This was more like a freaking luxury water park. It looked like something out of a five-star resort. Clear turquoise-tinted water filled three separate pools. Surrounded by lush trees that hid them from the main house, the pools were lined with cabanas on one side and a row of white sun loungers on the other. On every cushioned surface sat neatly arranged beach towels and ice buckets with bottled water. But none of that made me gape more than the sight of the person standing at the steps to the first pool.

My mouth fell open at the sight of Finch standing casually beside the sandstone steps. I managed to school my expression before she saw me, thank God. She wore a bright blue and green sports bra with a neon zipper up the front and matching board shorts that landed mid-thigh. In this outfit, I got the full display of her tattoos. Two full sleeves covered her from knuckles to shoulders while whirling black swirls intertwined with flowers across her abdomen, and the tip of a tattooed dagger peeked from her thigh. She looked like a tatted-up surfer with tanned skin and a lean, muscular physique.

She's mesmerizing, I thought, followed by an immediate: *Yeah, there is no way I'm taking this sundress off.*

"I don't think I can do this." I groaned aloud, staring beyond Finch to the deep water of the pool.

She appraised my dress as I approached her. "Well, I've found your first problem," she said. "You're still wearing clothes."

"I can swim in this," I said tentatively, wishing I could hide behind the cabana. I really hadn't thought this through. Going swimming together was basically being naked together, and I was not ready to be naked in front of anyone let, alone someone as attractive as Finch.

Finch gave me an exasperated look. "Please tell me you have a bathing suit under that dress."

"I do."

She lifted both hands up. "Then take the dress off."

"I'm good, thanks."

"Jesus, Goldilocks, I have *never* had such a hard time convincing a woman to take her clothes off in my life."

"I believe that." I snorted. "Why are we doing this again?"

"So if you ever decide to jump off a yacht in the future, you won't have a panic attack," Finch reminded.

"That seems very unlikely."

"Or if you fall in the water ever in the future," she countered. "It's important. Practicing is good."

I still wasn't compelled. "Maybe I should just steer clear of the water altogether."

"You live on an island," she deadpanned.

I pointed a finger to the sky. "Only for the summer."

"But you'll come back next summer, right?"

My head jerked back in surprise. "Do you want me to come back next summer?" I asked. "I mean, wouldn't it be complicated if we pretended to break up and then I was working here next year as your ex?" I tried to imagine what that would look like. "Would we have to pretend fight and things?"

"I don't think it would be weird," Finch said with a shrug. "I'm friends with lots of women I've hooked up with, and seeing as you and I have never *actually* been together, it'll be even easier."

"Okay . . . ," I hedged. "But how would—"

"Goldilocks, are you just trying to stall me?"

"Maybe."

Finch crossed her arms in a way that made her biceps even bigger, and my core clenched as I thought about being pinned down by those arms.

"You know, I *have* seen women in bathing suits before. I can control myself," Finch said pointedly. "I promise not to ogle you."

Ogling wasn't what I was worried about.

Still, I gritted my teeth. "Get in the water and turn around."

"What kind of G-string, crotchless panty, spaghetti strap getup do you have on that you don't want me to see?"

"I'm wearing a sensible black one-piece," I said, bristling and tossing my hair over my shoulder. "Timeless, elegant."

"And you think I won't be able to contain myself if I see you in it?" Finch's cheeks dimpled. "I promise to be on my best behavior."

"I have no doubt."

Realization dawned on her face, and it made me shrink an inch. "This is about that whole people liking your personality and settling for your body bullshit again, isn't it?"

"No," I said defensively. "I mean, Jake mentioned a few times that—"

"I really want to punch a hole in Jake's face, you know that?" Finch growled. "Fucking men! I can't believe he'd tear you down like that and, worse, you believed him."

I clenched my jaw. "I'm just being self-aware."

"This is the very opposite of that." She shook her head, waving between us. "I don't know how many times I need to tell you this, Goldilocks, and honestly, I don't mind telling you every damn day until you believe me, but your body is absolutely lovable exactly as it is." She pinned me with a stern look until I nodded. "Now stop stalling and take your dress off."

It was the first time I'd really considered that maybe Jake wasn't the most reliable person to believe about these things. The way Finch looked at me . . . How could two people have such differing opinions? And did either of those opinions even matter as much as my own?

I was all for body positivity. I'd seen women bigger than me, smaller than me, and every which size being absolute goddesses—with bodies I was personally infatuated with—but somehow I still couldn't quite translate that into the way I felt about myself. Why could I see it for others but not for me? It was only now with Finch so glaringly pointing it out that I was beginning to realize the thoughts weren't my own, that they were put there by society, the media, men, and most of all Jake. And I refused to let that bastard still have any control over me. With that anger now replacing my fear, I took a decisive step forward.

Like ripping off a Band-Aid, I whipped the dress over my head and chucked it on the sun chair beside me before quickly walking into the water.

"Oh look, a human body, how scandalous," Finch teased as she walked into the shallow end after me.

"Shut up," I shot back as I walked in to waist height. The

water was cool and refreshing against my heated skin. "Okay, so now what?"

"How about we start with dunking your head underwater?" I took a giant step back and Finch guffawed. "Not me dunking you." She laughed. "Just you on your own."

"I don't want to put my head underwater."

Her eyes narrowed. "Why not?"

"Because water might go up my nose and then I might panic and forget which way is up and—"

"And *this* is why we're practicing in the shallow end of the pool."

I nibbled the corner of my lip, watching the water like it might lurch up and attack me. "I don't know."

"Come on," Finch said, her hand swimming through the water and threading her fingers with mine. "We'll do it together. I promise by the end of the summer, you won't even be thinking about it anymore."

"Just a quick dunk," I confirmed, pinning her with a look.

"Yep." She gave me that carefree smile of hers, like everything was going to be alright, and I couldn't help but believe her. "On three, okay?"

"Okay."

"One, two, three." She started submerging herself, and for a split second I thought about remaining above the water, but her hand squeezed mine in reassurance and I decided to move.

I crouched down, submerging my face and then shooting back to a stand, frantically wiping the water out of my eyes.

"See?" Finch gave my hand another encouraging squeeze. "That was great. We'll just do that a few more times and you'll be Michael Phelps before you know it."

"You are annoyingly supportive."

"I know." Her dark eyes lit up. "I taught the twins and Wren how to swim. Although, those lessons were less patient and more me throwing them into the water."

I loved that cheeky smile she gave when she was being mischievous. How could someone be so sexy and playful all at once?

"Okay, well, don't do that to me or I'll fake break up with you," I teased.

"Wouldn't dream of it, Goldilocks."

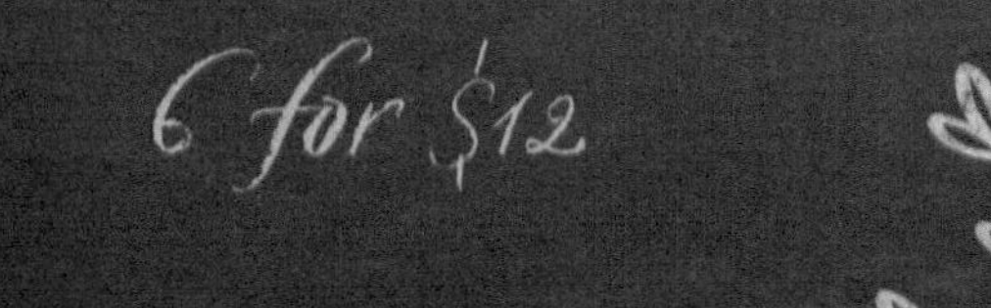

Daily Specials
kookaburra cucumber
sandwiches
$5.50
Macaw Macarons
6 for $12

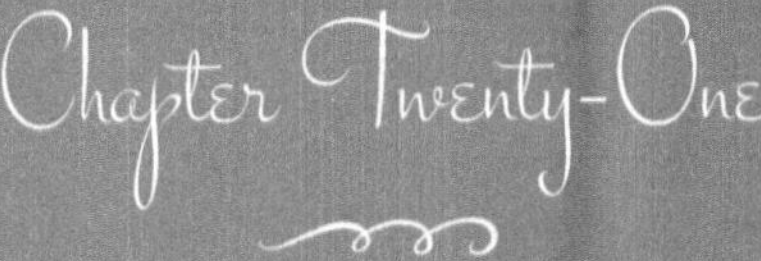

Chapter Twenty-One

Frankie

The torrential rain thundered against the slanted roof as I tossed and turned in bed. The storm lashed its way across the island, roaring so loud I could barely hear. I'd been wondering when our string of gorgeous summer weather would be interrupted, but I wasn't prepared for the ferocity of a storm rolling across a small island. The Salty Dog was all closed up for the night, no boisterous patrons or raving partiers. The darkened bar was eerily still, the only sound the roar of the gaping winds.

I grabbed my oversized hoodie and yanked it on, walking to the window as lightning streaked across the ocean. I stood there for what felt like hours, hypnotized, watching as the storm rolled away and the sun began to pink the sky.

Just as I considered getting back in bed, there was an explosion.

I ducked, covering my head and shrieking as the roof caved in. Water poured onto the floor and splinters shattered across the room as I gaped up at the boulder-sized hole above me.

Kirby and Aya came crashing in the door. "What the hell is . . ."

"Oh my god, are you okay?" Aya rushed over to me, checking me for injuries.

I stared at my now-soaking bed, my whole body shaking. "I'm okay." My voice trembled as adrenaline coursed through me. "I wasn't in bed, thank God."

Aya started sweeping around the room, picking up my things and tossing them into my open suitcase on the chair beside the dresser. "You can have our room. We can sleep on the couch and—"

"On the couch?" Kirby balked.

"Well, she can't stay in here," Aya shot back.

"Why doesn't she go stay with her girlfriend?"

"Isn't that too soon? They've only been dating for like a month."

"We're lesbians, Aya. That's a lifetime for us," Kirby reminded her, and I really liked that she'd included me in that statement. She seemed to know I would, judging by the look on her face.

How it had taken me this long to figure it out was a mystery, but now that I was looking back on my life with a fine-toothed comb, it was all starting to make sense. I was slowly coming to grips with the fact that I wasn't bisexual, but I still felt anxious to put a label on it, as if I weren't allowed. I felt like my relationship with Jake somehow negated this newfound awakening, like I wouldn't be welcomed into this community because I was only starting to wake up to these truths. But Aya and Kirby made me feel seen in a way I never knew I needed, a way that made me feel like I finally made sense to myself.

"Besides, Finch has two guest rooms if it's *too soon*," Kirby continued. "This is an emergency for fuck's sake."

"You have a point," Aya said, turning to me expectantly.

All the blood drained from my face as both of them looked at me. Everyone else had been fooled by our ruse, but I saw the skepticism in Aya's and Kirby's faces. Some things just weren't adding up for them. It was like a bullshit radar or something. I knew if I didn't move in with Finch now, it would be a surefire way of revealing the truth.

"Yeah, of course." I nervously bundled my hoodie sleeves around my hands. "I'll stay with Finch. No problem."

"Then call her," Kirby said, crossing her arms.

"What?"

"Call her and ask if you can stay with her."

Aya elbowed her wife as I swallowed thickly. "It's 4 am."

"So? If Aya needed me any day or night, she'd call."

"Yes, but I'm your wife of three fucking decades," Aya muttered. "They only just got together. Cut her some slack."

Kirby didn't budge, arching her brow at me and calling my bluff.

I grabbed my phone out of my hoodie pocket, feeling more trapped in this lie than ever before. I dialed Finch's number, and to my surprise, she picked up on the first ring.

"Hey, babe," I said, the word "babe" feeling strange to my ears.

"Babe?" Finch's voice was raspy with sleep as she chuckled. "I kind of like that." *Well, that made all sorts of Jell-O-y things happen to my legs.* "I'm guessing you're in front of someone? You okay?"

"I'm sorry to wake you—"

"I was up feeding Cranky Frankie," she said with a grumble. "The bird, obviously. I would never give you that nickname."

I chuckled. "Thank you."

"What's up?"

"Um . . . so . . . part of the roof kind of caved in at the Salty Dog and—"

"What?" She suddenly sounded more awake, clothing rustling like she'd bolted out of bed. "Are you okay? Are Aya and Kirby okay?"

"We're all okay," I assured her. "Don't worry."

"I'm coming over there."

"Seriously, no one's hurt," I pushed. Aya gave Kirby an "I told you so" look, as if Finch's response to the roof caving in was proof that our relationship was real judging by the vet's concern. "I just was hoping that maybe, I could stay with you—"

"Of course, you can." I heard the sound of keys jangling. "I'm bringing the truck over now."

"No, it's fine. Go back to sleep. I can walk—"

"You are not walking, Goldilocks," she insisted.

"Seriously—"

"Seriously, I'm on my way."

"Okay, thanks," I finally relented.

"See you in a minute."

"Okay, bye." When I hung up, I stared at my phone, smiling like an idiot for a second before I realized Kirby and Aya were still watching me curiously, like I was one of the exotic fish in the café aquarium. I put my hands on my hips. "If I didn't know any better, I would've said you orchestrated this whole implosion to force us to move in together."

"Listen, I'm invested in this thing," Kirby said. "But not enough to punch a bloody hole in my roof." She waved up at the jagged opening, roof tiles hanging onto the edges and spilling into the room. "I'll call Petey and see what he can do."

"Divine intervention," Aya said with a grin. She looked past me out the window, and I followed her gaze to the white vet truck that was whizzing down the road. "Well, if it isn't your knight in shining armor."

I glanced over my shoulder. "Not the first time I've called her that."

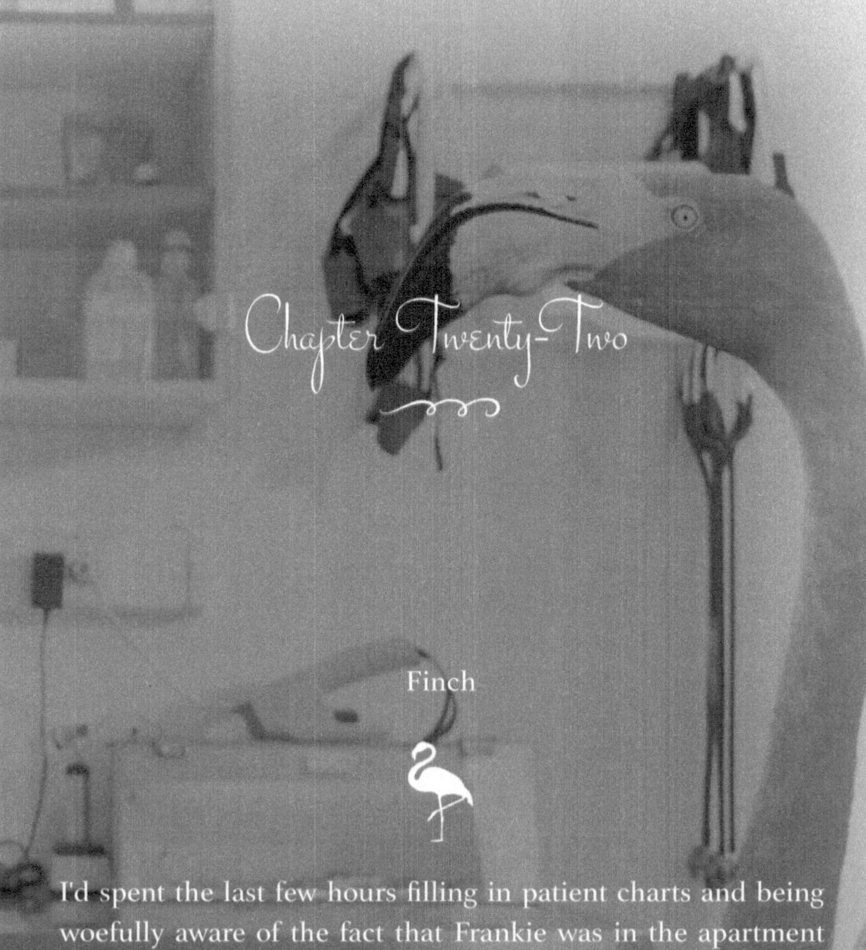

Chapter Twenty-Two

Finch

I'd spent the last few hours filling in patient charts and being woefully aware of the fact that Frankie was in the apartment above me. When I'd brought her back the night before, I'd made myself scarce so she could settle in, making up excuses of needing to start my day. But now I needed to face the fact that we would be sharing my apartment together for the foreseeable future . . . and I needed to not be super weird about it.

Frankie had seemed pleasantly surprised with the space at least, even though her bedroom was literally only a bed and an old banana box that Wren had converted into a bedside table as one of her many arts and crafts projects.

I spent my day thinking about Frankie, about how we were now roommates, and hoping that it wouldn't make our dynamic strained. At last, I decided it was time for bed. I checked on all the patients one last time before setting the alarms and turning off the lights for the night. When I entered the apartment, Frankie was sitting on the couch, watching TV, bundled up in wool socks, black leggings, and a gray hoodie. Her hair was still wet and that freshly showered smell filled the room.

"Hey," she said, sitting a little straighter.

"Hey," I added just as awkwardly. Why did this feel so different than the million other times I'd seen her? She was here, in my apartment, her presence feeling so much more intimate in my space. "How was your day?"

"Chaotic," she said, slumping back down on the couch.

I wandered over to the fridge. "Same."

"You hungry? I can cook something." Frankie was about to leap off the couch to help when I held up a hand, and she stalled, poised in a half-crouch.

"You don't have to earn your keep here, Goldilocks," I said, fishing around in the fridge. "You've been cooking all day."

"I just really appreciate you letting me stay here," she said. "I'm sorry if it's weird, me being here."

"Honestly, it's nice," I replied. "I don't necessarily miss living with all of my siblings, but I *do* miss having someone around at night." It was probably why I brought home someone several nights a week . . . I was too busy for a relationship, but I didn't really like being alone either, even if the rest of my family was literally only a minute's walk away.

Frankie hummed in agreement. "I understand. I've never lived alone."

I extracted myself from pilfering in the fridge to look at her. "You've never lived alone?"

"Well, I had roommates in college, and then I shared an apartment with some people for a while. Who can afford to live alone these days, you know? And then I met Jake so . . . yeah. After the summer, I might look at some shared apartment rentals or something. I don't really like the idea of getting my belt loop stuck on the door and dying before someone comes to rescue me."

I laughed as I opened the fridge again. "Knowing you, I think that's wise. Otherwise I'd have to sail to the mainland to rescue you." I pulled out a Tupperware container.

"Seriously, you don't have to cook," Frankie called from behind me. "You must be exhausted too."

"Mom's recipe," I said, waggling the container of spaghetti. "Is reheating acceptable, m'lady?"

She chuckled. "I'll allow it."

I started plating up the food. "Though, I will have you know I'm an excellent cook when I have the time to be. Nothing compared to you, of course, but I know my way around the kitchen."

"And *when* is this mythical free time you have?"

"Christmas maybe," I admitted. "When Lark and Logan come to visit and we have two extra pairs of hands, I enjoy some leisure cooking."

"Given your attention to detail, I bet you're a natural."

I gave her a wink. "I'm no Francesca Benedetti."

She laughed and toyed with her hoodie strings. "It's nice having someone cook for me for once. Jake never cooked anything. He said why would he when I was so much better at it."

"Every day, I become more and more confused how you ever were with a guy like that." I really wanted to stab him with a fork.

Frankie let out a groaning breath. "It's really only in hindsight that you see all of those things, you know?"

"I don't know," I countered. "He sounds pretty awful."

"To be fair, I really have no interest currently in sharing any of his good qualities."

"And *I* have no interest in ever thinking better of him," I said, "so please don't share them with me."

I took the hot bowls out of the microwave and stuck a fork in each, setting them at my four-seater dining table wedged into the corner of the kitchen, living, dining room.

Frankie got up and wandered over. "Thank you. I'll bring back some food from the Peacock tomorrow for dinner to make it up to you."

"You don't need to prove yourself to me," I reminded her, grabbing the bag of cheese from the fridge door without looking. I held it aloft. "Parmesan?"

"A girl after my own heart," Frankie said with a laugh. "Yes please."

I passed her the bag, and she dumped a heaping pile on her pasta before passing it back to me, where I heaped an even larger pile on mine. "I like my meals 50% pasta, 50% parmesan cheese," I told her.

She grinned as she swirled her spaghetti. "And this is why we get along so well."

"Want to put on a show?" I asked as I started Hoover-ing down my meal. "I've got a few queued up." I started scrolling through the thumbnails.

"Oh, *Deadloch*! I love that show," Frankie said as I scrolled past.

"I've been meaning to watch."

"You haven't seen it yet?" Her fork clattered against her plate. "We have to watch it." Her tired energy immediately sprung back to life. "But be warned, you will get addicted and want to binge-watch the whole thing, but we have to wake up at the butt crack of dawn so we have to swear only one episode per night."

"Does this show come with many more caveats and rules?" I teased.

She rolled her eyes. "Just hit play already, we're wasting time."

I laughed and put the show on, feeling Frankie's enthusiasm vibrating off her. It was infectious. I loved even more how much she wanted to share it with me. Maybe having a roommate slash fake girlfriend was just the thing I needed to get through the summer.

Chapter Twenty-Three

Finch

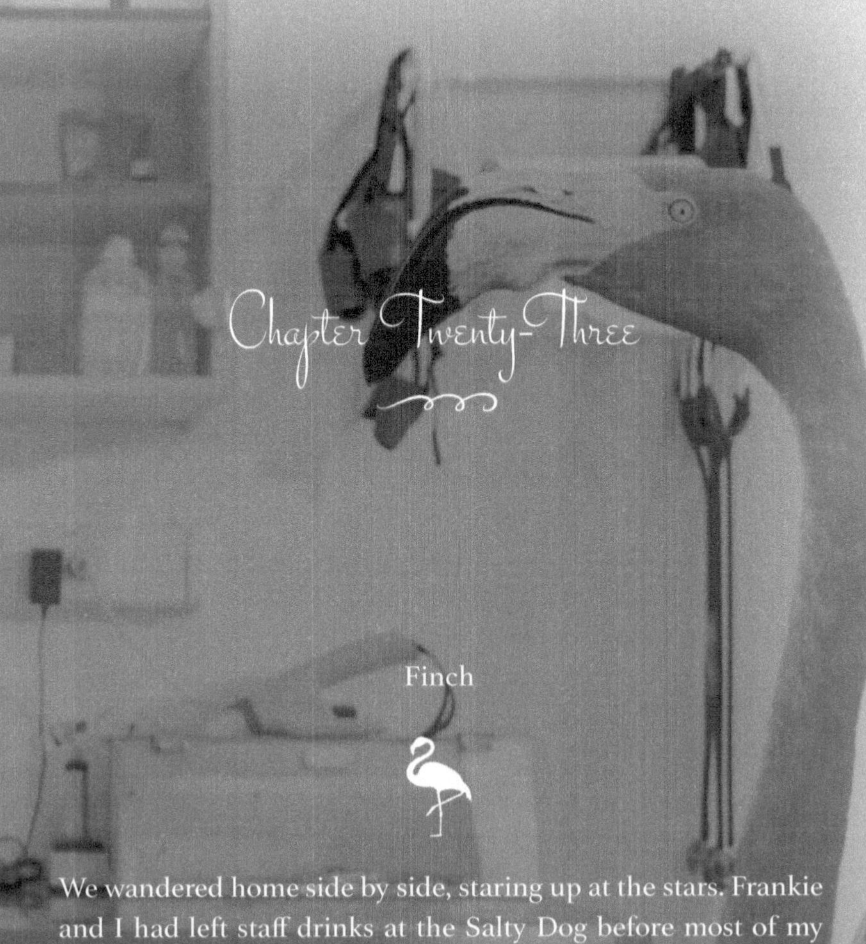

We wandered home side by side, staring up at the stars. Frankie and I had left staff drinks at the Salty Dog before most of my siblings, which had garnered a few curious glances. Normally, I was the last one to leave, but Frankie had looked tired and it had been a good excuse for me to make an early exit. After a slew of late nights feeding a baby bird, there was nothing I wanted more than to walk Frankie back to my apartment and watch TV until we fell asleep again.

"The girls were fawning over you hard in there," Frankie mused, staring up at the silvery, glowing moon.

"Apologies for using you like a human shield at one point," I quipped. "It's nice having a girlfriend to fend people off."

Her shoulders rose and fell with silent laughter. "I got a few pretty serious death stares, you know. I don't think the ladies of

Prickle Island are too happy about Finch Lachlan being off the market."

I grimaced. "Yeah. Sorry about that."

I hadn't expected so many women would be disappointed, but now I was coming to realize they viewed me as some sort of sapphic rite of passage. I hadn't thought about that before. They all just wanted one night with the zoo vet to tick off their summer bucket lists. It had seemed so fun a few years ago, and now it felt a little more like I was being used. But navigating the Salty Dog with Frankie on my arm had been a kind of relief. I hadn't needed to be on my game. I could just relax and enjoy the evening instead of jockeying around potential dates to see who I could take to bed that night. Although, I was *really* missing the having someone in my bed part.

"So, do you even need pickup lines, or do the girls just flock to you?" Frankie joked.

"Mostly flocking."

She laughed as she put her hands in her pockets. Frankie looked like some sort of 70s painter in her blue daisy-print overalls and a striped knit top. She had a cute, creative vibe—a little vintage, artsy, and colorful. Anyone could tell just by looking at her that she did something beautiful for a living.

Frankie's eyes dropped to my scrubs and she trailed a mindless finger over my arm. "The scrubs and vet jacket don't hurt, I'm sure. Everyone loves a woman in uniform."

I grinned, wondering if "everyone" included her too. "They love it a lot less when the uniform is covered in animal feces," I added with a chuckle. "All of us go to Tuesday drinks in our work clothes, my siblings in their khakis and me in my scrubs . . . unless I'm particularly covered in bodily fluids, in which case I change into a clean pair. Working with wildlife is a stinky profession."

"Good thing you naturally smell so good," Frankie said.

I'd wondered if she remembered the way she'd drunkenly

sniffed me on that yacht. There was something incredibly sexy about her liking my scent.

"I don't know, the smell of kangaroo piss can really get things going."

"Apparently. The girls seemed to be chasing you down like you're Harry Styles or something," Frankie teased. "Go on, tell me your secrets."

I shrugged. "I have a few charming lines in my back pocket."

"What is one of your tried and tested Finch Lachlan pickup lines?"

I paused and turned to her. "Did you know a group of finches is called a charm?" I waggled my eyebrows as Frankie laughed.

"*That* is your pickup line?" She cackled. "Does that even work?"

"Honestly, it's about 50/50."

We both laughed harder, wandering down the road to the zoo. "You're lucky you're gorgeous and smart and smell good," Frankie said through her belly laughter. "Because that's the only thing selling all that cheese."

I snorted. "I'm a cheesy person. What can I say?"

"Animal dork."

"Baking nerd."

"Here," Frankie said, passing me a plastic bottle that was tucked in the deep pockets of her overalls. "Water."

"Wa-ter?" I asked incredulously. "What is this mysterious liquid you speak of?"

Frankie rolled her eyes and playfully elbowed me. "Can I ask you something?"

I took a swig of water and screwed the cap back on. "Anything."

"Did you ever come close to a real relationship?"

I frowned at the bottle. "My life is too busy for real relationships," I said. "I can barely keep up with this fake one."

She hummed contemplatively. "Maybe one day you'll find someone who can keep up with you or, better yet, make you slow down."

"There is no slowing down," I said, the drinks loosening my tongue. "I'm going to work until it kills me according to my mother."

"That sounds very healthy."

I swayed drunkenly on unsteady legs despite only having three drinks the whole night. I hadn't slept more than two hours consecutively in weeks and the effects had me feeling like I'd just swigged down an entire bottle of vodka. "My job is my life. My life is me. It's all too intertwined to separate," I said. "That's why casual things are easier."

"How many casual things have there been?"

"You want my body count?" I asked with a laugh. "How forward of you."

"Well, seeing as you're my girlfriend . . ." Frankie gave me a little, secret smile as the ocean wind tousled her hair across her face. "It seems like the sort of thing I should know."

"Mm-hmm." I gave her a knowing look but finally gave in. "I really don't know. Somewhere in the mid three digits I'd guess."

"Oh dear lord," she said. "I don't know if I should be impressed or horrified."

I clicked my tongue. "We don't slut shame in this house."

"We're not in a house." I gave her a look. "And no shame," she added with a shake of her head. "I just . . . don't really see the point to it."

"What does that mean?" There was clearly some subtext there I was missing. "What don't you see the point in?"

"It just seems like a lot of effort on your part to be with so many people," she said. "I mean, no one actually enjoys sex—"

I jolted involuntarily, flinging the water bottle into the air like a haunted mansion clown had just jumped out at me. Frankie paused and looked at me, confused, as I scrambled to pick up the flung object.

"I'm sorry. I think I just had a stroke," I said, retrieving the water bottle. "*What* did you just say?"

"It's just movies and books where everyone is so turned on all the time," Frankie said with a shrug. "Like, sex isn't actually that much fun in reality. I don't get why anyone would choose to have it all the time."

My jaw unhinged, my mouth opened so wide at the statement. Snakes had nothing on me. I wasn't sure we were even speaking the same language. What sort of crazy pig Latin was coming out of her mouth right now?

Finally, I found the words. "Fuck, Frankie, what kind of sex were you having?"

She folded her arms defensively. "The normal kind."

"Not my normal," I said with a shake of my head as we carried on up the hill to the zoo.

"Maybe it's different with women—"

"I'm going to stop you right there," I said, holding my arm out to the side like Mom when she hit the brakes too hard. "It is most certainly different. Especially for someone who's gay, like me," I added quickly. I didn't want Frankie to think I was labeling her sexuality. There were lots of different corners of the rainbow community that she might belong to. But I *did* know many women with similar revelations as Frankie, myself included, although mine happened at sixteen and not twenty-nine.

"How do you know?" Frankie asked. "Have you ever been with a man?"

"A few times in school," I said. "Nice guys, but it was definitely not for me. I don't blame you for hating it."

"I just don't understand all the hype," she said.

"Well, we've got to find you someone to help you understand the hype then." The thought instantly made jealousy rise in my belly, something that was swiftly replaced by guilt. I had no right to be jealous of the person who got to rock Frankie's world.

"That sounds awesome for one day. I would very much like to be proven wrong," she added with a breathy laugh that made me ball my fists to keep from touching her. "But I'm not really thinking about dating again so soon after everything with Jake," she replied, chewing on her bottom lip.

"Who said anything about dating?"

That seemed to pique her interest. She looked at me sideways, a wry smile on her lips. "You mean just a casual hookup with someone?"

"Yeah." I playfully nudged her. *Keep your hands to yourself, Finch. Don't complicate this fake relationship!* "I think you'd enjoy yourself. A lot."

"Maybe." She chewed her bottom lip more, and I wished I knew exactly what she was daydreaming about. "I don't know. I wouldn't feel comfortable with a stranger."

"Well, if you change your mind, I've got a phone full of people who would definitely be interested," I said, feeling like I deserved a gold medal for not volunteering myself.

Daily Specials
kookaburra cucumber
sandwiches
$5.50
Macaw Macarons
6 for $12

Chapter Twenty-Four

Frankie

I bolted awake, hands thrown wide as if protecting myself from falling debris. My chest rose and fell in heaving breaths as I blinked away the dream and reality started to come back to my sleep-addled brain. The roof wasn't falling in on me. I was safe. My eyes took in the unfamiliar shadows of the room. All at once, I remembered I was in Finch's apartment, in her guest bedroom, with no roof caving in.

I let out a long, slow breath, trying to calm my nerves, when I heard another distant clatter of metal on a tiled floor.

I strained my ears to listen. It was probably Finch up for one of her nighttime feedings of that baby macaw. Maybe she'd dropped a bowl. But what if it wasn't? What if it was a burglar? Or worse, a loose tiger or something? What if Jailbreak finally figured out how to leap the visitor railing and there was a zebra wandering the halls of the vet hospital?

I knew I wasn't going to be able to fall back asleep until I investigated the source of the sound.

Throwing the duvet off me, I padded barefoot across the room. The space was easy to navigate in the dark since it was so sparse, with only a spare bed and a nightstand in the room. My suitcase lay open on the floor with stacks of clothes and toiletries mounded on either side. Finch had said she would get me a dresser, and I'd told her not to worry about it, that I'd be out of her hair in no time. But now that we were pretending to live together, would it be weird if I moved out again? Did I even want to? I supposed if anyone came over, I'd have to quickly move all my stuff into her bedroom across the hall, otherwise they'd suspect something was up. This snow-balling secret was getting hard to keep up with.

The sound of another clatter came from the distance, and I pulled a hoodie on over my tank top and baggy sleep shorts, letting it fall to the top of my thighs.

"Finch?" I called, opening my door and peeking a head out. I turned on my phone flashlight and swept the beam up and down the hall. Feeling like a member of a SWAT team, I kept my back to the wall and flashlight held high as I traversed the hallway to Finch's door.

I gently rapped on the freshly painted wood and opened it, only to find Finch fast asleep, mouth agape and arms curled around a pillow as if holding someone in her sleep. I smiled at her shadowed figure and tiptoed backwards, slowly shutting her door.

The sweetness of her sleeping was quickly replaced by a terrifying question: if she wasn't the one making the noise, then who was?

I turned to the kitchen, then the bathroom, inspecting the

rest of the apartment. Another clatter rang up the stairwell, and I realized the sound was coming from the hospital below.

I turned my phone flashlight to the front door and crept silently down—which was no small feat in an echoey, tiled hallway with no soft furnishings to dampen the sound. There was no dim lighting in the vet hospital either, and I knew if I turned the bright fluorescent lights on, all the animal patients would probably think it was morning and expect food. That was the last thing Finch needed. As I passed through the darkness, I checked Finch's schedule on the whiteboard in the hallway. She'd be up in half an hour to feed the chick again. I couldn't wake her.

Something caught my eye in the shadows, sliding across the floor, and I nearly jumped out of my skin. Every horror movie that had been permanently branded into the ridges of my brain flashed through my mind in rapid succession.

Don't be ridiculous, Frankie. It's probably just a cute, escaped baby monkey or something, the sensible part of my brain thought. But the louder part of my brain screamed, *Or it could be a hell beast sent to disembowel you! Run for your life!*

Another clatter made my blood run cold, followed by the sound of scratching that made bile rise up my throat.

"Finch better kiss my freaking ass for this," I whispered as I followed the trail of overturned bowls and baskets.

My heart slammed into my sternum with every step. I grabbed a pair of suture scissors off the drying rack and held them aloft as I kept walking. It was the least practical weapon I could've selected. What was I going to do, suture the burglar to death?

I turned the corner, scissors raised, ready to attack, when I saw the culprit: a tortoise slipping and sliding across the tiles.

"Oh shit," I said, dropping the scissors and giving chase. "Stop!"

The rebellious leopard tortoise must've escaped his carrier and decided to go gallivanting around the closed hospital in search of midnight snacks. I thought for a second about waking up Finch to catch him, but she already was so sleep-deprived .. . and it was a tortoise, not a cheetah. Of all the animals, I could handle this one.

I went to pick up the escapee and he skidded across the floor with surprising speed. "You're supposed to be slow," I gritted out, chasing him down the hall before finally grabbing him by the shell and hoisting him up. His little legs kept scrambling under him for a few seconds before he resigned himself to the fact he'd been caught.

I surveyed the damage as I walked him back to the reptile care room in Ward A. Luckily, there hadn't been many breakable things at ground level for him to knock over. If he had gotten up on the countertop, that would've been a very different story.

I placed the shelled fugitive back into his carrier and carefully latched the door. It was fiddly, rusted on one end, and easy to mistake for shut when the latch was still only half in the lock. I rattled the wire door a few times to make sure the escape artist was well and truly stuck for the night before turning to clean up the trail of overturned bowls and crates.

"Frankie," someone whispered into the darkness.

My brow furrowed. There was no way I could've heard that, right?

I spun, searching the darkness with my phone light. It probably was just the whir of the air filter.

"Frankie," a voice whispered again, clearer this time.

I froze, my arms rippling with goose bumps as I searched the shadows. Was I still asleep? *No*, my logic told me. This was very real. And I did hear someone whispering my name from the shadows, not a figment of my imagination.

I tiptoed into the next room, debating whether I should investigate the sound or run upstairs and hide under my bedsheets until morning. Was this place haunted? The only logical conclusion was I was down here, alone, with a freaking ghost. I suddenly realized I was standing in a dark hospital ward like every fucking slasher movie, and now some rogue spirit was whispering my name.

Well, at least this is an interesting way to be murdered. Francesca Benedetti, death by poltergeist.

"Frankie." I shuddered as the voice called again. "Frankie."

Creeping through the next room, I headed toward the sound when a hand landed on my shoulder. I shrieked, dropping my phone.

"Frankie," Finch said, holding me out by both arms. "Jesus. Are you okay? What happened?"

"I . . ." I spun around, my whole body shaking. "Were you . . . Oh god, you're going to think I'm crazy, but I think I just heard a ghost."

Finch was clearly not expecting that response. "A ghost?"

"Yeah." I glared into the darkness at the end of the hall. "It was whispering *my name*."

Finch's concern morphed into a smile as recognition lit up her face. "Ah," she said. "Come this way."

She threaded her fingers through mine, lifting my hand to kiss the back of it, which I told myself was just out of friendly reassurance and nothing more. As she pulled me down the hall in the direction of the sound, I practically hid behind her as we moved farther into the darkness. We stopped at the mesh of an aviary door, coming face-to-face with a very awake scarlet macaw.

"This is Monty," Finch said, making introductions. "Monty, this is the other Frankie, the one I was telling you about."

The macaw's pupils widened as he spotted Finch and he whispered again, "Frankie."

I gaped at the bird. That sound was coming from him?

"It was a macaw?" I whirled to Finch for confirmation. "How does he know how to say my name? Why does he whisper it so creepily?"

Finch chuckled. "When I come down here to feed the baby bird, Frankie—complicated, I know. You can blame Dove for that—I whisper to her so I don't wake up all the other patients." She tipped her head to the macaw. "Monty must've learned the whispering from me. He also knows how to say "hot stuff" and can whistle a bunch of TikTok sounds that Dove taught him. He's a big fan of Billie Eilish if you have any requests."

"It was a macaw," I said again, still in bemused disbelief. Who would've ever thought *that* could be the reason? I didn't blame myself for thinking ghost. Really, that still made more sense. My panic finally eased. Finch released my hand as if suddenly realizing she was still holding it.

"What are you doing down here anyway?" she asked.

"Your tortoise got out," I said, waving down the hallway behind me. "He's fine. I put him back. I was just cleaning up his disaster trail."

"Scooter," Finch muttered. "Never has a tortoise given me as much trouble as him." She folded her arms and looked at me. "That was thoughtful of you, but you should've just woken me up. I could've handled it."

"I know, but I wanted you to get some sleep," I replied. "If it was anything more formidable than a tortoise, I promise I would've asked for your help."

Finch wiped the sleep from her eyes and checked her watch. "It's almost time for Cranky Frankie's feed so I guess I'll get a head start on that." She swept her hair out of her eyes, her gaze lingering on my hoodie then moving down to my bare legs and feet. A smile formed on her lips. "Of all the things I expected to find coming down here."

"Living above a vet hospital must be an adventure," I said.

"Only with you in it." Finch shook her head. "When you're used to living with six siblings, you'd be surprised how calm and organized this place is by comparison, even with wild animals as housemates."

My chuckle was cut short as she touched a gentle hand to my forearm. "Go back to sleep," she said and rocked forward for a split second before immediately rocking back again like a neurotic seesaw. The way she leaned in, it was as if she were planning on kissing me. Maybe her sleep-drunk brain still thought we needed to pretend.

She tried to play it off by shifting her weight back and forth a few more times and stretching her neck side to side, but I caught the way she'd dipped her head ever so slightly.

"Do you want me to help you?" I asked. "I'm up now. My heart's still racing. Let me tidy or wash up or something."

Her face softened at the offer. "That is very kind of you, but I'm okay," she said. "I make the summer volunteers do a lot of the cleaning anyway. They get experience around a vet hospital and a letter of recommendation from me in exchange, so I'd say it's a fair trade."

"Probably a good way of weeding out the ones not cut out for veterinary medicine too," I mused. "Very perceptive."

I'd certainly be deterred by spending my days cleaning up bodily fluids. I had no idea how medical professionals did it. I'd gagged when I'd found a batch of moldy raspberries in the fridge yesterday, and here Finch was just casually surgically removing gecko tails and shit.

As we walked back down the hall, Finch's eyes fell to my weapon of choice—the discarded surgical scissors. She picked them up and put them into a tub of soapy water in the sink. "I will be putting these through the sanitizer again. No more scissoring random ghosts," she scolded then laughed to herself. "At least not this kind of scissoring."

My cheeks burned furiously at that comment. I looked everywhere but at Finch. "Okay, uh, goodnight again then."

"Goodnight, Goldilocks," Finch said as I scampered back down the hall and away from the creepy macaw who knew how to whisper my name.

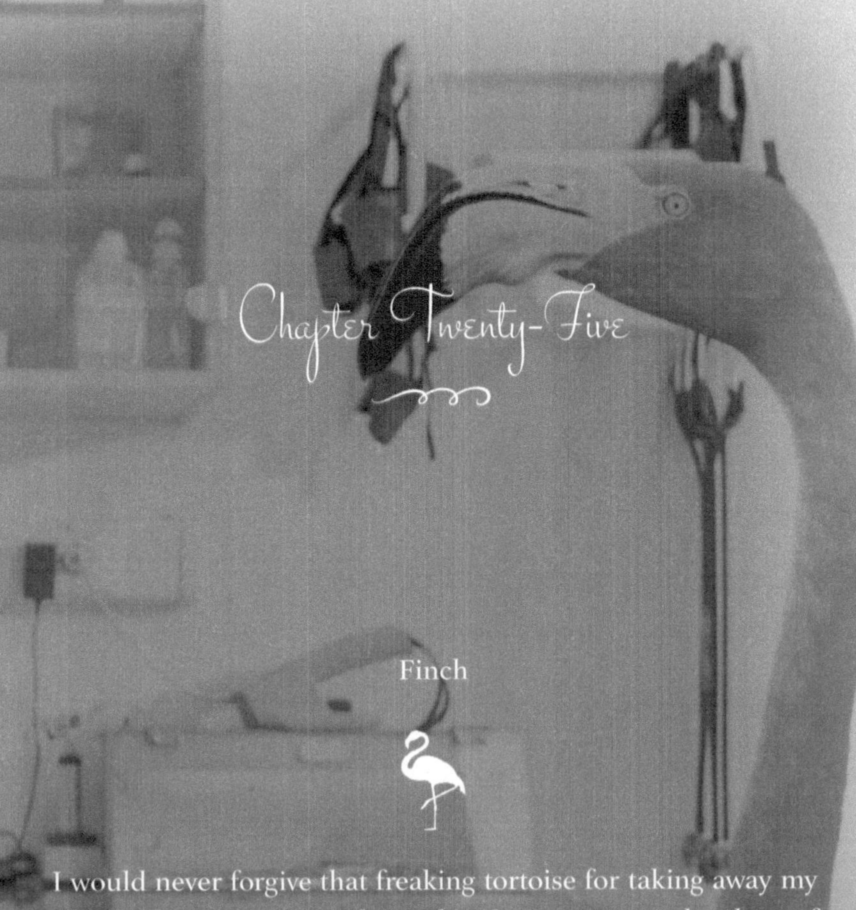

Chapter Twenty-Five

Finch

I would never forgive that freaking tortoise for taking away my evening hangout time with Frankie. Scooter was on day three of being on my shit list. He seemed determined to ruin what little social life I had left.

By the time I got upstairs, I wondered if Frankie had already gone to bed, but the light in her room was still on . . . as well as the light to the third bedroom—the bedroom where I had a leather chest of sex toys.

As realization dawned on me, I practically sprinted the rest of the way down the hall to find Frankie gaping down at the opened chest.

"Oh!" she exclaimed, shooting backward. "Sorry. Sorry. I was just looking for an extra pillow, and sorry—"

I let out a sharp laugh. "You found my sex toy treasure chest."

"I can't believe how many . . . uh, *things* you have," Frankie commented, clearly trying to keep her tone neutral. "I'm pretty sure I don't know what half of them even do."

"Want me to show you?" I loved how easily I could turn her redder than a scarlet ibis. I thought maybe she'd stopped breathing entirely as I leaned in and added, "That was a joke."

"Oh right." She let out a shaky laugh. "I knew that."

But did she? And did I mean it as a joke? I had no idea. The thought of her splayed out naked on my bed while I used these toys on her had flashed through my mind before . . . especially during my solo fun times in the shower, which had been happening a lot since my involuntary vow of abstinence.

"What are these?" Frankie asked, lifting up a pair of latex panties between pinched fingers as if they were dirty underwear.

"Those are for oral *things*," I taunted. I was normally very cavalier with these sorts of things, but showing them off to Frankie was different. "Gone are the days of dental dams," I added with another awkward chuckle. "These you don't have to hold in place and they don't slip around as much."

"Oh," she said, retuning them to the box. "You have like, fifty pairs of them."

"They're disposable," I said.

"Do you always use them?"

"Often." I shrugged. "If I were with the same partner for a while, I probably wouldn't, but I think it would be irresponsible of me to be deep sea diving with every girl on the island and not use protection, you know?"

Frankie's mouth bobbed open and then quickly shut at that comment. "Right." She looked like her brain was spiraling out. "And the rest of these things?"

I made a half sigh, half grumble sound that caught at the

back of my throat. "Well, they've certainly come in handy for solo adventures while I've sworn off casual sex for the summer."

"Yep," Frankie said, popping her P as she swayed, unable to stand still. "I sympathize with your current predicament."

"Well then, here," I said, diving into my treasure trove and producing a brand new, still wrapped, purple bullet vibe. "A gift for you."

Her laugh was too loud as she stared at it and then up at me. "I don't know when I'd use it with you right next door but—"

"I don't care," I offered, sounding overly casual. Frankie knew me too well by now, and judging by her expression, she knew I was lying. Still, I continued, "There's no point in leaving a brand-new toy just sitting around. You should have it."

"Really?" she asked incredulously. "That wouldn't be weird?"

"We're grown adults, Frankie," I scoffed, really laying it on thick. The truth was, it shouldn't bother me at all, and if we were actually just friends like we said we were, I wouldn't be flustered by it. "What you do behind your bedroom door is your business. Have fun."

"Fine," she said, squaring off at me, a challenge in her eyes. I had a terrible feeling she was going to try to prove just how "weird" it could be. She started opening the packaging. "Maybe I'll go have some fun right now since you aren't bothered."

My eyes widened, and when she flashed her defiant smile in response, I knew I'd just given myself away.

"Fine," I gritted out, trying to sound flippant. "I'm going to do a final check on my patients anyway. Enjoy."

She smiled at me smugly as she took her new vibrator and disappeared behind her bedroom door. Flustered and, let's be honest, horny, I stormed out to the stairwell and back down to the vet hospital.

There's no reason I should be thinking about this, I told myself over and over again. *Solo fun times are great. Important, even. I'm a sex positive person. This is a public service. This is all cool. I'm definitely not thinking about Frankie fucking herself right now, and I'm definitely not wishing I could be a part of it . . .*

With my mind split in two, I fed Cranky, turned off all the lights, checked the doors, and then took one last peek at the corn snake who was spending a night of observation in the hospital. Nothing out of the ordinary. If anything, apart from the baby bird, the hospital was relatively quiet this summer.

Still, I decided to make myself another cup of decaf coffee and update all my charts, check my emails, do some admin I'd been putting off, and give Frankie some space. She'd have to charge the thing first anyway. I was probably fine to go back up there. I'd fall asleep before she could even turn it on, but I couldn't bring myself to get up. Flashes of her fisting her sheets, trying not to moan too loud, burying her face in her pillow as she came undone—

Fuuuuuuuck.

I wanted to storm up there, spread her legs, and lick her sweet pussy until her thick thighs were trembling around my ears.

Dammit, Finch! This is no way to think about your friends, even the ones you are pretending to be in a relationship with!

This was bad, so torturously bad. Frankie obviously didn't feel about me the way I felt about her. I should've never agreed to enter this ploy with someone so ridiculously beautiful. I should've known I wouldn't be able to keep my strap-on dick in my pants. This was agony, and I was beginning to suspect Frankie knew it, knew how touch-starved I was, knew how much I just wanted another casual fling of spending all night making a hot girl come.

But I couldn't risk sneaking out to the mainland. If my family found out . . . it would be bad. They'd murder me if they thought I was cheating on Frankie. They all loved her, and they'd probably boot me out of the zoo before her. I couldn't do that to them, or to Frankie.

But Frankie had only had really disappointing sex her whole life so she probably didn't even miss it, whereas *I* knew how great it could be between the two of us. But if I did seduce her into bed, what then? She'd probably want something more and I definitely didn't. That would be the shittiest thing I could do: sleep with her, lead her on, and turn her pretend feelings into real ones. No. We couldn't cross that line. It would just make all of this even messier.

I drank the last of my coffee and left it on my desk to clean up in the morning. Frazzled and frustrated, I walked back up the steps, resolute in my decision. But when I reached the kitchen, I heard the buzzing sound.

That fucking buzzing.

Fuck. Fuck. Fuck.

I was so screwed.

I grabbed my hair in both hands, yanking it in frustration.

I wanted to go to her door, press my ear against it, hear her soft, frantic breaths in my ears, hear the sounds she made as she came undone. I wanted to watch as she touched herself, as she came apart and surrendered to her own pleasure. I wanted her to look me in the eyes and finally know what it could actually be like...

This was well and truly hell. This was a mythological torture that would put Sisyphus to shame. I didn't know if I was strong enough to survive it.

But instead of storming to Frankie's door and throwing it open and fucking her like I wanted to, I turned to the bathroom for an ice-cold shower.

Daily Specials

kookaburra cucumber
sandwiches
$5.50

Macaw Macarons
6 for $12

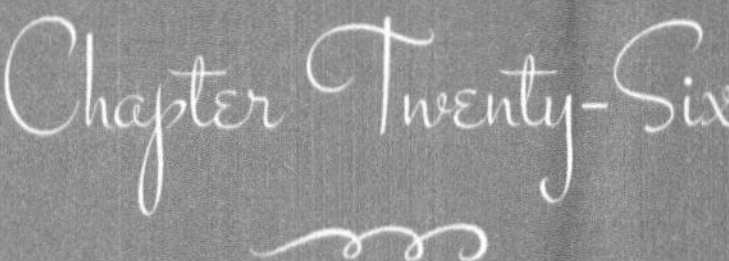

Chapter Twenty-Six

Frankie

Finch was still pulling her shirt on when she walked into the kitchen and paused at the sight of me.

"Morning," I said through a mouthful of fried egg sandwich. "I brought you some breakfast."

I felt like I needed to clear the air after last night, and also, while I was . . . having fun with myself, an idea had popped up in my mind, one that I was still debating if I was brave enough to voice aloud.

"Hey," Finch said, her voice still raspy with sleep as she wandered to the coffee pot, and upon finding it already brewed, she added under her breath, "You're my favorite person."

I chuckled. "So easily won over. Excellent."

"Sorry, I would've emerged fully clothed if I thought you were still here. Usually, you're gone by now."

"It's fine," I said, remembering the planes of her tanned stomach and the way she wore her scrubs so low on her hips. "I had just finished prepping for the morning and I thought I'd come back and change before the zoo opened so I wasn't covered in flour and oil stains." I nodded to the plate across from me. "And I figured you'd want some breakfast too."

She murmured something sleepy and unintelligible, but it sounded grateful so I took it. She groaned as she bit into her egg sandwich. She licked the runny yoke from her thumb in a way that had my eyes snagging on her mouth.

I took another long sip of coffee. "Thanks for the gift last night," I said, adding that goading back into my tone. "I *definitely* enjoyed it."

Finch folded in half, collapsing to lean her forehead against the wood of the kitchen table. "Uncle. Mercy. Whatever you say, just please stop."

I laughed at the dramatics. "What?"

"You're trying to kill me, aren't you?"

"Whatever do you mean?" I asked coyly.

"You know exactly what you're doing."

I'd seen the look in her eye when she'd given me that vibrator. I'd read the barely restrained lust on her face. "I thought you didn't care," I taunted.

"I don't," she blustered, lifting her head to look at me. "I mean, I don't in the way that you're meaning. I'm not bothered in a "wish my roommate wasn't getting off with me in the house" kind of way. It's just . . . I haven't been laid in a really long time and I have needs, and I just . . . am a little sexually frustrated at the moment," she admitted.

I bit my lip, trying to contain my grin. "Just a little."

"The tiniest smidgeon," she joked, pinching her fingers together. "And I don't want to be sneaking off with someone else and have people thinking I'm cheating on you, but the last thing I want to do is complicate things between us either by sleeping together."

"Maybe we should," I said, and Finch choked on her food, lurching forward.

Gasping, she asked, "What did you just say?"

"Maybe we should sleep together. I mean, if you want to?"

"Jesus, Goldilocks, I'm not awake enough for you to joke with me like this."

"I'm not joking," I said, pushing through my rising nerves. "Look. I've never been with a woman, and after I finish this job this summer, I think I'm probably going to want to be with women, only women, and I don't want to have absolutely no idea what I'm doing. So . . . maybe you could teach me?"

"*Teach* you?" she spluttered, snatching a paper towel to wipe her yolk-covered fingertips. "Believe me, you absolutely have nothing to worry about in that department."

"Still, I'd feel more confident, and you could take the edge off. It seems like a win-win."

"But what if—"

"There will be no feelings attached," I vowed, crossing a hand across my chest. "My heart is still all trampled out of shape. I think the only thing it'll be feeling is wild rage and vengeance for a long time still. You don't have to worry about me. I know you're not into relationships."

"No feelings," Finch echoed, as if confirming my position.

I nodded. I didn't want to have feelings for anyone for a long, long time. And it seemed like too good of an opportunity to pass up. I could be free to ask questions, make mistakes, and be awkward, and I knew Finch wouldn't care. I couldn't believe I might have casual sex at all, let alone with someone as glorious as Finch.

She took another sip of coffee and weighed her head back and forth, and I was so excited she was even considering it.

"You told me you'd show me how all those toys worked," I goaded.

She guffawed. "Well, a promise is a promise, I guess." She bit her lip in the sexiest way before asking, "Do you know your status? I get tested with a certain amount of regularity." She laughed softly, as if she were suddenly a little shy, which only made her even more endearing. "No STIs to disclose."

"Me either," I said. "I mean, I've been with the same guy for eight years so . . . Actually, let's not mention him."

"Hard agree." She finally met my gaze as the haze of sleep lifted off her. "No feelings, only fun. Just a physical, casual thing, yes?"

"We'd be doing each other a favor, nothing more," I agreed, feeling like I'd solved an impossible riddle. *Ask and you shall receive*, I supposed. "Just another natural evolution of our arrangement."

Finch grinned at me. "Well, Goldilocks, you've got yourself a deal then."

"Really?"

"Yeah, I think it's a good idea actually," she said. "Maybe I might be able to relax a little bit."

I felt like I'd fallen through a portal to another dimension where it was totally normal for hot friends to sleep together just for fun. Maybe they did and it was just another thing I knew nothing about? Why did I feel like I'd just pulled off the most incredible heist?

"Okay, so, uh, tonight?"

"Tonight," Finch said with a wink, rising to a stand as she took a giant mouthful of sandwich. It was only once she left to the stairwell that I suddenly realized that I'd actually have to go through with what I'd just proposed. She'd actually taken me up on the offer. I was actually going to sleep with the hottest woman I'd ever seen in my entire life.

Holy shit. I was going to sleep with Finch! Tonight!

There was no way in hell I wasn't burning every bit of baking in anticipation of tonight. And I couldn't seem to find a single fuck to mind about it. Oh my god. I was about to sleep with Goldfinch Lachlan. What had I gotten myself into?

Daily Specials

kookaburra cucumber
sandwiches
$5.50
Macaw Macarons
6 for $12

Chapter Twenty-Seven

Frankie

I had never shut down for the day so quickly in my life. You could lick the floor, that was how perfectly shined the front café and Peacock were. Both spaces were locked promptly at 5 pm, and I moved in a haze through the zoo back to the vet hospital. I was barely able to lift my hand to wave at Hannah as the keeper wandered past.

I was levitating, practically jumping out of my skin. What would it be like? I couldn't even begin to imagine, but I had a feeling it would be really, really good.

When I entered the back of the vet hospital, Finch must've heard because she called from the treatment room, "Have a good day, babe?"

"Babe," I heard Dove snicker.

"A great one, love," I called back, and I knew Finch would

be smiling. How? I had no idea, but I would've bet good money she was currently wearing that cheeky, lopsided grin, the one that made her cheeks dimple.

There was something incredibly fun about sneaking around, about fooling everyone. It was like we were playing house and no one knew. I hoped tonight wouldn't change that. I'd promised Finch I could handle casual sex and I needed to not let it get weird between us. This felt like a good stepping stone into a real relationship with a woman.

"I'm almost done here," Finch called. "Looking forward to tonight, babe."

My heart punched a hole in my ribcage at that.

"I am literally standing right here," Dove muttered. "Control yourself. You're worse than Loki."

"Comparing me to a teenage baboon, nice," Finch replied.

"I'm hopping in the shower, see you in a bit," I called as I raced the rest of the way up the stairs and fled to the shower. I needed to shave everything from below my eyeballs all the way down to my hobbit toes. I would buff my skin raw and scrub my much-neglected pussy until she was fucking pristine because *oh my god,* Finch might be touching her tonight.

When I emerged from the bathroom, I leapt backward. Finch stood in the middle of the kitchen, dropping her phone onto the magnetic charge stand.

"Uh." Finch looked at me with a confused laugh. "Boo?"

She sat backwards on the kitchen chair, still in her scrubs, a stethoscope still hanging around her neck, and she looked like the sexiest fucking doctor I'd ever seen. *I wished she'd straddle me like that,* I thought, making my blush even more furious.

"Sorry, I was in my own world," I said with an awkward laugh. It was only then I realized I only had a towel wrapped *mostly* around me, the slit rising all the way up to my hip. "Um, I'll go get changed."

"Why?" Finch asked. "I'm just going to take your clothes off again." My mouth fell open. "Unless you're having second thoughts, which is seriously fine. I'm only into what you're comfortable with—"

"I'm not having second thoughts," I cut in, practically leaping forward at that. I would never forgive myself if I chickened out now. "Are you . . . having second thoughts?"

Finch's eyes trailed down my body, snagging on the bare skin of my hip where the towel didn't completely close over, and my heart lurched into my throat. "Absolutely not."

"Okay."

"Okay," she echoed with a rueful smile. "So you want to go my room?"

"Yeah," I said, straightening my towel and trying to walk with some modicum of confidence to her room, even while it felt like my chest was vibrating with nerves. I flicked the bright overhead lights off when I walked in and headed straight to Finch's bedside lamp.

"What are you doing?" she asked before I could reach it.

"Turning the light off?"

"Why?"

"I . . ." I shrugged. I really didn't want to be butt naked with a whole ass light on. Shadows could conceal a lot of my anxiety. "You want it on?"

"Goldilocks." Finch swept a hand through her hair before taking off her stethoscope and hanging it over the back of her door handle. I knew that tone, and my gut clenched because it was hard to hear it. "I have no idea how to say this without just saying it, but since we're just messing around casually, no feelings," she said carefully, "I'm just going to be blunt and tell you."

My pulse ratcheted faster. "Tell me what?"

"I really, *really* want to see you naked."

My mouth fell open. "Oh."

"Respectfully," she said, holding out her hands.

We both gave each other a perplexed look before erupting into laughter. The absurdity of the moment caught up with us, and I couldn't stop the rolling belly laughter until Finch took a step toward me. When her hand touched my bare arm, I sobered up real quick.

Nerves wobbled my voice as I said, "Okay, well, you have to get naked too then."

"I mean, I was planning on it." She grinned, reaching back without hesitation and removing her scrubs top. She stood before me in a black sports bra, her scrubs low on her hips as she kicked her wool socks off to the corner of the room.

"Thank you for showing me what this is all about," I said, my voice coming out all breathy.

Finch laughed again, a sexy, rasping laugh that was better than foreplay. "The pleasure is all mine, Goldilocks," she crooned. "But being with a woman isn't like being abducted to another sex planet," she teased. "I don't think you're going to require any instruction, other than maybe a reminder to get out of your head and have some fun?"

"Right," I said, forcing my shoulders down as she hooked her hands into her pants and pulled them down.

She stepped out of them, revealing her black boxer briefs. I could feel the heat rising through every cell in my body as I took her in. Her skin was a beautiful, smooth olive tone, muscled and athletic in a way that made my mouth go dry. She was masculine and feminine in all my favorite ways, this beautiful cocktail that seemed mixed especially for me, like she'd walked right out of my most secret fantasies.

She took a step back to me until she was a hair's breadth away. "Is it okay if I kiss you now?" she asked tauntingly.

"Uh-huh," I said, barely able to get the words out.

"Get out of your head, Goldilocks," she said, leaning down and brushing a light kiss to my lips. "If you want to stop, just tell me, okay? If you want to change things, just tell me. If you want more..."

"Just tell you?"

She nodded, her eyes transfixed on my mouth. "These lips," she murmured as if speaking only to herself.

This time, I decided to be bold and bridged the distance between us. I kissed Finch with more eagerness. I'd never felt anything like when I kissed her. It was as if my heart were exploding and I *liked* it.

Finch's hands slid up my sides, one hand tangling in my hair while the other snaked around my back. The little sound that caught at the back of her throat set me on fire. My hands that had strained with the effort of not touching her were finally released and they roved over her sides and down to squeeze her firm ass and rove up her sides. She groaned into my mouth.

"Take your towel off." She pulled me back into a kiss before I could reply, as if she couldn't keep her lips off me. "Please," she begged against my mouth.

I smiled and our teeth knocked together. We both laughed as she took a step back. My pulse galloped through every vein as I dropped my towel. I stood there for a second, terrified, feeling like I'd just leapt out of a plane without a parachute. I wondered if every stretch mark and dimple was being scrutinized. I kept my gaze downcast, heat building in my cheeks, my eyes pricking with unwelcome tears.

Before I could spiral out though, Finch's body came into view and her fingers lifted my chin gently to meet her eyes. When I looked up, she was wearing that roguish grin, her eyes hooded with lust.

"Frankie?"

"Yeah?"

"You are so fucking beautiful," she whispered. "I'm going to worship every inch of your body until you believe me."

Air stole from my lungs as I finally rasped out, "Okay."

Finch's smile grew as she closed the distance again, kissing me with growing intensity as her hands smoothed over my skin. I gasped each breath between our kisses as her hands skimmed over my ass and up to cup one breast. Circling my nipple with her thumb, she rolled it into a peak as my breath hitched.

I was flooded with desire, kissing her like I might be able to consume her very essence into me. Desperate. This was meant to be casual, fun, but Finch matched my intensity, kissing me as if she needed me just as badly. I gave in to the intoxicating rush. She spun me to the bed and prowled on top of me, kissing me again before dropping her mouth to one breast and then the other. I writhed beneath her as she kissed across the dips and valleys of my belly to the top of my thighs.

"Open your legs," she commanded, and I did. "Wider." She grabbed me by the knees and bared me to her. "Every sweet inch. I promised you, didn't I?"

I couldn't reply, breathless and trembling with anticipation.

She kissed up the inside of my thigh, nibbling at the dimpled skin and licking her way higher until I was practically floating off the bed in a heady cloud of desire. She traced a finger down my center, parting my flesh, opening me wider to her as her mouth dropped to my clit.

The garbled moan I let out made her hum against my pussy, pleased with my sounds. She licked me up and down in slow, measured strokes, as if she had all the time in the world to feast on me.

"That feels so good." I panted, barely able to get the words out as she licked me over and over, building me higher. "Oh god."

Finch grabbed my wrist and brought my hand to her head. I grabbed a clump of her hair, holding on for dear life as I began moving against her mouth. It was already too much. I was going to shatter apart. Just the thought of the most stunning human on the entire planet devouring me had my core slick with desire.

As if hearing my silent thoughts, Finch's fingers circled my entrance, dipping in and out of me deeper and deeper as her tongue continued its trail up and down, up and down.

"Yes," I moaned as she hooked her fingers, massaging my inner walls.

She did it again, and before I could control myself, I was breaking. My orgasm exploded through me, my sound a rasping gasp, so sharp and all-encompassing, I couldn't control the sounds escaping me. Every cell in me tingled with that sweet ecstasy, wringing me out and making me whole again. When my pussy finally stopped clenching around Finch's fingers, she released me.

I thought she might just walk away, might go wash her mouth out like Jake used to . . . before he gave up entirely. Thought she'd maybe give me a high five and say goodnight. Was that how casual hookups ended? Instead, she slowly trailed kisses back up the way she'd come, as if she needed to taste every stretch mark and freckle, worshipping my body just as she'd promised she would.

When she reached my mouth, she kissed me deeply, the taste of my own release on her tongue.

"Oh, sweet little Goldilocks," she purred. "You and I are going to have all sorts of fun together, aren't we?"

My tentative hands strolled along her sides as she lay next to me. I strayed my fingers to the waistband of her boxers. Emboldened by her reverent touches, I dipped a finger beneath the band suggestively. "Do you want me to . . . ?"

A wicked curve graced Finch's lips. "Do you want to?"

My mischievous smile matched her own. "Show me what you like."

She took my hand and guided it into her boxers, skimming over the trimmed hairs between her legs.

"I don't think I'm going to be able to hang on very long." She groaned as she slid my fingers across her clit. She led me, circling them, her hand over mine, showing me exactly what she liked. I could feel she was already dripping wet. The thought had my pussy clenching again. That she was so turned on by eating me out . . . I didn't know that was possible.

"Like this?" I whispered into her ear, kissing down her neck.

She only let out a confirming groan before releasing my hand, letting me fly solo. I continued circling her as she ground her hips up into my touch, her breathing growing ragged.

"Fuck, Frankie, yes." She moaned, turning and burying her face into my shoulder. "Yes."

She lifted her chin, claiming my mouth right as she came. I kissed her back, consuming her every desperate breath as she rocked beneath my touch. Our mouths fused as I circled her through the last echoes of her orgasm before finally releasing her.

She collapsed back down, sweat slicking her brow, a sated smile on her face, and I felt a strange sort of pride that I was the one to make her come undone like that.

"That was an excellent first lesson," I said, sweeping the tangled hair off my face.

Finch chuckled, a sleepy smile on her face. "I am an excellent teacher," she teased, rolling onto her side and propping her head up with her hand. "But this lesson isn't over yet."

My eyes widened in surprise. "No?"

Her eyes dropped back to my mouth as she shook her head. "Welcome to my world, Goldilocks," she said. "Our night has only just begun."

Chapter Twenty-Eight

Finch

I didn't know how I was going to get through this without touching her. Especially when she dropped her towel and revealed a coral pink two piece that sat high on her hips, the neckline cut like something a 50's pin-up might wear. Immediately, I had flashbacks to when she'd dropped her towel the night before, of how she'd been shy and nervous, of how by dawn, she hadn't hesitated at all. Now she walked around like she knew exactly how gorgeous she was. And I felt glad that I got to give her that little nudge she needed. The confidence already existed in her, but I loved that I could be a part of getting her to finally reveal it.

"Finch?"

"What?" I realized I hadn't been paying a lick of attention to what she'd asked.

Frankie's cheeks dimpled as if she knew exactly where my mind was. "What are we doing today?"

"Um." I clapped my hands together, trying to formulate a game plan. "You know, I think we're ready for the deep end."

Her smile fell. "I don't know . . ."

"It's just the same as the shallow end."

Her face scrunched. "Except it's not."

"I think you should jump in."

Frankie's eyes flew wide at that. "Have you lost your ever-loving mind?"

"It'll be good practice if you fall in the water," I pointed out. "You've already practiced kicking up to the surface. It's just now you won't be able to put your feet down."

"Yeah, I don't like the sound of that."

I took a step toward her and extended out my hand. "Come on, Frankie," I prodded. "You know I'd never let you drown, right? I'll be in the water, ready to grab you if you freak out."

"I'm freaking out right now," she countered, waving to her feet. "On dry land."

"Okay," I said, easing off. "It's your call. Let's start in the shallow end again then."

Instead of taking my hand, Frankie squared her shoulders and said, "No. I can do it."

"There's my girl," I said with a laugh. I had a sneaking suspicion if I called her bluff, she'd agree. I knew that kind of stubborn determination all too well.

Turning, I dove into the deep end. When I emerged, I slicked my hair back and smiled at Frankie as she stood at the edge of the pool. Her toes gripped the tiles as if she might inadvertently fling herself off at any moment.

"Okay," she said, her shoulders rising and falling with resolution.

"Remember to turn around and kick back toward the wall," I called encouragingly.

"Yep.” She nodded.

"You've got this."

"Uh-huh," she said, biting her bottom lip. But she didn't move.

"If you jump, I promise to feast on you tonight."

She let out a nervous laugh. "You would've done that anyway," she countered.

"Good point." I laughed. "Okay, how about I show you my strap?”

“Is using sex as a reward part of the casual hookup guidebook?”

“It is if it's working.”

She laughed a little lighter this time. "You make an excellent argument."

"I'm very compelling." I splashed water at her playfully. "Come on, Goldilocks. You jump and I'll give you a record-breaking number of orgasms tonight, seems like a fair deal—”

She jumped before I could even finish my sentence. Water sprayed the air as I laughed. I watched the foaming bubbles, waiting for her to reemerge. She kicked upward and tilted her head back in anticipation of breaking the surface, but she'd misjudged the distance and was still underwater. It all happened so fast. I saw the moment she panicked and started flailing instead of kicking. I shot over to her, grabbing her by the upper arm and hoisting her the rest of the way above the surface.

"You're okay, you're okay," I said as she wheezed and coughed. I swam us over to the steps that lead out of the deep end and sat her on the top step.

Her eyes were so wide, searching, panicking. "Breathe," I coached. “Listen to my voice, take a deep breath."

But instead of her breathing steadying out, it just grew more ragged. She began hyperventilating. I'd seen it before in both human and animal alike. This kind of panicking was not good.

"Breathe, Frankie," I commanded, holding her cheeks in both hands.

She didn't hear me, didn't even give the subtlest of nods, lost in her own hysteria.

"Fuck," I gritted out, doing the first thing I could think of.

I pulled her face to mine and kissed her. At first, she didn't reciprocate as I worked my lips over hers, but then she started moving, started responding, her breathing steadying to match my slow, luxuriating kiss. We kept kissing as her hands clinging to me eased, her shallow pants turning into soft, gentle breaths.

I pulled back just enough to lean my forehead to hers. "You okay?"

She swallowed and nodded. "Do they teach you that in vet school?"

"It was an oversight on their part to omit Making Out with Animals 101," I teased, leaning in and kissing her again. Her once clinging hands now pulled me closer through the water as my hips settled between her thighs. My tongue dove into her mouth and I kissed her deeper before realizing what I was doing.

I pulled away instantly, searching her eyes. "I was just trying to steady your breathing," I said, clearing my throat.

"Really?"

"Not really," I admitted with a chuckle. "I just got, uh, caught up in the moment and decided to kiss you again."

Her eyes searched mine as if she might find answers there. "Like a casual friends who kiss friends thing?"

"No, yes, I don't know." *Shit.*

"Thank you for clarifying," she quipped.

My jaw clenched. Now it was my turn to panic. I shouldn't have done that. It was reckless and stupid and blurred the clear lines we'd admirably drawn. I was spinning something that didn't have to be complicated into an intricate spider's web. We weren't dating but we pretended like we were. We weren't hooking up until we did. I had no idea what friends who were fake dating but also casually having sex looked like. Maybe this was it?

"I'm sorry. I—"

"If there's anything you've taught me, Goldfinch Lachlan, it's that we don't always need everything figured out," she said. "Now, I'm going to go again."

I raised my eyebrows at her. "What?"

"I'm going again."

"I'm impressed." I knew she wouldn't believe me, but I added, "You're braver than me."

She was. She asked for what she wanted in a way that I admired. She faced her fears head-on in a way I never had.

"*But*," she added as she squeezed the water out of her ponytail, "you have to kiss me again after I jump." She arched a wicked eyebrow. "For safety purposes, of course."

"You drive a hard bargain, Goldilocks," I replied. "But I agree."

Daily Specials

kookaburra cucumber sandwiches
$5.50

Macaw Macarons
6 for $12

Chapter Twenty-Nine

Frankie

Finch's voice echoed through the apartment. "Where are you?"

"Where do you think I am?" I called, chucking my phone on the nightstand and pulling the sheets up to my chin.

"Marco!"

"Polo!"

Finch laughed and wandered into her room. When the door opened, she leaned on the frame. "Just letting ourselves in now, are we?"

I shrugged. "Wasn't it you who texted me that you were thinking about me in your bed all afternoon long? Or was that the other Goldfinch I'm currently sexting with?" I eyed her up and down. She'd just gotten out of the shower. Now, she wore a baggy black T-shirt and gray sweatpants, her wet hair slicked off her face. "I thought you'd be too desperate to fuck me to shower." I pouted.

She sighed and folded her arms across her chest. "I had a toucan vomit on me today, so I thought I'd do the courtesy of showering first."

"Okay, fine," I amended. "For vomit, I'll allow it."

Her eyes dipped to the sheets lifted to my chin. "I like the sight of you in my bed," she confessed.

I pushed the sheets down, revealing the lacy black bra I was wearing, and Finch froze, her eyes taking me in.

"Do you like the sight even more now?" I teased.

"You vixen," she said with a shake of her head. "You have no idea what the sight of you like that does to me."

She yanked her shirt off and tossed it on the floor, revealing her sports bra and the top lines of her strap peeking above her low-slung gray sweatpants.

I gulped. "And you have no idea what the sight of you like that does to me."

"I want to see more," she said, her eyes lingering on my chest.

I rose up onto my knees, revealing my black lace panties that matched my bra, a crisscross leather harness belted across my waist down to the top of my thighs. I swore I saw the moment Finch's soul left her body and reentered again.

She shook her head. "The student has become the master," she said, prowling forward. "I have no more to teach you. My work here is done."

I chuckled, crawling toward her as she crossed the distance and captured my lips.

"You want me to fuck you so badly, don't you?" she murmured against my mouth.

"So, so badly," I said back between deep, desperate kisses.

Her hands were everywhere, tangled in my hair and skimming over my ass. I threw my head back as she kissed over the lace of my breasts, nipping at my sensitive flesh. Trailing down my belly, she hooked her fingers in my underwear and slowly pulled it down.

She shoved me back onto the mattress, and I gasped as she whipped her pants off and revealed the ribbed purple cock she'd been hiding under them.

I licked my lips.

"You want this?" she asked, stroking a hand over the purple shaft.

I nodded, biting my lip as she prowled over me. I knew what she would do, all of the foreplay and slow building before she'd take me, and I was way too turned on to accept the level of teasing I knew I was in for. I was already dripping wet, and I needed her to take me fast and rough.

I grabbed for the ribbed head and positioned it to my entrance. "I am so ready." I groaned. "Fuck me. Please."

Finch was more than happy to indulge me, slowly pushing in. My head fell back as I relished in the sensation.

"Faster," I begged.

She started moving, slowly at first and then increasing in pace. In and out, she found this sweet rhythm that had my eyes crossing, reading my every breath as she rode me harder. I tried to focus, to get lost in the rhythm, knowing I only had a little bit of time before . . .

I realized it all at once and let out a surprised laugh.

Finch paused, lifting up on her elbow as a confused smile spread across her face. "Why are you laughing?" she asked even as she started laughing too, like she couldn't help it. "Care to share with the class?"

I loved this. I'd always thought sex had to be so serious. I never thought we could chat or laugh or take breaks, easily floating in and out of these different states of being. We could be everything at once. There was an inherent safety and comfort with Finch that I didn't know existed before her.

"I just realized something," I said as Finch studied my face with a playful expression.

"What?" She rocked her hips again, and I gasped as each ribbed nub trailed over my inner walls.

"Before." I didn't specify, but I knew she knew who I was talking about. "I felt like I had to focus, like I knew I only had a few minutes before he finished, but—" My laughter consumed my words.

"But we can go all night, love," Finch said, nibbling her way up my neck as she read my thoughts.

"Yeah, we can."

I rocked my hips, a silent plea, and Finch started taking me faster again.

"One of the many wonderful things about sex with women you'll find, Goldilocks," Finch said, kissing her way up to my ear and making my skin tingle. "Our cocks are always ready to go."

My laugh was cut off as she started moving faster, morphing into a moan. "Yes." I panted as she hit a spot that made my eyes roll back. "Oh god, yes. I . . ."

My fingernails raked down her back, and Finch moaned into my mouth, her tongue battling my own as she fucked me. It was all too much, too good. My orgasm took me by surprise, roaring through me before I could rein it back in. I cried out Finch's name as she buried her head in my neck, taking me deep and rough, fucking me through every last echo of pleasure. When I collapsed back onto the bed, breathing ragged, Finch propped herself up on her elbows and smiled down at me.

"That's one," she said.

"One?"

Her devilish smile widened. "I believe I promised you a record-breaking number of orgasms tonight."

I gulped. "You did."

My pussy fluttered around the ribbed cock as she slowly

pulled out of me, prowling down my body. "I believe I promised to feast on you too."

Her hot breath skimmed across my mound, and she poised above my pussy, waiting.

"You di—"

My words were cut off on a moan as she dropped her mouth to my clit, burying herself between my thighs and devouring me.

My hands fisted in the bedsheets, holding on for dear life as the euphoric wave started cresting in me again. I didn't know what kind of heaven this was, but I was pretty sure nothing better in the world existed than the magic of her and me.

Daily Specials

kookaburra cucumber
sandwiches
$5.50

Macaw Macarons
6 for $12

Chapter Thirty

Frankie

I'd never been so happy to be tired.

I hadn't even thought it was possible to have so many orgasms in one single night. Finch had treated our latest escapades like her own personal challenge, and I was *more* than happy to be her guinea pig. *Target that competitive nature at my pussy all day long please!*

I still couldn't believe everything we'd done together. Was this real life? It felt like a fever dream. What was more, Finch had seemed to savor every single climax she'd given me, as if each one had gotten her off too. It was truly a mind-blowing experience, spiritual even. My entire perceptions about sex and intimacy had radically shifted in just two nights.

Normally, I had to put every ounce of my effort into orgasming when I was with a partner. If they changed rhythm even slightly, if my mind started to wander, if the anxiety started mounting with every minute I didn't climax, I knew it was game over. Most of the time, it was easier to just fake it. I didn't want to be a disappointment even to myself, and then it could be done and I'd get to go to bed.

But with Finch . . .

She was truly like a gold medal level lover—not that I had much to compare her with, but I was fairly certain it would be impossible to best her. Better than last night would probably kill me. Finch might actually be magic. No wonder queer women were so into crystals and witchy shit. Two nights with a woman and I was ready to believe in fairies and unicorns if it meant experiencing that again.

Finch loved my body. She *loved* it. My body was lovable. That was such a radical notion, I hadn't fully comprehended it until now.

Never had someone so deftly touched me, as if she knew my body even better than I knew it myself. Not just pleasure, not just satisfying, it was something so grounding and gratifying. I hadn't thought sex like that was real. She'd completely revolutionized and reawakened everything I thought I knew in a couple nights.

Of course, I'd said none of this reverie to her, only a simple "That was amazing" because such adulation was so far from "casual" that I didn't know what to do with it.

We'd barely slept. Never in my life had I wanted to have sex more than sleep, but I was already eager and willing for another sleepless night.

With wobbling legs and a happily sore pussy, I worked with a song on my lips. I marbled the croissants, filled the puff pastries with buttercream, and decorated the quiches in the cabinet with parsley garnishes before prepping the bread and pizza dough that I would bring up to the Peckish Peacock.

Someone let out a wolf whistle, and I looked up to see Hannah.

"I know that look," she sang as she skipped over to me.

"What look?" I asked but was still flashing a megawatt smile.

She grabbed a clean spoon from the drawer and helped herself to a scoop of leftover buttercream. "The 'just had really great sex' look."

"You're not wrong." I couldn't deny it even if I tried, and considering Finch and I were already pretending to have sex anyway, it wasn't really breaking any codes. My cheeks hurt from smiling like a deranged clown all morning and I didn't care.

"You and Finch are so cute together." Hannah swooned, fluttering her lashes. "I knew it would take a miracle to make Finch want to settle down, and you, Frankie, are truly miraculous." She went to pat me on the shoulder but missed and swatted a tray of muffins. I managed to catch them before they plummeted to the floor.

Hannah did a 360 spin, taking in all of the baking laid out across the bench tops that I hadn't put in the cabinet yet.

"I probably shouldn't be in here," she said with a sheepish smile. "The farm animals are the only ones that seem to tolerate my clumsiness. And the penguins," she added, "but that's a story for another time."

"I've got time," I said as I plated up a tray of tiger strip cupcakes. "Maybe we can grab a coffee on my lunch break?"

"Really?" Hannah beamed at me. "I'd really like that!" She was practically shimmering with excitement. "I mean, I love all of the other keepers and Hawk, obviously, but they're all siblings so they have this shorthand with each other, and even though they are super welcoming, I always feel like an outsider kind of, not that they mean that, but—" She sucked in a gulp of air and kept going. "But the only other person dating a Lachlan lives in New Zealand so Logan and I are not very close, and it would just be really cool to have a buddy who was also dating a member of the family, so yes to coffee."

A bemused smile formed on my face. I wondered if Hannah remembered she'd already said all of this to me before, when she came to interrogate me about the yacht party. I wasn't going to mention it. She was chaotic but also kind to me, and I enjoyed her pandemonious company.

"Sorry, I'm known to ramble," she added with a tight smile.

"You would make an excellent free diver or wind musician with all that breath control."

She laughed and managed to actually pat me on the shoulder this time. Hannah was like a full-on tornado of energy, but I kind of loved that about her. She was just as warm and welcoming to me as she claimed the other Lachlans were to her. I hadn't had much time to get to know any of them except Dove and Wren, who both were really awesome. But Hawk and the twins always seemed off building something or doing a project. I was grateful for the Sunday dinners, when they all got together to catch up each week.

I realized Hannah had said something to me but I'd been too busy thinking about the Lachlan clan to hear. "Sorry, what?"

Her already wide smile broadened even further, making her smile lines deepen. "I said, could I grab two blueberry muffins? Evelyn and I have an accreditation meeting and I want to bring something."

"Oh yeah, sure," I said, bagging up two muffins for her. "Enjoy."

"Coffee at 11?"

"Sounds good," I replied, waving to her.

She wandered off through to the gift shop to go chat with the gift shop manager. I heard a clang of a baking tray falling from the kitchen and I turned to hustle from the counter to behind the scenes.

"Alex, is that you?" I called out to the day's rostered barista.

"I've got the cupcakes ready for the cabinet. Do you know where that giraffe-print cloche is?" When I looked up, I didn't see anyone. "What the . . ."

I spotted the fallen tray and kept walking around the kitchen island, only to come face-to-face with a flamingo. My eyes fell to the freshly bandaged foot.

"Ron," I snapped. "What the hell are you doing here? You seriously are the most meddlesome, feathered, little bitch that has ever existed! *How* did you get from the aviaries to my kitchen?"

It was only then I realized I was scolding a lanky pink bird and decided I'd better radio for help. I turned back to the counter and realized I hadn't picked up my radio from the docking bay in the gift shop yet.

"Shit," I cursed as Ron tried to hobble to the front. "No. No. No." I ushered him to the back door, but I didn't want to shoo him outside either. What if he ran off and fell into the lion enclosure and got eaten? I'd never forgive myself. I grabbed my phone and dialed the first person I could think of.

"Hey, Goldilocks, miss me already?"

"Ron," I said, the word frantically sputtering out of my mouth.

"Strange pet name, but I'll take it."

"No, like, Ronald, Ron."

"What?"

"There is a flamingo in the café kitchen. Help! Please!"

"I'm on my way," Finch said, and I heard her radio clip and the door open over the phone. "Sit tight."

"Thank you."

"And don't let him get away."

She hung up before I could reply. Ron started limping to the back door again.

"Don't move," I commanded, but the stubborn bird wouldn't listen.

This was probably violating a million health and safety codes. No one could see a fucking exotic bird in *my* kitchen.

"Okay. It's okay." I blew out a slow breath as I stretched my arms out wide and cornered Ron against the cabinets. I'd held him before when Finch was bandaging his foot. I'd just do that again. It would be fine.

I bent over and gently held his oval body. He started clicking his beak up and down my legs like he was grooming me.

"I'm not trying to hit on you," I muttered to the horny bird. "I just need you to not run off anywhere."

Ron took that opportunity to stick his head up the wide leg of my high-waisted chino shorts.

"Oh my god," I hissed. "Ronald! Get your fucking beak out of my shorts right fucking now."

Finch chose that moment to burst in the back door. "Whoa!" she jeered. "Am I interrupting something?"

"Help me!" I demanded.

She doubled over laughing at the sight of the disappearing flamingo head, whose beak now made it look like I was packing a hard-on. She whipped out her phone, but I shot her an "I will murder you" look and she put it back down.

Crouching, she grabbed Ron's neck. She slid her hand up my shorts as she went, and I cleared my throat as her hand grazed over my panties. She ferreted around before finally finding Ron's beak and gently extracting him.

"Thank you," I said, fanning myself with a dish towel as she pulled the gangly bird into her and tucked him under her arm.

Before she stood, she leaned in and kissed the inside of my knee. "You are most welcome."

I shuddered at that kiss, remembering all the ways she'd touched me the night before.

"I'm thinking all the same things, Goldilocks," she said with a chuckle. "Believe me."

I cringed. "Was it really so obvious what I was thinking about?"

"Well, you weren't thinking about the flamingo." She shrugged as Ron kicked his legs like an obstinate toddler. "Or at least, I hope not."

"I wasn't thinking about the flamingo," I said, feeling like a giddy schoolgirl twirling my hair.

"Last night was amazing." Finch smiled, ignoring her flailing captive. "We should probably take a break tonight though, hey? Get some sleep?"

"Oh. Yeah, probably," I said with a nod.

Her smile widened. "But for some reason, I have a feeling class will be in session again tonight."

I bit my bottom lip. "I concur with that assessment."

"I think we're going to have fun with this new arrangement."

"Uh-huh," I said. "Same." I could barely get any words out.

Ron let out an indignant honk and Finch rolled her eyes. "Alright, alright, come on, you miscreant. I was going to catch you to take this bandage off anyway, so might as well seize this opportunity."

"I'd offer to help you," I called, "but you might want to ask someone wearing full-length pants."

"But I have so much fun rescuing you, Goldilocks." She winked at me and wandered off, leaving me hot and flushed. If I was frazzled by her before, it was nothing compared to now that I knew what she could do in bed.

I felt the butterflies swarming in my stomach and I clenched my jaw, trying to push them away. We agreed on no feelings. And I definitely, definitely wasn't going to break that promise.

Definitely not.

Chapter Thirty-One

Finch

Frankie kissed her way down the swirls of my tattoos, tracing each pattern with her tongue. She hummed at the taste of me, like I was the most delicious flavor. I'd never hooked up with someone where we were mutually obsessed with each other; it was always skewed to one side. But with Frankie, we were both equally ravenous for each other. Our energy together had created a spark all its own. One I was too afraid to name.

My chest rose and fell in panting heaves. I was still lost to the sensations of our last bout as Frankie mindlessly ran her lips over my skin.

The little noises she made as she kissed across my body were my new favorite sound. I brushed her hair over her shoulder so I could get a better look at her swollen lips as I trailed my fingers down her arm, unable to keep myself from caressing her.

"Look at you," I said with a smug shake of my head. "Gone is the timid, little bedroom mouse."

"I've had an excellent instructor," she purred, kissing up my ribs and over the blank spot I was saving for my "work hard, play harder" tattoo.

"You're a quick study, Goldilocks," I joked. "You already know exactly what I like."

She hummed, the feeling vibrating across my flesh and making my skin prickle. "And what exactly do you like?"

You, I thought before I could suppress the idea. *Everything about you.*

Frankie seemed like an impossible gift from the universe. I'd never felt this kind of familiarity with someone before . . . hadn't *wanted* to because I didn't want things to get complicated. The longer I slept with someone, the more likely they'd catch feelings, and I couldn't let that happen. No one fit into my life. My puzzle piece was a circle. I'd either neglect them or my animals, and I refused to do either.

But with Frankie . . . It was the best arrangement I'd ever had. My family left me alone, I wasn't waking up hungover in strangers' beds, no messy drama with girls who wanted more from me, and nobody's feelings were going to get hurt in the fall when it all ended. There was no commitment. Only fun. We could call it a day at any time, but I really didn't want to think about it ending just yet.

"My turn," I said, flipping Frankie over.

She yelped, her hair splaying across the pillow as she sunk further into my mattress under my weight. I loved the way she grinned in sleep-addled surprise.

"It already was your turn," she said with a mock pout. I instantly had to kiss that frown away, sucking her full bottom lip into my mouth. When I released her, she added, "You've had several turns in fact."

I kissed down her neck as she reached for her phone on my bedside table. "It is 2 am!" she exclaimed. "I need to be up in three hours, Finch." She moaned, slinging her forearm over her eyes. "Can we just have a storm for the love of God so we can sleep in for once?"

I laughed, continuing to trail kisses toward her breasts. God, her breasts. The greatest pillow to rest my head. I wished I could sleep every night nestled between them.

"You still have so much to learn though," I murmured, trailing my index finger down her side. "Class is still in session."

"Finch," she reprimanded, playfully shoving my shoulder.

I huffed and lifted my head up, resting my chin on her belly and arching a brow at her. "Do you want me to stop?" I asked as I slid a hand up her inner thigh.

Her eyes hooded with desire, and I already knew I'd won.

"You know at some point, we're going to need to sleep," she said, the cutest little frown lines bracketing her mouth.

"Sleep is for the weak," I countered, my hand trailing up to cup her pussy, and she tilted her hips into my touch.

"Twenty minutes," she said breathlessly. "Then we sleep."

Daily Specials
kookaburra cucumber
sandwiches
$5.50
Macaw Macarons
6 for $12

Chapter Thirty-Two

Frankie

"Hey! I have a question for you." I slid into the vacant office chair beside Finch, rolling the rest of the way to her. "I brought you a scone."

"Thank you, goddess," she replied, leaning in for a split second before leaning back in her chair. She seemed to be doing that a lot lately, catching herself at the last moment.

The lines were being muddied even further between what happened in her bedroom and what happened outside of it. But Finch seemed to think affection in the bedroom was for fun and affection outside was for show. We didn't need to kiss when no one was looking, but damn did I want to. Her mouth was just so irresistible.

"I can see the wheels in your mind spinning," Finch said.

I nibbled at my lip and her eyes dropped to my mouth. "It just looked like you wanted to kiss me."

"I did," Finch admitted, averting her gaze from my mouth. "Sorry. I'm getting all my wires crossed. I blame the lack of sleep."

"Even casual hook-ups kiss outside the bedroom," I said, trying to feel out her response. "Especially when they're pretending to be dating, right? Like, if someone walked in and saw, it would just lend credibility to our lie, so . . ." When Finch didn't respond, I shook my head. "Ugh, sorry. This whole thing is turning into a lasagna of secrets and I'm just trying to keep up with all the layers."

"A lasagna of secrets?" she asked incredulously.

"I'm tired!" I said as Finch held a hand to her mouth to contain her laugher. "I would have better metaphors if I had more than two hours of sleep."

"Worth it though," Finch whispered conspiratorially.

"Definitely," I added with a mischievous smile.

Finch licked the jam from her thumb. "So you said you had a question for me?"

"Yeah." I swept a strand of hair behind my ear. "So tops and bottoms." Finch's cheeks dimpled as she took another bite of scone. I swatted at her. "Don't laugh at me."

"I'm not laughing at you," she said even as her shoulders continued to shake. "Go on."

"You're a top, right?"

"Yep," she said immediately and then weighed her head side to side, considering. "Well . . . yes, but you know I like being taken care of too."

"Oh, I know." I smiled around the lid of my coffee. "I like taking care of you."

I couldn't believe I'd just said that out loud, but it was true. I loved when I made her come. It felt like a victory every time I brought her pleasure. She was still the commander of our ship in the bedroom, but I loved making her fall apart too. Before her, I'd always thought sex was a chore. And I definitely didn't think I'd enjoy giving as much as I enjoyed receiving, but Finch had changed my mind about everything, and yet, there was still so much I didn't understand.

"So does that make me a bottom?" I asked, scrutinizing the ceiling. "I'm clearly not a pillow princess, but—"

"Somebody's been spending too much time on Google." Finch chuckled. "And we will be taking no pillow princess slander in this house. They're an important part of our community."

"Wouldn't dream of it." My lips curved up. "I just want to understand everything."

"There's not as much to understand as you think," Finch said. "We don't all worship at Sappho's shrine. This isn't a standardized religion. Each person is different. Each couple is different. If there's anything I can 'teach' you, it's to have the confidence to ask for what you want."

I swallowed thickly. "I'm just trying to understand where I fit in to all this. What's expected of me."

"What's expected of you? *Expected of you*?" she repeated pointedly. "You're still talking like you're sleeping with a man."

I laughed. "Right."

Finch ran a hand through her short hair, sweeping it back off her face. "Honestly, I don't think I'm a very good instructor for you, Goldilocks. Everything you do turns me on."

A wicked grin stretched my lips as an idea popped into my head. "You said I should have the confidence to ask for what I want?"

"Uh-huh."

"Will you teach me how to go down on you?"

"Whoa!" a voice barked from behind me, and I whirled to find Finch's little brother spinning and running out the door.

"Crane!" Finch shouted. She pointed at me. "We will definitely be finishing this conversation, Goldilocks." She ran out the door. "Crane, get your ass over here. Do not pick up your radio. Put the radio down!"

The radio on Finch's desk crackled, and I heard Crane's voice saying, "Hey, Heron, do you still have my power drill with you? I need to perforate my eardrums immediately." Then I heard Finch's voice in the background of his radio call saying, "Get over here, you little shit!" as the sound of stampeding footsteps echoed up behind him.

I buried my face in my hands, horrified.

"Put it in the group chat before Finch murders you," Dove replied. "Don't let your death be in vain."

"Do *not* put it in the group chat!" Finch shouted at the same time Crane said, "Done!"

"Okay, well, that's actually kind of cute," Dove said over the radio.

"Still not as bad as what happened with Hawk and Hannah," Heron chimed in.

"I will remind the keeper team once more that the radio is for work-related matters," Evelyn jumped on. "Unless you're all done for the day already and need some more tasks to be assigned to you?"

The radio waves went silent at Evelyn's threat. I had a sneaking feeling that the conversation was still continuing on in the group chat though.

I decided I didn't want to be around when Finch returned from whatever sort of telling off she gave her little brother and headed off back to the Peacock. It was my fault. I should've been more discreet. I'd just gotten swept up in trying to learn everything there was to learn about being with a woman. But so far, Finch was teaching me to forget everything I'd learned and just focus on her. And God did I want to just focus on her.

Chapter Thirty-Three

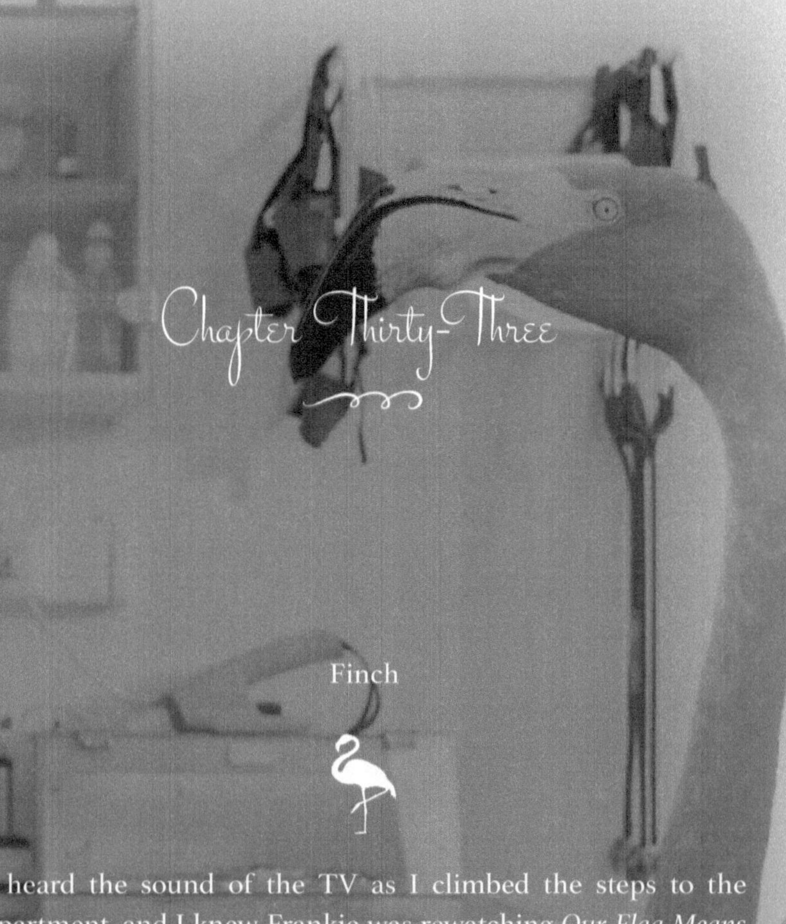

Finch

I heard the sound of the TV as I climbed the steps to the apartment, and I knew Frankie was rewatching *Our Flag Means Death*—her favorite comfort show. When I opened the door, she was bundled up in a hoodie and leggings, a fleece throw blanket over her lap. Where did that come from? I didn't even know I had throw blankets in the apartment. Mom probably stashed it in the linen closet without me noticing.

"Hey," Frankie said with a wave of her hoodie-covered hand. "Popcorn?" She offered out the giant red bowl.

I reached over and took a handful. "So did you kill your brother today? Am I going to find bits of Crane floating around the crocodile moat?" she asked. "'Cuz if you need an alibi, I'm your girl."

I loved the way she said that. I had no doubt that Frankie

had reached the "help me bury the bodies" level of friendship. She'd probably be the first person I'd call too.

"Sadly, no alibis will be needed," I said, rubbing my twitching eyebrow. The little muscles in my face had all started betraying me with the lack of sleep. "I just gave him a stern talking to about knocking. I think he learned his lesson."

"A stern talking to. How ominous," Frankie joked.

"I can be intimidating when I want to be," I protested. My mask of bravado quickly slipped as I let out a long, weary sigh.

Frankie curled her knees up. "Long day?"

"Yeah." My shoulders drooped and my arms hung limply by my sides, as if it were too much effort to stand straight.

"Do you want to talk about it?"

That took me by surprise. I had a lot of listening ears in my family, but no one asked me if I wanted to talk about my long days. We all had long days, after all. "Nah, I'm okay."

"If you ever need to, I'm here," she said with a shrug. Easy as that. Everything with her was easy, as if she'd always been here with me. It didn't feel like weeks, but decades, lifetimes, and in every one of them she had been mine.

"I am, unfortunately, very crampy," Frankie said, curling tighter under the blanket, "so I'm thinking I might need to take a rain check on tonight's extracurricular activities."

"No worries," I said. "You need painkillers? I've got just about everything under the sun. How about some tranquilizers?" I tapped a thoughtful finger to my lip. "Although, I might struggle calculating the dosage for a human . . ." Frankie's gullible eyes widened. "I'm joking."

"Oh, right." Her head reared back as she waved a hand at me. "I knew that."

"I do have the regular human painkillers in the cabinet above the sink though." I hooked a thumb to the bathroom door. "Want a hot water bottle?" As I turned toward the kitchen, Frankie grinned at me. "What?"

"I don't know." She shrugged. "You're just being really nice."

"You say that like you're surprised," I hedged.

"Not surprised, just happy," she amended. "I'm not used to being taken care of like this, so thanks."

"What are fake girlfriends for?" I said with a wink. "Periods are the worst." I walked to the freezer and produced a bar of chocolate. I tossed it to Frankie, and she caught it one-handed. I gave her a polite golf clap which made her chuckle. "Chocolate," I instructed. "Doctor's orders."

"Do you prescribe chocolate to all of your patients?"

I winked. "Only my favorite ones."

She started attacking the foiled edge, opening the top corner. "Why do you keep your chocolate in the freezer?"

"That is for another night for you to find out," I said. "One when you're feeling up to some more adventures in the bedroom."

"Intriguing." She opened the chocolate wrapper, broke off a square, and slumped down on the couch.

If I was being honest with myself, I was looking forward to a long night of sleep too. Between bird feedings and "lessons" with Frankie, I was becoming chronically sleep-deprived. Some days, I was seeing double, and that would not do, especially when I still had to perform surgeries and think strategically. A few days off our nighttime gymnastics would probably be a really good idea. But if Frankie hadn't suggested it, I would've never taken the break. If she wanted me, she could have me, always. I could deny her nothing. Not when every night with her felt like a reawakening of something I'd long lost, like her and I were made of all the same ingredients, an unspoken connection that I was too afraid to name.

Frankie sucked on a square of frozen chocolate and murmured, "I'm sorry."

My brow furrowed. "Why are you sorry? Because you have your period and are not in the mood?"

"Yeah," she said, putting on an adorably mopey Eeyore voice.

I shrugged, looking at the date on my phone. "I'm going to be right there with you in like two days."

Frankie pulled the drawstrings of her hoodie tighter, looking like a cozy couch gremlin. "I just figured you were a sex goddess every day of the month."

I grinned at the way she said *sex goddess*. "Sometimes," I said. "But most of the time, I'm not really feeling it either. Even God rested on the seventh day."

She snorted. "Well in that case. Want to watch an episode with me?"

Frankie looked up at me with saucer-like puppy-dog eyes, drawing me in. I never thought I'd enjoy being wrapped around someone's finger. Maybe I'd just always picked the wrong fingers.

"I'll be your hot water bottle," I offered as Frankie lifted the blanket for me to crawl under.

I cuddled into her warm side, her body molding into mine. My sleepy head dropped onto her shoulder. The comfort was instant and overwhelming. I managed to watch only five minutes before I fell asleep.

I didn't know how long I was out before Frankie started moving beneath me. My arms shot out without me opening my eyes, holding her to me like a teddy bear. "Don't go."

She laughed. "We should get you to bed, Dr. Lachlan."

"Here is fine," I murmured into her hair, burrowing further into the softness of her body.

My cheek rose and fell with her laughter. "You're going to have a wickedly sore neck in the morning."

I let out another unintelligible grumble, but I let her pull me to a stand and walk me to bed, my eyes barely open.

She pulled the sheets back over me, and I smiled at the way

she lovingly tucked me in. When she turned to leave, I reached out for her and clumsily grabbed her wrist. "Don't go."

"Finch, I think you're asleep," she whispered.

I shook my head into my pillow. "Not asleep. Stay," I said. "Please?"

"You are adorable when you're half comatose," she said. When I didn't let her go, she laughed and said, "Okay, fine."

She went around to the other side of the bed and climbed in, folding me into her. I was always the dominant one, in charge, but as she wrapped me up in her arms, it felt like she was taking care of me in a way I seldom allowed. She was as much my protector as I was hers. I could let go and just melt into her embrace. Frankie lifted a hand and tenderly swept the hair off my face as I drifted back off to sleep. She made me feel safe and warm and . . . loved. She made me feel loved. And I had no idea what to do with that thought.

Chapter Thirty-Four

Finch

I wasn't prepared for this. Not at all. What I'd thought was confidence was now so obviously foolish arrogance.

I'd thought we could keep it casual. That I could sleep with someone as beautiful and funny and kind and warm and sexy and exciting and world-rearranging as Frankie and still not catch feelings.

I laughed to myself as I filled a syringe of antibiotics, going through the motions like a practiced dance.

What had I been thinking?

I'd been the one adamant that *she* not develop any feelings, but after a week with her, I was starting to recalibrate my entire belief system about relationships.

I shook out my arms and slapped my cheek.

"No," I growled at myself.

I couldn't do this. Not to either of us. I was just deliriously exhausted, that was all. So many hours I'd spent sneaking downstairs in between heavenly bouts of sex to feed Cranky in the night. I didn't think I'd gotten more than a single hour in a row in a long, long time, and I knew that couldn't be good.

"Look who's so smug," Hawk said with a laugh as he appeared in the doorway. "Things going well with Frankie then I take it?"

"Knock," I snapped.

"What?"

"You didn't knock."

"Well, I'm in here now." I tipped my head back to the door as I capped the syringe. Hawk huffed. "You're seriously not going to talk to me until I knock?"

"It's a new rule I've instituted of late," I said, thinking of the way Crane had barged in the other morning. "And I'm very strict about reinforcing it."

Hawk chuckled. "This is about what Crane said in the group chat, huh?"

"Yep."

"Still not as embarrassing as what happened to Hannah and me last summer."

"Accurate."

"So—"

"Nope." I jutted my chin toward the door. "Knock first."

From my periphery, I watched as my older brother rolled his eyes and walked out the door, pulling it shut behind him and waiting a beat before knocking.

He knocked again. I didn't reply. He knocked louder. I ignored it.

My radio scratched to life. "Carnivores to Vet team."

"Creative." I chuckled and picked up my radio, looking at my brother glaring at me through the treatment room window as I said, "Vet team, go ahead."

"Will you please say 'come in' so I can carry on with my very busy work day?"

I laughed and set the radio down. "Come in."

"Thank you," Hawk said as he reentered the room.

"No problem, thanks for knocking," I said smugly, passing him the syringe. "For Ptolemy. Keep an eye on that wound. If he doesn't stop licking it or it starts looking infected, we're going to have to dart him, and that's the last thing either of us need right now."

"Agreed," Hawk said. "I've got tickets to this Broadway show for Hannah's and my anniversary and—" I mock gagged, and Hawk bristled. "You are in a relationship too. Need I remind you?"

"Yeah, I know. Just not as cringey, sappy sweet as you two."

Hawk leaned into me and whispered, "Your girlfriend just asked you to teach her how to go down on you while the two of you were having an office picnic. *That* is vomit level inducing sweet too."

I stared at him flatly. "I would very much like to go back to five minutes ago when you were standing on the other side of that door."

Hawk snickered. "You get used to it."

"Used to what?"

"Being in a relationship," he said. "After a while, you stop really caring what other people think. I don't. I'm happy. Like, 'feel like I won the jackpot every fucking night' kind of happy, and I know it sounds sappy," he cut me off, already knowing exactly what I would say, "but I don't care because until I met Hannah, I really didn't think it was possible to feel this way."

"You've made your point," I muttered.

Hawk clapped me on the shoulder. "It's probably going to be even worse for you since this is like, your first ever actual relationship," he added with a chuckle. "I look forward to it."

I shrugged off his hand on my shoulder. "So how long will you be gone in New York?"

"Just two nights," he said.

"Just?" I scoffed. "You would've never done this two years ago."

"I'm not the same me as two years ago," he countered. "Crane is going to cover my animals. He's been angling to do more carnivore work, anyway. And Mom and Aya are pitching in. Wren's taking Hannah's schedule since she's been doing it since she was like seven. And the summer volunteers this year are surprisingly useful and abundant thanks to Hannah's article last year. We've got all our bases covered."

"Sounds like it."

"You and Frankie should take a weekend off—"

"That's not going to happen," I cut in. "At least not until the off season."

"Why not?"

"Because unlike *you*"—I shoved the tiger's file and dosage instructions at Hawk—"there's only one vet here and none of you can cover my shifts."

Hawk gave me that brotherly look like he wanted to give me a dead-arm punch. I angled my body away just in case.

"The rest of us can take care of the animals in the ward just fine," he said, annoyed. "And we can reschedule any nonessential surgeries. You know, some baboons don't ever have their teeth cleaned, let alone annually."

I gave him a stern look. "We take care of our animals better than they'd live in the wild. I have a duty of care and I won't delay it to go watch a Broadway show."

Hawk's smile softened and he shook his head. "You look happy, Finch, but exhausted," he added quickly. "And it's going to break you if you never rest or take a day off. The zoo is ours; no one is buying it out from under us anymore. We have the most money in the bank we've ever had, plans for expansions, off-season deals. Hell, we even have a movie shooting here in the spring. Things are good. We don't have to keep living like there's an emergency around every corner. The adrenaline crash is going to kill you."

I let out a long breath through my nose. He wasn't the first person in our family to tell me that. Even Lark had been up my ass about slowing down, the traitor.

I really wanted to slap someone and settled on my older brother, but Hawk anticipated the move and dodged out of the way. "Maybe if you took a break every once in a while, you'd have quicker reflexes."

My nostrils flared. He didn't have the slightest clue what it took to live my life and I wasn't about to share it with him. Everyone thought I was this fun-loving party animal. They had no idea of how much weight was truly on my shoulders.

"Well, you've got one thing right, bro," I said, forcing my patented Finch smile.

"What's that?"

"I'm happy," I said. "Now, if you'll excuse me, I'm taking Frankie to the Holloways' pool for a *restful* afternoon."

He smiled at that and stepped back to make way for me to pass. "I'm glad. Have fun."

"Oh, I will," I gritted out. "Keep an eye on that sore. Text me if anything changes."

I shouldered my way past him and out into the hall, still fuming.

Daily Specials

kookaburra cucumber
sandwiches
$5.50
Macaw Macarons
6 for $12

Chapter Thirty-Five

Frankie

I strolled down the Prickle Island shops, snacking on red licorice and boiled candies from Johnny's Rockin' Candy Emporium. The main street was a zany mix of old-timey New England shops, ocean-themed cafés, and luxury boutiques. It was like a rich, nautical Disney World where the old-money New Yorkers came for the summer along with an abundance of summertime staff to keep their estates running. I'd made friends with a few private chefs who frequented the Salty Dog. Maybe they'd have job recommendations for me after the end of the summer season, when everyone went back to the main-land and the population dwindled to only the Lachlan family and about 50 others.

I sucked on an aniseed candy from my waxed confectionary

bag. It made my tongue all fizzy and wasn't entirely pleasant at first, but I couldn't help but keep going back for more. I loved the care with which Norbert—the proprietor of Johnny's Rockin' Candy Emporium and not, in fact, a fellow named Johnny—made these. He was always willing to indulge my curiosity when I peppered him with culinary questions. And he'd throw in a few extra candies for me whenever I visited.

Probably six months ago, I would've never allowed myself to indulge in a bag of sweets—or at least allow myself to enjoy it. I felt like I was always constantly on a half-diet, always waffling between ignoring a scale and hyperfixating on one. But since moving to Prickle Island, my life wasn't controlled by numbers anymore, nor the judgement of a body-shaming partner.

I'd never felt such freedom. And everything with Finch . . . the way she looked at me like I should love every inch of myself . . . I was starting to see a different person in the mirror. I was starting to like myself exactly as I was without caveats and conditions.

Nothing needed fixing.

It was such a radical notion to me that I laughed every time I thought about it, as if I'd unlocked some secret code. It was only now that the veil had been pulled back. I was wildly aware of everything, from the advertisements on my phone to the shows I watched to Jake's passive-aggressive comments. They were all designed to make me hate myself. And I was wildly aware that hating myself would make me spend more money. And then whatever outcomes from spending that money wouldn't be good enough, so they'd change the rules to the game again forever and ever, always stacking the cards against any kind of self-love I could win if I kept playing their game. There was no winning unless I opted out of the game entirely, and I had finally, *finally* found the escape hatch.

I knew that everyone else could be loved at any and every

size, but I finally believed that I wasn't the exception to that rule too. I'd always have Finch to thank for helping me truly see that. More than just understand it conceptually, but actually believe it.

Finch had made it abundantly clear we were just fooling around. But our version of "fooling around" felt a lot like something real. We liked to flirt with that line, blending fiction and reality. We blurred the truth to the point where I didn't really know if I was acting anymore. And maybe, just maybe, I could convince Finch to be something more—or at the very least try. It was probably foolish to even attempt it, but the way she made me feel . . . it made me want to be brave and bold. It made me want to confess all of the feelings building inside me. Even if she didn't reciprocate them, I wanted to tell her, *needed* to tell her.

And I had the perfect plan to confess the true feelings in my heart: I'd been orchestrating a day off for her behind the scenes already. I was going to make her favorite pesto sandwiches and take her to the beach for the day, and after few summer drinks, I was going to confess that I didn't want to pretend anymore. I was falling in love with her for real.

I was so caught up in the daydream of our romance potentially becoming real that I was nearly bowled over by a man walking in the opposite direction.

"Whoa!" he said. "Frankie?"

I looked up to see Jake's wide blue eyes, a bemused smile curving his thin lips, and for the first time since he'd ended things, it didn't hurt to look at him. I braced for the pang of sorrow, for the fire of revenge, for the nagging nostalgia, but nothing came. Not even the smallest melancholic ache. He was just a person who'd once meant something to me...and didn't anymore.

"Oh, hey, Jake," I said, straightening my top. "Sorry, I was lost in my own little world there."

"I can see that," he said, shoving his hands in his jacket pockets. "I nearly knocked you into the street."

"Luckily, there are more bicycles than cars on the island." I swept a windswept lock of hair behind my ear, and his intense eyes tracked the movement. "So, how are you?"

"I'm doing well." He tipped his head to a shop across the street. "Olivia is just at the salon, and I'm in charge of buying drinks for our tennis match."

I eyed the bag in his hand, revealing what appeared to be a six pack of bougie cans. "You need watermelon hard ciders for tennis?"

"The club is having the Shoreline Philharmonic play on the green," he amended. "We sit out on the grass and listen. It's pretty boring, hence the drinks."

"No, it sounds fun," I said and honestly meant it.

"It won't be the same without the spread you put on. You always made the best food. I would pay good money for one of your quiches again."

"You can." My smile was tight as I jokingly added, "You can always buy some from the zoo café. They box the food up in cute little eco-friendly boxes. Perfect for picnics."

"Thank you for the tip," Jake replied, and I started wondering if he'd ever release me from this drawling conversation. "So, how are you, Frankie?"

I loved that I could answer honestly. "I'm doing really, really well actually."

"I can see that," Jake said with a chuckle. "You seem happy. So you and Finch are still together I take it?"

"Yes," I said with a secret smile. "I wasn't planning on falling in love with her so quickly, but here we are."

Jake's smile faltered for a second, his only tell. "That's wonderful."

"I guess everything worked out for a reason," I said, patting his arm. "Olivia seems delightful, really. Hang on to her."

The lines between his brows deepened into a V. "You want me to *hang on* to my mistress?" he asked skeptically.

"She's your fiancée now, isn't she?"

"She is," Jake quickly corrected. "That's just very big of you, that's all."

"I see how happy she makes you," I said with a shrug. "And it all worked out in the end for both of us."

He was still a grade A asshole for cheating on me, but I was struggling to find that righteous anger. All I could think about was how much better my life was now that he wasn't in it. In many ways, him breaking up with me saved me from a lifetime of hiding who I truly was. If we'd stayed together, I might've never known my life could be so much better.

"It worked out for the best," Jake echoed, but I could tell he was feigning nonchalance.

"You and I never really made sense," I said. "I think we tried our best, but it was just never truly right, don't you think? Like, everything with Finch is just so easy, so right, and I see you have that with Olivia too. I'm happy for you, Jake."

I meant it, but I still deserved a quadrillion gold stars for being the bigger person.

He looked me up and down, hesitating for a second before finally closing the distance and hugging me. "I'm happy for you too, Frankie. You deserve someone amazing."

I hugged him back, knowing this was something final. We'd had our closure; we'd said our goodbyes. The greatest gift to myself was not thinking about him at all after this. I thought I would go on hating him forever, but I couldn't bring myself to feel that way, not when he'd freed me from a relationship I was bound to be unhappy in, not to mention from really unsatisfying sex. Now that I knew what it could be like, I was never going back.

Jake gave me a final nod and headed past me. I looked at him one last time over my shoulder and my eyes snagged on the figure walking up the steep hill to the front entrance of the zoo.

A smile split my lips as I saw Finch walk up the hill, backlit by the morning sunlight. Tomorrow. I'd tell her all these new revelations. Tomorrow, I'd ask her to stop pretending.

Tomorrow, I'd tell her I loved her.

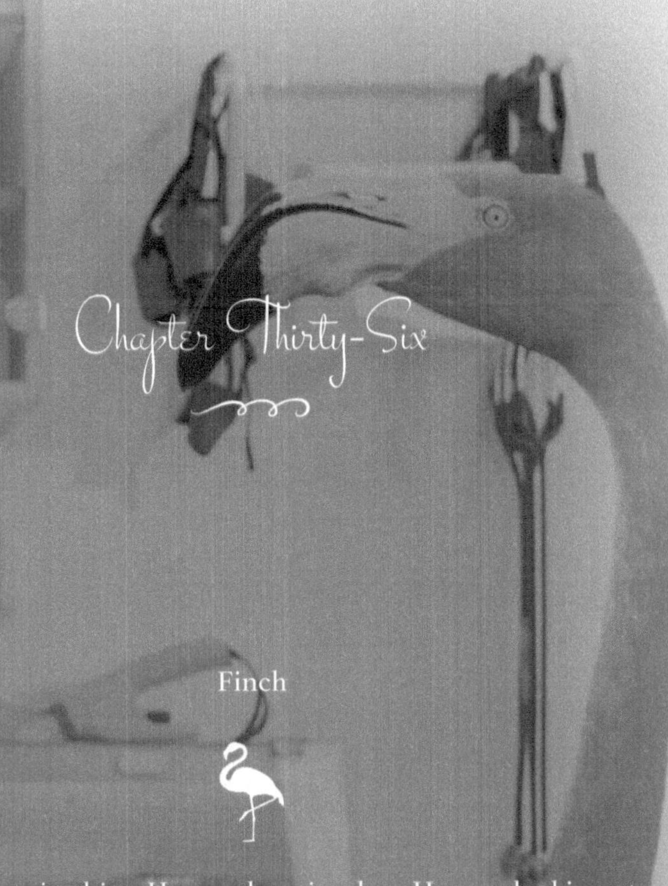

Chapter Thirty-Six

Finch

She was *hugging* him. He was hugging her. He was looking at her like he still loved her, and even though she had her back turned to me, all I could imagine was her looking back at him the same way.

Fuck, why had I gotten so swept up in this lie? Wasn't this the plan all along? To make Jake jealous? To get revenge? Although, I'd really thought Frankie wouldn't go back to him. *Was* she going back to him? From my vantage point, it seemed like it.

I balled my hands into fists as I stormed through the rear pathway to the vet hospital. We'd always agreed to use each other to our own ends. There had been no mistake, no miscommunication. I'd been the one who'd been so fucking adamant about it in the first place. Would she still be hugging her ex like that if I hadn't? I'd been the one to keep her at arm's length, but dammit, I thought she'd have at least told me she was going back to him.

I had no right to be angry. We weren't really together. It wasn't like she was cheating on me. I'd made my position very clear: I didn't do long-term relationships. But after the last few weeks we'd spent together, office lunch dates, cuddling on the couch, falling asleep tangled in each other's arms . . . I was starting to rethink all of my previous misguided sentiments.

Frankie made me rethink everything I'd ever wanted. Maybe I didn't want a long-term relationship, but I didn't want this thing with her to end, and I certainly didn't want her going back to fucking Sgt. Douchebag! That professional level shit stain was so unworthy of her.

"Hey, Finch, I—"

"Not now," I growled at Crane as he tried to flag me down in the middle of the back pathway.

"Jeez, what the fuck has your panties in a twist today?"

I stopped and turned, a murderous glare on my face, and my little brother had the good sense to flee. He knew the ass-kicking I could give him—as was my ordained right as eldest sister. Someone had to put the little scoundrel in line. And I was in no fucking mood to put up with his shit.

Crane took a Hail Mary pass through the recently trimmed hedgerow, probably garnering scratches all up his arms and legs. Good. Let that be a fucking lesson to him to never mention my twisted panties ever again.

I kept storming up the hill to the vet hospital. I'd feed Cranky and then get the tranquilizers ready for the howler monkey castration. And then I had the dental check on Guava. And then I'd feed Cranky again. And then I needed to draw bloods on Ptolemy. And then I needed to feed Cranky again . . . on and on and on forever. The work would keep me sane, and I'd forget about the way Jake had hugged Frankie, pressing himself against her beautiful body like she belonged to him. I'd work straight through the night until I forgot about how fucking happy she'd looked in his arms, when I could've sworn she'd looked just as happy in mine just last night.

Maybe I'd been seeing only what I wanted to see.

Maybe I just wanted to be loved, even when I didn't have the capacity to give it in return.

I threw open the door to the treatment room, waiting the hear the chorusing squawks of Cranky . . . but heard nothing.

My heart dropped into my boots. I practically ran the rest of the way to the incubator and threw the blanket off the top.

Relief flooded through me as I saw Cranky's chest rising and falling. Her little heart was thumping through her translucent skin. She was alive.

But the relief was short-lived when she didn't perk up or start flapping her wings again. She didn't start bobbing for food, wiggling her cute little porcupine-esque feather sheaths that had begun to grow. The little, lethargic baby bird simply lay there.

"Fuck!" I shouted, the frustration of the day already compounding.

Hawk came running in like he was ready to wrestle a crocodile. "Finch? You okay?"

"Yeah," I said, scrubbing a hand down my face. "The chick isn't looking too good. Again."

"No lemon zest?"

"Zero zest."

It was something my siblings and I said when an animal was particularly lacking in gusto. When Wren was a little kid, she'd thought that zest for life meant lemon zest, and we'd never really stopped saying it after that day.

"This is one of those ones that's really going to hurt," I said. I'd put so much into this little bird. With some animals, I could handle their deaths with a level of professional detachment. It was part of the job, unfortunately, when you dealt with sick and injured animals all day. But some animals' deaths wrecked you, even with all the experience in the world. I leaned on the bench top and hung my head. "I don't know if she's got it in her to keep fighting."

Hawk wandered over and put a conciliatory hand on my shoulder. It was all he needed to do. I was used to this part of the job, used to having my heart stomped on, but it still hurt just as badly. I fought tooth and nail for every animal, even when their chances were slim. But Cranky, I'd fought harder for. She'd become my reason to keep moving forward, and I couldn't let her go.

"Is there something you need? Carnivores okay?" I asked, shedding off the momentary slip on my emotions and focusing back on the work.

"Actually, Hannah asked me to ask you if you and Frankie would want to go on a double date to the Salty Dog?"

I shot my elder brother an incredulous look, and he held up his hands defensively. "I know, I know."

"As opposed to the other times we all hang out in the Salty Dog?"

Hawk rubbed the back of his neck sheepishly. "There's not a lot of other couples around. It could be fun?"

"Maybe another time," I said. I didn't want to say it out loud, but I didn't think Frankie and I would be carrying on this fake relationship for much longer. Not after what I'd seen with Jake.

"Everything okay with you two?"

"It's fine," I snapped and then smoothed over my rotten mood with a cheeky smile. "I'm just tired and keeping her to myself for now."

"Fair enough," Hawk said. "Look at the two of us. Who would have ever thought," he added, and it was like a knife twisting in my gut. "I never could've imagined I'd find someone like Hannah."

I wanted to tell him that his relationship was *very* different than mine. His was real, for example. But I just smiled and nodded.

We were interrupted by Dove on the radio asking me to come take a look at a sun conure whose mate was over-plucking her feathers. I was grateful for the reprieve.

"Double date rain check?" I asked. "When it isn't baby bird season?"

I grabbed my jacket as I headed out the door. Hawk laughed and nodded. "I like that you're planning that far in the future."

I rolled my eyes. "Spare me the sappy love stuff, bro. Especially today."

He held a hand to his chest and laughed. "I may be spouting *sappy love stuff*, but don't think I won't be chasing you for an incident report on what happened with Ron in the bakery."

I slung my go bag over my shoulder and headed to the door. "Nothing happened with Ron in the bakery."

Hawk gave me a deadpan look. "I saw the tapes, Finch. You didn't report one of the flamingos almost managed to escape the zoo because you were too busy making googly eyes at your girlfriend. I expect the report by the end of the week."

"There's the Hawk I know and love," I called with a wink, ignoring my brother's request and heading out to the aviaries.

Daily Specials

kookaburra cucumber
sandwiches
$5.50
Macaw Macarons
6 for $12

Chapter Thirty-Seven

Frankie

Finch looked exhausted, dark purple bags under her eyes, that kind of zombified glaze over her slow movements. She trudged down the hallway from the first room, and I knew it was Cranky she was worried about. I refused to ask aloud. It felt like saying Macbeth in a theater, but I was starting to wonder if the little chick wouldn't pull through. It hurt to even think about after all the hard work that had been poured into her survival. I couldn't imagine how Finch did it day in and day out.

I hoped today would be the levity Finch needed. Some sunshine and sea air and my famous picnic spread would do her good.

As Finch reached for her lab coat, I stayed her arm with a gentle touch. "You won't be needing that today," I said, trying to contain my smile.

It took her tired brain a second to catch up. "Huh? Why?"

"You're taking the day off!" I excitedly announced, flourishing jazz hands. "Well, we both are. I've packed us a picnic lunch, and we're going to this private beach by the Holloways', Hannah organized that for us, and then I'm taking you to—"

"What?" Finch's eyes were searching her calendar behind me, her voice sounding like she was underwater. "I can't take today off. I have Jailbreak's procedure and—"

"We rescheduled it."

Her bloodshot eyes dropped to me and my gut plummeted. "Who's we?"

"Heron said it would be okay if we moved it to tomorrow," I offered tentatively, shrinking an inch at her glare. Had I just gotten Heron in trouble?

"And what about the procedures I have tomorrow?" she grumbled, leaning against the whiteboard as if she were too tired to stand. She folded her arms, her stare piercing. "Are we pushing those back too?"

"Your siblings said they could take on some of the work." My voice was laced with nerves.

"So now you're mounding more work on my siblings?"

"It's not like that. I . . ." I thought this was going to be a sweet gesture, now Finch was looking at me like I'd ruined her life. "Your mom said that it would be okay?"

"You should've asked *me*," she fumed. "I would've told you no."

"But I wanted it to be a surprise."

The muscle on her jaw popped out, and I could tell she was trying to contain her anger. "I don't like surprises. Not when it comes to my job."

"It's just one day."

"It is not one day!" she erupted, balling her fists like she might punch a hole in the wall. "This is my life! You're fucking with *my life*."

I inched away from her, my eyes flaring at her outburst. "I'm sorry. I thought—"

"You thought wrong," she cut in, seething. She rubbed her red-ringed eyes. "You don't know me, Frankie. You've gotten too comfortable with this little game."

"Game?"

"It's all pretend! That's what we agreed, isn't it?" Finch shouted. "You are not my girlfriend. You have no right to do this."

"I'm your friend at least—"

"You mean nothing to me."

I stumbled a step backward. Her words stung worse than being slapped in the face.

"I see." I set the basket of her favorite foods down, trying not to cry but being unable to stop the welling of tears. "Here I was thinking we might be friends after everything we've been through. But if you want to pretend we're no more than strangers, then fine. I guess we're nothing to each other. My mistake."

"Frankie." Finch reached for me, but I side-stepped her and stormed down the hall. "I'm sorry. I'm delirious. I didn't mean it like that."

"You meant it exactly like that," I spat.

"Goldilocks, please," Finch called as she rushed after me.

I spun and pointed a finger at her, choking on my words. "*Don't* call me that." I turned and kept moving, letting the fire door slam between us and forcing Finch to shove it open again.

"I'm just tired and I snapped and—where are you going?"

"I won't keep *fucking with your life*, Finch," I said, heading toward the stairwell. "The roof at the Salty Dog has some temporary patchwork on it now. I'd rather sleep under a tarp than live with someone who fucks me then treats me like a meaningless stranger."

Finch grabbed my wrist and I whirled on her, ripping my hand from her grip. "You're not a meaningless stranger to me."

"I mean nothing to you." My voice broke. "Even casual hookups mean *something* to each other, even when it's only friendly fun. But that's not ever what this was between us, was it?"

"I . . . We . . ." Finch shook her head, reaching out to wipe my tears, and I took another step out of her reach. I could see in her eyes that she felt it too, that there was something more between us, something we'd both avoided acknowledging. Or there had been for however brief a moment. But I knew Finch would never admit it because whether it had been real or not, she never wanted it to be.

"You're right," I said, wiping the tears from my eyes. "I overstepped and I'm sorry. I'll get out of your way."

I started climbing the stairs.

"Frankie, please! I don't want to lose you."

My blood boiled as I stopped on the second step, gaining a couple inches of height on Finch. "You never had me," I hissed. "Why do you care about losing someone who means nothing to you?"

"I didn't mean it like that—"

"You never wanted me to be yours."

"I can't," Finch rasped, emotion constricting her throat. "I can't care about you. I can't have relationships and this job. Look at me!" She waved a hand across her exhausted body and up to her bloodshot eyes. "I'm falling apart. Who would want someone like me?"

"I would," I said, a tear slipping down my cheek. Finch's eyes bracketed with pain, and I wondered if she knew she was breaking her own heart right now just as much as she was breaking mine. Did she even know that she cared? Or were her lies so convincing even to herself? "What do you want, Finch?"

It took her a long moment to answer, and the whole time I

silently begged: *please, please, please say me. Just say me. It's all so close, within reach. You just have to say me.*

But when she rubbed a hand across her forehead, Finch said, "I want to be good at my job and I don't want to hurt you."

"Too late." I turned and kept climbing the stairs.

"Frankie," Finch called after me. "I don't want you to go."

"You don't know what you want!" I shouted back, finally allowing my anger to match her own as I stormed up the stairs. "But you've made it very clear that it's not me."

Finch's radio scratched to life from the waistband of her pants. "Carnivores to Vet team."

Finch took a step toward me, as if she might ignore it and follow me, but then stopped herself. Growling, she answered her radio. "Vet team, go ahead."

I jogged up the rest of the stairs and out of sight but could still hear the conversation echoing up behind me.

Hannah jumped in. "Finch is off for the day, Hawk," she reminded him.

"No. I'm not," Finch cut in, and more hot tears streaked down my cheeks. "I'm here and I'd appreciate if you'd all stop fucking up my schedule."

I winced as Evelyn jumped on. "Language, Goldfinch. And you're off roster for the day. Go have fun."

I grabbed my things and hastily tossed them into my suitcase, uncaring if everything broke and got covered in lotion and toothpaste in my haste. In less than a minute, all of my belongings were in my bags and I began dragging them out of the bedroom.

"I'm not off roster," Finch said, her voice growing louder again as I descended the stairs. "Heron, I'm coming up with the endoscope. Get Jailbreak in the crush."

"But you're going to the beach with Frankie?" Heron asked, and more tears poured. I angrily wiped my sleeves over my eyes before I turned the corner.

Rolling my suitcase past Finch, I snatched the radio from her hands. "No, she's not," I said, proud I didn't sound like I'd been crying. "It was my mistake. I messed up our plans. Sorry, everyone." I passed the radio back to Finch, and she looked at me with bleary eyes, a confused look on her face. "I'm not going to put you in shit with your family just because you're being an asshole," I said and kept walking.

"Let me drive you to the Salty Dog at least," Finch called, her fingers grazing my arm and falling away.

"You've got a zebra waiting," I called over my shoulder with a wave, even as my heart was breaking. "I'm not your girlfriend, Finch. You don't owe me anything. Now go deal with Jailbreak then take a fucking nap."

She didn't reply, and I stormed out the back door as more tears streamed down my cheeks. I thought I'd known what it felt like with Jake, but I had no clue. This feeling of shattering into a million pieces as I walked away. *This* was what it felt like to have my heart broken. And I had no one to blame but myself.

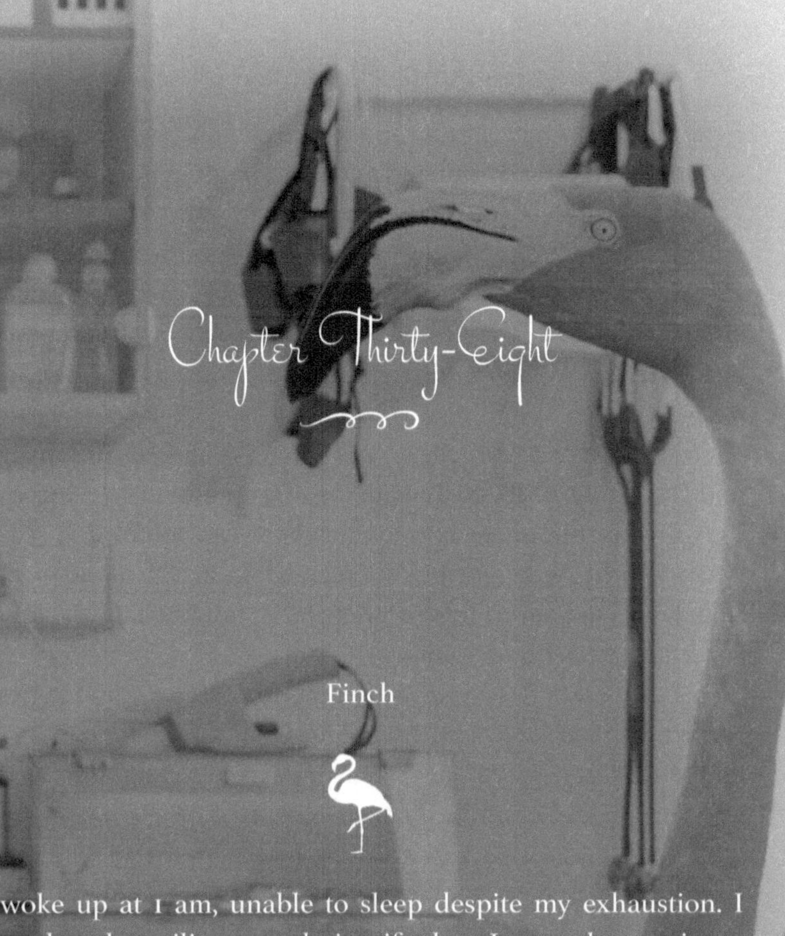

Chapter Thirty-Eight

Finch

I woke up at 1 am, unable to sleep despite my exhaustion. I stared at the ceiling, wondering if when I went downstairs to feed Cranky, I'd find her gone. I'd started checking on her before mixing her feed. I didn't want to waste the stirring time if she was already gone. It was a morbid thought. One I'd had many times before in my life. But something about this stupid, fucking, little bird . . .

Death was a big part of animal medicine. Whether by old age or illness or some mysterious inability to thrive. Some animals were just never meant for this world. But this little bird, I *needed* to survive. I needed it so badly. But if she didn't gain weight again today, if she didn't have the strength to lift her head, it might be time to let her go. There was a time to fight tooth and nail and a time to not prolong suffering, and I was afraid I'd already tipped the scales too far in one direction.

And then there was Frankie and the way she'd looked at me with those big, excited eyes. It would've been a beautiful day together and I'd fucked it all up. I should've gone with her. I should've picked her. And yet, I wasn't sure if it all happened again right now, I wouldn't still make all the same cowardly decisions.

My white-knuckle grip on this job was going to ruin my life and I *still* couldn't let go. I would be forever haunted by the way I crushed her spirit. I stomped her back down into that small person she'd once gloriously emerged from. I was no better than Jake. Fuck, I was *worse* than Jake. At least he had given her something real, however briefly.

And Frankie deserved something real, something magical, something extraordinary. Someone who would light her up and make her smile, not someone who strung her along knowing I could never be what she needed.

The fact she wasn't here in my bed . . . as if she'd always been there, as if in my arms had always been where she'd belonged. And I threw it all away because I was too afraid that if I took a break, if I stopped, I might never start again.

One of the worst things about having a vast amount of medical knowledge was that I was wildly aware of how bad my lifestyle was for me. I knew what the partying and lack of sleep would do to my body, but I still didn't stop. It was how I survived. Work and play.

Work hard, play harder.

And right then, I didn't want to stare at my bedroom ceiling and think about how I'd screwed up the greatest friendship I'd ever had, which hurt even more than the romance simmering between us. Frankie knew me in a way I rarely let people see. She saw right through all of the bluster and bravado and right to the heart of me. When she spoke to me, I knew she spoke to that heart. And I'd told her she meant nothing to me.

"Fuck it," I muttered to the darkness. I'd go weigh the chick now. I couldn't stay there waffling between thoughts of Frankie and thoughts of a dead patient.

I stumbled numbly out of bed, stomping into my boots without doing up the laces, and trudged down the stairs, only to find a note taped to the door: *Fed at midnight, go back to sleep —Dove.*

Great. My sister being thoughtful had foiled my plans to pretend I was awake to do my job, and not because I was thinking about that crushed look on Frankie's face.

Turned out, I was Sgt. Douchebag after all.

I shoved open the weighted door to the break room and fished through the cabinets for the still unopened bottle of tequila. Grabbing it by the neck, I entered the code to the back door, resetting the alarm behind me, and stormed off in an unknowable direction.

I roved the island, necking the bottle until everything began to blur, the sharp edges to the world blended, and I thought maybe it would ease this weighted pain in my chest.

"Dr. Lachlan!" I heard someone call from above.

I craned my neck up to see the lighthouse—the converted staff dormitory where many of the gift shop workers lived. Two girls in their early twenties leaned over the balcony that ringed the top floor, their limbs loosened with drinks.

I squinted up at them, trying to focus my tired vision. "What?" I barked, which was *apparently* hilarious, judging by the way the two of them tittered with laughter.

"We're having a flashlight party," the other one goaded. "Come drink with us."

I took a step toward the lighthouse door out of muscle memory alone. This had been my world, but suddenly, it didn't fill me with any excitement. I wanted to be in sweatpants cuddled up next to Frankie, trying to convince her to let us watch one more episode before bed. I still wanted these parties sometimes too, but not every fucking night and not without Frankie by my side. Everything was better when she was around. I suddenly realized I needed to tell her that—immediately.

I frowned down at the bottle of tequila in my hands. "Can't," I called, and they let out moping sounds in unison. "But I've brought a bottle of tequila for you." I set the bottle on the rickety table out the front door and waved to the girls. "Have fun."

I headed away from the raucous sounds of the party and down the street toward the Salty Dog that sat on the corner overlooking the docks. One of the benefits of living on an island was that everything was in walking distance. I started crunching across the gravel of the parking lot—a few stray cars still left behind from drunk people who needed a lift home.

The lights were still on upstairs and I scoured them, searching for which room was Frankie's. Was she still awake? I nearly stumbled, bending over to pick up a stone, but before I could throw it, the front door to the bar opened.

"If you throw a rock at my window, you're going to need all that fancy medical training to put yourself back together once I'm done with you," Kirby growled.

I dropped the stone. "You're going to kick my ass, Kirby? Really?"

"Worse." Kirby turned the porch lights on and walked out to stand across the threshold like she was a bouncer. Arms folded, a scowl crossed her face. "I'm going to tell you that you fucked up."

"I don't want to hear this from you." I groaned, waving a hand and letting the momentum nearly topple me over. There was no way I was that drunk, but the sleeplessness blurred with the alcohol made the world spin.

"Go home, Finch."

"I need to see her," I said, half demand, half plea.

"Not right now you don't," Kirby scoffed.

"I need to apologize."

"You need to leave her alone until you know what you want from her," Kirby said, and in my gut, I knew she was right. "This isn't like you, Finch. You know this isn't the way to do this."

"I need to tell her I'm sorry for today," I begged. "I just really need to see her."

"Can't you see all this hot and cold is hurting her? I thought you were better than that." Oof. I wished she'd just punched me in the chest. It wouldn't have hurt half as bad as saying that to me. Kirby didn't move from the threshold. Her eyes narrowed at me. "Do you even know what you want from her?"

I hated that question. I just wanted things to go back to the way they were, but I was terrified of what it would mean to turn this fake thing into something real. Look how I'd already messed it up! I wasn't the sort of person who could handle relationships. I wasn't good enough for Frankie. I couldn't give her all of me in the way that she deserved. I didn't want to hurt her again, but I wanted us to be together too.

Why couldn't we just keep pretending? But I knew that was cruel and selfish in a way that scared me to think I was even capable of.

So what did I want? And was I brave enough to admit it?

"No," I finally relented, feeling Kirby's knowing eyes on me. "I don't know what I want."

Kirby walked down the steps and crossed the last distance to me. She grabbed me by the shoulder and pulled me in to a tight hug. I wanted to fall apart in her grip, wanted to sob because I knew she was sending me away because she loved me and she loved Frankie and it was the right thing to do. I felt so small in that moment, stripped of that faux confidence. I thought about the million ways I would've fallen apart if not for these people, these mentors and guides, this family who kept me from imploding. When my arms finally loosened, Kirby released me.

She held me by the shoulders and said, "Go home, Finch. And think really long and hard about what it is you want your life to be before coming back here."

Chapter Thirty-Nine

Finch

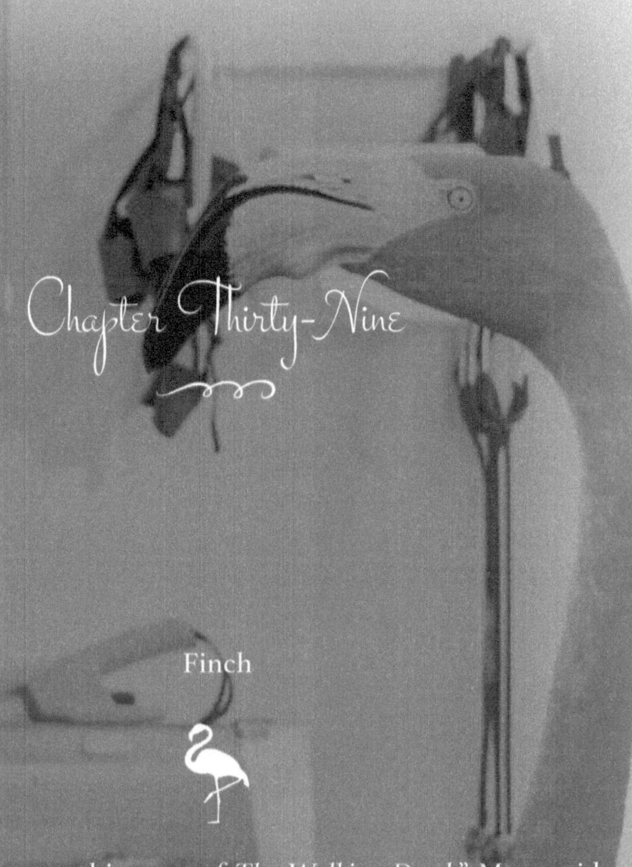

"You look like something out of *The Walking Dead*," Mom said as she flopped her stack of manila folders down on the desk between us.

"Thanks," I muttered, rubbing my eyes. "Is that what you scheduled a meeting during lunch to tell me? That I look awful?"

"Well, seeing as you are refusing to take your scheduled days off—"

"I have better things to do than have you berate me." I started to rise, but Mom held up her hands, her mouth tight, and I sat back down.

"That's not why I'm here," she said, "but don't think we won't be talking about that."

I didn't have a witty retort. I was grumpy and bitter and sad about what had happened between Frankie and me, and I couldn't seem to juggle that with my usual carefree persona. "So this is an interrogation?"

"No," Mom said evenly, but I knew she was pissed at me. She'd probably heard about everything that had happened with Frankie—or at least that we had broken up. The fact that I wasn't currently eating lunch with the zoo chef was her biggest clue. "I called this meeting to tell you the good news. We're starting a new vet program."

I lifted my head out of my hand. "What?"

Mom slid a stapled packet across the desk to me. "We're starting a new vet program," she repeated as my eyes frantically scanned over the proposal that she'd already drafted and signed, making it official before even announcing it to me.

"You've sent these out already?"

Mom nodded, ignoring the way I glared at her. "Funding is secured. We've already had the green light that Tufts will be sharing this with their students. Three different programs will be contributing, and we're looking into bursaries for top students."

"Mom," I groaned. She'd pitched this plan to me before and I'd immediately nixed the idea. But now it seemed she was willing to go ahead without my blessing—which she could of course do, being the CEO. I knew what this ambush announcement was though: a punishment.

"They'll stay in the dorms in the off season, two new graduate vet students and two vet nurses for 3-month rotations, all acting under your supervision," Mom continued, undeterred. "The best ones we will offer generous contracts to for another rotation over the summer months. It means valuable experience for many of them who are looking to get into wildlife medicine. As well as a potential letter of recommendation from one of the most preeminent zoo veterinarians in the country," she added, trying to sweeten the deal, but my vanity was not so easily flattered at present.

She'd floated this idea to me many times before, but I liked running the hospital the way *I* wanted, and the idea of constantly training people up sounded exhausting, just another thing to add to my day, despite the fact Mom insisted it would mean more help and fewer work hours for me.

I was going to open my mouth to protest when Mom placed her elbows on the desk and leaned in—one of her classic power moves. "I don't care if you don't want to save yourself, Goldfinch," she said, a bite of mama bear seeping into her business voice. "I will do it for you. I love you too much to see the thing you love break you."

"It's not breaking me—"

Mom scoffed and whipped out her phone, flipping it around for me to stare at myself on her camera. I rolled my eyes, not wanting to look. The last thing I needed was an intervention from my mother.

"We have the zoo gala tomorrow," Mom said, frustration mounting in her voice. "I expect you to show up looking more human than this. People will want to talk to you, and you look like you're seeing double."

"Nothing a shower and a well-tailored suit can't hide," I muttered.

"And your animals? Are they getting the best of you?"

I held a hand to my chest like I'd just been shot. Damn, that was rough, even if she was right. It seemed my mother was going to use every weapon in her toolbox to cut me open today.

"After your father died—"

"And there it is." I threw my hands up. "I knew you'd pull out the big guns eventually."

"After he died," Mom pressed on, "I kept myself so busy with work and raising all of you. It's only now that I'm starting to lift my head up and think about all the things I missed, all the things I should've done sooner if I'd been braver." I wasn't expecting that. I peeked back up at her, confused as she kept going. "I've chosen to be busy and lonely for thirteen years." That felt like a gut punch. Had it really been that long? I had never stopped to consider if my mom was lonely. I knew she missed my dad, but I never really thought about what it must be like to go so long without someone.

"I'm starting to regret burying myself in work," Mom whispered. "I don't want to see you do that too."

"Maybe it's too late for the both of us," I said with a weary sigh.

"I don't think so, but if it ends up that way, at least we'll have each other to commiserate with." Her eyes crinkled in a sad smile as she swept her hair back. "I probably pushed you too hard into this thing with Frankie, and I'm sorry for that."

"You didn't push me," I murmured. "I pushed myself. And I can't decide if I'm glad or angry that I did."

"You've always acted like you didn't have a heart so no one could break it, too busy being the fun life of the party, flippant, uncaring." Mom shook her head. "But I *know* you. You probably have one of the biggest hearts of any of my children. You just bury it down so deep because you're afraid what will happen if you let someone in like that."

"Mom, please," I choked out, my emotions spiraling out of control again. "Just stop."

"Is it worth it?" Mom asked, giving my arm one last squeeze before rising to stand. "Is guarding your heart really worth it? Is feeling this way really any better than the fear of heartbreak?"

No. It wasn't. The truth was, Frankie had snuck into my life without me realizing, right into my very soul, and now I was heartbroken before I even realized she had my heart to begin with. And maybe I was too spineless to ever rectify that.

Mom shrugged as if hearing my unspoken thoughts. "You're

braver than you know, Goldfinch. You're my daughter after all," she said a gentle laugh. "And whether you use that bravery right now or not, I love you regardless. But she's right there." Mom nodded out the window in the direction of the Peckish Peacock. "If you have the courage to go and get her."

Chapter Forty

Finch

Another year. Another fucking zoo gala.

And this year in particular, I *really* wasn't in the mood. I donned my navy suit, the same one I'd worn to the yacht party with Frankie. I didn't even want to put it on, as if the fabric were still infused with the memories of us. I owned two suits—one for events and one for funerals—and wearing my funeral suit felt a little too on the nose. I was mourning the death of a friendship and possibly something more. I was mourning the death of that brief blip of happiness too, so careless to squander it. Some things just weren't appreciated until they were gone.

I paired my suit this time with a skinny tie and shined brown dress shoes that matched my belt. When I opened my dresser drawer to grab my watch, I was careful to avoid the box that held the pocket square from Frankie. How pathetic was I that I couldn't even touch it.

I put myself together as best I could, not relishing in the opportunity to dress up like I usually did. The annual gala required more effort than a normal party. It was one of our biggest fundraising events of the year, one when we'd dazzle all of the island's rich summer residents and show them cute baby animals to goad them into opening their wallets. We relied on the whole Lachlan family showing up in force for this one night. I couldn't let everyone down . . . well, at least not more than I already had.

When I left the apartment, I put on my best Finch swagger, schmoosing with guests as they wandered up the mason jar lit path to the Peckish Peacock. I always had ten anecdotes in my back pocket for such occasions, but the delivery was far more strained than usual. I was grateful when I got up the hill to the reception area. My siblings were all on form at least, milling about and chatting up the rich patrons. Crane carried around a blue-tongued skink. Heron was showing off our sulfur-crested cockatoo, flying her over the coiffed heads of the guests. Mom was moving from guest to guest, shaking hands and taking photos as if she were a celebrity, her smile extra wide. When the crowd parted around Dove, I saw that she sat on a stool holding Ron by the chest as guests took turns stroking a hand down his eager neck. It took everything within me not to burst into tears at the sight of him.

I grabbed a glass of wine from a passing tray and drank it back in a single gulp. I needed to get my shit together, but my mind was far from the event. Every tray of food that passed by made me wince. I knew how much thought and time Frankie had put into this carefully curated menu.

I stuck to the far edge of the party, only chatting with people who spotted me. I was keeping my distance from the Peacock, and from Frankie, trying to give her space and not step on her toes during this important event. It had been three days since I'd spoken to her, and it felt like a tortuous eternity. She was probably behind the scenes supervising the waitstaff, which meant we shouldn't awkwardly bump into each other. But I still found my eyes searching the crowd anyway, desperate to find her amongst the throng of rich patrons.

"You know," Hawk said, sidling up to me with Hannah on his arm. "We wouldn't blame you if you wanted to sit this one out."

I swapped my empty wine glass for a full one as I rolled my eyes. "I'm fine."

"It's just, things between you and Frankie seem kind of tense," he hedged. "We know she moved back into the Salty Dog and . . ." I shot my brother an "I'll kill you" look and he held up his hands in defense, taking a half-step behind Hannah because he knew I wouldn't smack her. "Alright."

"The food is amazing," Hannah added, not-so-subtly moving the stilted conversation onward. She snagged a miniature quiche from a passing tray and shoving the whole thing in her mouth. Hawk grinned at her like the action was adorable, the insufferable oaf. "Oh, sorry," Hannah said as if catching herself. "I didn't mean to mention Frankie."

I shot her a sideways look. "You hadn't until now."

"Well, the catering was done by her," Hannah amended. "So good food to the head chef to Frankie to you is only like a few degrees of separation, and I'm going to stop talking now."

"Seriously, you two, it's fine," I muttered.

"So you wouldn't mind bumping into her at this event?" Hawk asked, and it was clear he already knew the answer.

"Nope."

"Good 'cuz there she is," Hawk said, tipping his head across the crowd.

If I had more willpower, I wouldn't have looked, but no sooner could I have stopped the world from spinning. I spotted her instantly and the force of seeing her collided into me like a zebra kick to the gut. She looked gorgeous in a glittering champagne dress, sweetheart neckline with draped half sleeves. Her hair was pinned back off her face in a chic bun, highlighting her diamond chandelier earrings. She looked like a model, like a queen. The world around her faded into shadows until she was all I could see. It felt like my soul was ripping away from my body, reaching out to her, but I didn't move, like my mind was screaming for her to look my way, but I remained silent.

"Wow," Hannah said, giving voice to my own thoughts. Her jaw dropped open as she appreciatively took Frankie in. "She looks amazing. Damn."

I watched as Frankie took a dainty swig from her glass of wine. Her glittering gaze searched to and fro. Was she looking for me? There was a pinch of concern in those smoky eyes. Did she want to see me, or was she afraid to?

I felt torn in two directions, unsure if I should go to her or retreat away. This was her night. Her catering was truly the star of the show, pulling the whole event together. She deserved to be in her element. An elderly couple approached her, and I could tell from Frankie's reaction that they were complimenting her on the food. The concern in her expression faded and she morphed into that beaming, confident person so few rarely got to see. It made everything in me ache that she'd shown that side to me before anyone else.

I took a step forward then lurched to a stop. No, I couldn't ruin this night for her. I couldn't ruin one more thing in her life.

I cleared my throat. "I'm going to offer to take the Holloways on a tour of the new savannah walkthrough," I said, clapping my brother on the shoulder.

He looked at me curiously for a second, and I knew he was going to ask something taunting, like why I didn't go talk to my gorgeous girlfriend, but Hannah came to my rescue.

"Come on, dance with me," she said to Hawk, tugging him away before he could question me.

"Thank you," I mouthed to her and turned to find a quiet place to hide.

But as I turned, I saw a crumpled flash of white shirt, my eyes tracking the fast walker, and when I recognized who he was, I started moving before I could stop myself.

Daily Specials

kookaburra cucumber
sandwiches
$5.50

Macaw Macarons
6 for $12

Chapter Forty-One

Frankie

It was a skill, I realized, to smile when you wanted to cry, but after a few glasses of wine, I thought I performed admirably. The gala was a success—glitzy patrons were descending on my cooking like ravenous wolves. I had several people even come up to me and ask if I had ever been a private chef and others ask if I'd be interested in catering more of their own glamorous events.

I handed out all of my business cards in the first hour. I couldn't believe how many job offers I'd gotten before the patrons even had a chance to get really drunk. That was when I started sending out more greasy and nostalgic—but still dazzling—finger food. It was what really set me apart from the average event fare. My cuisine evolved along with the guests' palettes.

I was glad I'd forced myself to come and see the fruits of my labor. Getting dressed up was a Sisyphean task of redoing my eyeliner again and again because I kept breaking into tears. But I was pretty proud of my efforts considering. I'd never chosen such a glittering ensemble before, preferring to fade into the background, but right then I'd wanted to finally show off my revenge dress. I'd bought it with Jake in mind, but now all I could think about was showing Finch what she was missing.

I had a feeling that my honorary aunties, Aya and Kirby, were intentionally shielding me from Finch. The pair had kept within a few paces all evening. Still, I couldn't help but keep checking from my periphery, wondering if every flash of dark hair and peek of tattooed skin was Finch.

I was so focused on trying not to search for Finch that I managed to entirely miss a person walking up behind me until he was speaking.

"Can I talk to you?" the voice asked, and my stomach sank at the sound.

This was the last thing I needed right now. I turned to see Jake. He didn't look his normal, suave self. His shirt was wrinkled, his sleeves clumsily rolled up, his pants stained with mysterious dirt marks, and his breath reeked of stale beer. What had happened to him? I wondered if he'd slept in those clothes or if he'd just been out on a two-day bender. Judging from his breath, I guessed the latter.

"Whoa, Jake," I said, concern crossing my face. "Are you okay?"

Pinching his side, Jake had to catch his breath before he spoke. "Can we talk?"

"Yeah, over here," I said, leading him down the alley between the toilets and the Peckish Peacock. I didn't want all of the people who'd just asked for my business card to see me with this drunken, disheveled man. Once we were behind the restaurant, out of view, I turned to Jake and asked, "What happened? Are you okay?"

"You look so beautiful, Frankie." His speech was slurred as his unfocused eyes dropped to my cleavage and just lingered there, as if he were entitled to the eyeful. "So, so beautiful."

Seriously, what did I ever see in this man? I really didn't know anymore. But he looked in distress, and I felt some strange sort of obligation to still help him.

"What's going on with you? Why are you drunk?" I asked. "Where's Olivia?"

"Gone," he said, dramatically waving a hand to the ocean behind him. "I ended things with her."

"You what?" My eyes bugged. "But— But she's funny and gorgeous and way too good for you. Wh-why? You broke up with her? What the hell is wrong with you?"

"I had to." Jake swayed on his feet as he spoke. "I realized I was still in love with someone else."

I held up a hand. "Jesus fucking Christ, Jake, if you say me—"

"I love you, Frankie." He stepped into me, clouding me with his stench. I backed into the wall, leaning against it to keep some distance between the two of us. "I never stopped loving you."

"Yeah, you really loved me so much while your dick was in someone else."

"It was a mistake," he said. "I don't know what I was thinking. I'm sorry. Forgive me?"

"I forgive you, Jake, even if you don't deserve it." He reached for me, and I shoved him away, hard enough he nearly toppled backward. "But I don't want to get back together with you. I've moved on. I thought you had too."

I debated explaining in more detail, but now really didn't seem like the appropriate moment to come out to him. I didn't owe him an explanation. I was never getting back together with him or any man.

"Frankie, please," Jake begged. "It's still us. Our life. Our plans. Let's get married and move back upstate and have some kids and go on adventures and do all the things we said we'd always do."

The tears that I'd been forcing back all day started to well in my eyes again. They welled not for our abandoned plans, but for the woman I was when I'd made them in the first place. It felt like a lifetime ago that I'd wanted all those things with him. I mourned the person I thought I was. I wished she'd known herself sooner, wished she'd never let a man like Jake cut her down.

"I'm not the one for you, Jake," I said with a shake of my head. "I never really was."

"You are," he pleaded, closing in on me again and puckering his lips.

"Jake, stop." I turned my head as he tried to kiss me, wrinkling my nose at his awful breath and shoving on his chest. "This isn't what either of us want anymore. You need to let this go."

"I want you, Frankie," he whispered, balling my dress in his hands and lifting the hem as I shoved him harder. He tripped backward, nearly biting it on the pavement, but he righted himself and charged back toward me. "You're never going to do better than me."

"I already have," I hissed.

"With that fucking vet bitch?" He reached for me, grabbing angrily at the air. I easily dodged out of his flailing hands, but the fact he even thought to reach for me had my stomach curdling. There was an uglier underside to him that I'd never seen before now.

"If you ever call her that again, Jake, I'll punch you in the fucking nose," I snarled. "Now walk away now before I make you."

"So tough now, huh?" He scoffed. "You think I can't make you leave with me, Frankie?" Jake insisted as he shot forward again. "A few weeks with that stupid cunt and you think—" Without a second's hesitation, I lifted my fist and punched him square in the fucking nose. I might have called for help to manage him, or ran back to the crowd, or done a million other de-escalating things, but he'd insulted Finch and I couldn't let it stand. Jake's head snapped back, but before he could recoil, another fist collided with his jaw.

Jake toppled to the side as Finch stood there, shaking out her hand.

Her eyes fixed to mine. "Are you okay? You hurt?"

I shook my head. "I'm fine." I couldn't feel my hand, couldn't feel anything, so much adrenaline was racing through my veins.

Jake spat blood onto the brick as he stood. "Frankie, let's go."

"No," I snapped.

"Frankie—"

Finch shot forward, grabbing Jake by the collar, yanking him to stand, and shoving him roughly against the wall. "She said no."

Hatred clouded Jake's expression as he stared daggers into Finch. "She's mine."

Finch twisted the fabric in her hand, squeezing Jake's collar tighter and making his already flushed face turn even more red.

"Listen to me right now," she snarled, leaning into Jake. "She does not belong to you or anyone but herself."

"I'll just come back again, Frankie. I won't give up."

When he had the gall to still struggle, Finch's grip tightened. "Look at me," she seethed, and Jake's bloodshot eyes slid back to her. "Do you know how easy it is to dispose of a body in a zoo? I could end you before you could even step one foot outside these barbed wire fences. I can think of a dozen ways just off the top of my head. I could throw you in the industrial composter and not a single hair follicle would be found. I could bury you under a tree in the lion enclosure. What about a live feeding? Excellent enrichment for the animals." Jake shuddered. "Did you know the hyenas just love to eat bone? Have you ever seen a crocodile death roll?"

Jake went still in Finch's grip, the blood draining from his sweaty face.

"No," Finch hissed. "Your flesh is too rotten for my animals. I know what I'd do. I have a loaded tranq gun that could take down a fucking bear. I'd dart you, take you down to my friend Petey's boat, and head all the way out to sea before chumming the water and tossing you overboard. Your body would never be found. And even if it was, it would never come back on me. I have industrial-grade cleaners at my disposal and I am *very* thorough about sanitizing everything I touch." She leaned in closer, her voice getting low and lethal. "Remember that the next time you think it's a good idea to come close to Frankie. Got that, Jake?"

His eyes were impossibly wide, all of the blood drained from his face as he nodded. "Good," she said, finally dropping her grip. "Now get the fuck out of my zoo. You're banned for life. I never want to see you on my island again."

"You can't ban me from the island," he blustered like the absolute fool he was.

"You really want to test me?" Finch's eyebrows lifted. "I know everyone from the ferry driver to the marina workers to the owners of every fucking store on Prickle Island. You'll be turned away everywhere at my request. Don't test me," Finch growled. "Now, you've got one hour to get off this fucking island before I call my friends at the Coast Guard."

Jake ran, the coward, not even bothering to look back at me, and honestly, I couldn't blame him. Finch was fucking terrifying in that moment, but in one breath to the next, her mask slipped and she turned to me. "Jesus, Frankie, are you okay? Did he hurt you?" She frantically checked me over, all that steely anger ebbing to fear. "Do we need to call the cops?"

"I'm okay," I said. Finch kept scouring every inch of my exposed skin. "I thought vets were supposed to be calm in an emergency?"

"Not when the emergency is about you," she replied instantly.

I put my hands on her forearms, stilling her. "Really, Finch, I'm fine."

But we both knew that was far from true.

"What did he say to you?"

"That he broke up with Olivia," I said. "That he still loves me and wants to get back together."

Her face paled. "And what did you say?"

"Besides fuck no?" I asked, crossing my arms and taking a step out of her touch. Finch instantly dropped her hands, clearly devastated at my retreat.

"Frankie, I'm so sorry," she said, her eyes welling, and mine instantly did the same. I'd never seen her so instantly overcome with emotion. "I'm so incredibly sorry. I was scared, and I didn't mean to push you away. I just have this death grip on my job and I don't know how to let go of it. I *can't* let go of it, but I never wanted to hurt you."

I shook my head. "It's my fault," I said. "You told me the way things were from the start. I should've paid better attention." My laugh was half-hearted, barely able to conjure a smile. "I never should've pushed us to be more. You were right. Your job is your life."

"Oh."

That "oh" contained multitudes I couldn't parse apart. Was she relieved? Disappointed? I had no idea.

"We should've just kept it pretend," I continued, resolute to make things okay between us again, even if it stomped all over my delicate heart. "I think we need to go back to just being the normal kind of friends. I regret making this something physical."

"I don't." She took a step toward me, pain in her eyes. "But I can't give you what you deserve. I can't give you something real," she murmured, taking another step closer. "But I don't want to let you go either, and I know that makes me the worst sort of person." She took another step, searching my eyes, waiting for me to retreat, but I held fast to that spot, my gaze dropping to her mouth. "I'm going to keep my distance for now. I have to," Finch whispered, her breath hot on my lips. "Because when I'm near you, I have no self-control."

I bridged the gap between us, lifting on my toes and kissing her. Finch groaned, pulling me closer, her fingertips pressing into my skin, holding onto me as if she were afraid I'd evaporate into thin air. She licked into my mouth, tasting me, her kisses frenzied and desperate.

All at once, Finch took a giant step backward. "I'm sorry," she said, her voice cracking. "I'm so sorry for everything. I won't do that again."

She balled her hands into fists, as if forcing them to remain by her sides and not reach out to me again.

"Finch," I called, reaching for her, but she didn't stop.

And if she did, what would I say? That I could just go on pretending I wasn't in love with her? That I was willing to let her break my heart just to be with her? At least Finch had the strength to end things, while I was willing to let her burn me just to be close to her flame. That was how much I wanted to be with her. And we both knew that was a mistake. She'd been honest with me when she'd said this thing between us could never be anything more. And it was my fault that my traitorous heart had fallen for her anyway.

My eyes misted. She disappeared around the corner as I tried to keep my heart from shattering into a million pieces all over again.

Chapter Forty-Two

Finch

Knuckles rapped on the wall and Dove appeared in the doorway with a bottle of whisky in her grip. "Courtesy of Kirby."

I dropped my head back into my hands. "Did she also say 'I told you so'?"

Hawk appeared behind her, and they both let themselves into my office. "No, but she should have."

Dove claimed the office chair beside me, and Hawk perched on a filing cabinet. I had a feeling this impromptu visit had nothing to do with their animals.

"If you came to gloat—"

"Your sleep deprivation is making you paranoid. Have we ever gloated about stuff like this?" Hawk asked. "We came to bring you your favorite drink because we had a feeling you're

295

avoiding the Salty Dog right now, specifically a certain chef that lives there."

"Right."

It still stung to think of Frankie living over there. A tarp covering a hole above her bed was better than staying with me and I honestly didn't blame her. I gave her no good reason to stay. In fact, I'd practically driven her away. I couldn't give her a relationship, but I still wanted her in my bed, and until I could bear the thought of not kissing her every time I was near, I needed to stay far, far away. That last kiss we'd shared still echoed in my mind. The way we'd fused together as if we'd both known it would be our last. It ripped my heart in two walking away from her, but that didn't mean it wasn't the right thing to do.

Dove grabbed three mugs from the dwindling supply shelf above my desk and poured us each a drink.

"How is she?" I asked to the room, knowing I sounded as pathetic as I was.

"Hannah's down at the café now," Hawk confessed. I looked at Dove, hoping she'd checked in on Frankie and had something to report. But what did I want her to say? That she was happy? That she missed me? I didn't know which was worse. I'd barely left the vet hospital because I was such a fucking coward.

"Don't look at me, I have no idea," Dove said, grimacing at a sip from her mug. "I was always bad at reading these things. It's probably why I've bailed on the idea of a relationship altogether. I'm too neurospicy for dating."

I chuckled. "You just need to find the right kind of neurosparkly person for you," I countered. "Find someone where everything just clicks. Then it'll all feel easy."

Hawk raised his eyebrows at me, and I dropped my head back into my hands. "Yes, I can hear myself." I groaned.

"Yeah . . ." Dove clinked her mug with Hawk's and they both

took long sips. "This"—she waved me up and down—"isn't really selling me on the whole *love* thing."

I peeked up at my siblings through my disheveled, greasy hair. "Did she tell you?"

Hawk cocked his head. "Which part?"

I eyed him, knowing he was gauging me, trying to get me to reveal more than I was willing.

Finally, I let out a frustrated sigh and said, "That it was all pretend." Dove threw her head back and cackled. Hawk immediately followed suit, spitting his drink back into his mug. "*Why* are you laughing?" I snapped.

"Other people I can't read for shit, but you, big sis, I can read like an open book," Dove said through deep belly laughs. She took off her wire-rimmed glasses and wiped her eyes.

"I really don't get you," I muttered.

"It so *obviously* wasn't all pretend," Hawk said. "I think everyone knew it except the two of you apparently."

I wiped the sleepy grit from my eyes. "Yeah, well, she doesn't want anything more from me now. She said being together was a mistake and she just wants to be friends."

Dove snorted. "I thought you were supposed to be the smartest one of the Lachlan clan."

My frown deepened. "What's that supposed to mean?"

"Uh, she's clearly in love with you," Hawk said incredulously.

I blanched. "Did she tell you that?"

"Anyone with two eyes can see it from a mile away." Dove leaned in conspiratorially. "And I hate to be the one to tell you this, but you're in love with her too."

"I'm—"

"I swear to fucking God, Finch, if you say you're not, I'm going to put you in a chokehold until you admit it to yourself," Hawk said in his aggressive, brotherly way.

"Someone needs to," Dove muttered, taking another sip of her drink.

"Can you two just go? Please?"

"Why can't you two work it out?" Hawk pushed. "You can't just end things like this."

There were times when having a big family was beneficial, but this wasn't one of them. Each of my siblings felt like they could meddle in my life, and I was too exhausted to handle it anymore. "That's exactly what I'm going to do."

"Why?" Dove said, exasperated as angry heat rose across her cheeks. She seemed more frustrated about this than even me. Curse my siblings and their misguided supportiveness. "Why can't you just be with her? You clearly want to be."

"That's rich coming from someone who's never been in love," I snapped.

"And maybe I never will be!" she shouted back, leaping from her seat and making the office chair skid backwards and bang into the wall. "But if I *was*, I wouldn't be such a coward that I'd let them get away instead of fighting for them."

I curled my lip at her, and Hawk held up a "time-out" hand. "You're meant to be helping here," he said out of the corner of his mouth.

"Good cop, bad cop," Dove spat back.

"Aw, man," I grumbled. "You're trying to good cop, bad cop me?"

"We rock/paper/scissored for who had to come talk some sense into you."

"Gee, thanks," I muttered. "Here I was thinking you'd come out of the kindness of your own fucking hearts."

"The twins are useless at feelings," Dove said. "And Wren is too introverted. You would've been able to evade her prodding too easily. And Lark would totally be the one telling you off right now, except it's the middle of the night in New Zealand, so I'm filling in."

"So I'm stuck with Big Brother and hothead? Great," I muttered.

"And Mom's afraid that any time she tries to talk to you about relationships, you just become more resolute never to have one," Hawk added.

I pursed my lips. He wasn't wrong. "You know, I really love when you all talk about me behind my back."

Hawk crossed his arms. "That surprises you?"

I huffed, not surprised in the least. I'd been involved in these splinter family groups my entire life. When Logan had left and we'd convinced Lark to go after him. When Hannah had left and we'd convinced Hawk to go after her. But Frankie was *still here,* and we'd never had a real relationship. All the feelings with no backbone, doomed before we could start because I refused to delude her and myself.

This thing between Frankie and me was different. I wasn't going to go after her because if I did, I would just trap her into another few months of sleeping together and nothing more—nothing real. Frankie had said that she regretted us sleeping together and that we'd be better as friends and then she'd kissed me, and I knew we were both utterly fucked. There were no big gestures to be had. The best thing I could do now was let her finish out this summer in peace.

"I appreciate the moral support," I said, standing and stretching my tired arms above my head. "Really. But this is different."

Hawk let out a long sigh. "Is it?"

"It is." I shot him a look, drinking the last of my mug and leaving it on a stack of half-filled-in paperwork. "I can't be in a relationship with anyone right now, let alone someone as good as her."

"Listen," Hawk said with a frustrated sigh. "I know how fucking scary it is to be in love with someone. I'd take getting dropped in the tiger enclosure before confessing my feelings any day, but if you don't tell her how you really feel and give this a real shot, you'll regret it for the rest of your life."

"I need to feed Frankie," I said wearily.

"I can do it," Dove said. "I am the bird keeper, after all. I *can* be doing more than you're letting me."

"Nah, I've got it," I muttered. "Thanks for the pep talk, you two." I waved without looking and headed into the hall.

"Will you at least think about what we said?" Hawk called after me.

"I'll think about it," I called back.

"We love you, you stubborn asshat," Dove sang.

"Love you annoying pieces of shit too," I said and wandered off down the hall.

I slipped into the first room and shut the door. Leaning against it, I let out a long sigh as I stared up at the ceiling. A little groaning squawk like a creaking door was let out to my left, the sweet sound so much smaller than the racket of an adult. I looked over to my left at Cranky's incubator. It was the first time she'd made a sound in days.

I pushed off the door and got out her weighing bowl. I put it on the scale and tared it before plucking up my prickly pink friend and putting her in it.

"Come on, come on, come on," I begged, watching the numbers dance across the screen.

Before they even stopped moving, I doubled over, a sob pulling from my lungs as tears streamed down my face.

Dove exploded into the room at the sound of my cries, followed closely by Hawk. "What is it? What happened?"

Dove started looking around the room like a snake might fall from the ceiling—which wouldn't have been the first time.

"Is she okay?" Hawk asked, just as confused.

"She gained weight," I croaked, a river of tears streaming down my face. "She's doing better."

Hawk looked at me, confused for a second, but Dove just

launched herself at me and wrapped me in tight koala hug. The relief that this little bird might be okay was so huge that it swamped me with emotion. I'd hung on to her survival like a lifeline, and now that she was starting to grow, all of the things with Frankie came crashing down on me. It was like the dam had broken and every held back emotion came flooding out of me.

Hawk didn't seem to instinctively understand like Dove did, but he wrapped his arms around both of us anyway. Emotions ran high when working with animals. It wouldn't be the last time. But I knew they were holding me together in the comedown of the hollow life I had built and the life I now realized I wanted—if I was only brave enough to admit it.

I knew Cranky wasn't out of the woods. Animals got better sometimes right before they died too, but I had this gut instinct that she was going to be okay. This was a positive turning point, an upswing. This little bird would make it. And whether I fed her every time or let my mom and Dove do it wouldn't matter to her survival now. I knew then that this game of fate couldn't be controlled by bearing witness to it. I couldn't be here for every single moment forever.

I needed to let it go. Needed to live instead of hovering in this limbo. Needed to go tell Frankie everything that I'd been pushing down for so long now.

"Finch—" Heron's voice was cut off as they walked into the room, Crane murmuring something beside them.

"Don't just stand there, hug her!" Dove demanded.

And suddenly, there were more arms around me, keeping me together, and I was so fucking grateful for each and every one of them.

Daily Specials

kookaburra cucumber
sandwiches
$5.50
Macaw Macarons
6 for $12

Chapter Forty-Three

Frankie

I stared down at the burnt scones, black char circles across the cinnamon crumble tops. I'd set the oven to broil. BROIL! It felt like I could only use 2% of my brain and the rest was just reliving the last few days over and over. Violent flashes of Finch and I rolling around in bed together, of her telling me I meant nothing to her, of Jake attacking me like he'd never done before, and of Finch kissing me that one last time. I hadn't seen her since, not even a glimpse, and if I was being honest with myself, I actively avoided anywhere I thought she would be too.

I glared at the black polka dots of burnt dates. I couldn't let this affect my job. It was the one thing that was well and truly mine, and I wouldn't let a broken heart take that from me. Groaning, I headed back to the pantry to start all over again. But when I turned the corner, I stopped short.

A flamingo was standing in the back doorway.

I didn't know what came over me, but I instantly lost all control over my tear ducts. Hot streams of tears flooded down my cheeks.

"How the hell did you get in here?" I sobbed, swiping away my tears as fast as they fell. "My hormones are a fucking mess right now." Ron just stood there, cocking his head at me with curiosity. "And now I'm talking to a freaking bird again."

I took a step back and Ron took a step inside. How was he getting down here? I corralled him into the corner like I had the previous time he'd escaped. But this time I had no idea who to call. If I put out a radio call, Finch might hear, and if she came down and saw my sobbing face and burnt scones, it would wreck me. Now, Jake wasn't the breakup I wanted to win. Even though Finch and I had never actually been together, I needed her to think I was doing just fine without her. The last thing I could let her do was see this mess I'd become.

All at once, I had an idea. I picked up my phone and rang the only non-Lachlan zookeeper I knew. The words were barely understandable as I sobbed through the phone, but Hannah understood enough to come running. It was early, even for a zookeeper, but at least she sounded like she was awake.

A few moments later, she appeared in the doorway, the top three buttons of her khaki shirt still undone and her pink bra on full display. "Sorry, I dressed as I ran," she said, making quick work of the last few buttons. The image of her running in just a bra and cargo pants made a half-laugh break through my tears.

"I can't stop crying," I admitted, sniffling pathetically.

"Okay," Hannah said, holding her hands out and triaging the situation. She went and picked up Ron first, detaining him easily by tucking him under her armpit. Ron happily snuffled his head down her shirt, seemingly content to remain that way.

"Is this a 'want me to hold space for your emotions' kind of crying or 'help me stop crying' kind of crying?"

My shoulders rose and fell in a silent laugh as I grabbed a fresh dishtowel to wipe under my eyes. "Tell me something else so I stop crying kind of crying."

"Oh, thank God," Hannah said. "I'm much better at that. If you want the holding space kind of friendship, I suggest Wren," she added with a chuckle. "So." She wandered over and casually leaned against the table next to me as if she didn't currently have a flamingo motorboating her. "Did you know that Dove used to be best friends with Deacon Harrow?"

My bleary eyes widened in surprise. "As in movie star, heartthrob Deacon Harrow?" I asked. "Isn't he filming a movie here next spring? I didn't know they were friends."

"Childhood besties apparently," Hannah said. "Dove says they fell out of touch, but obviously they're still in contact considering she was the one that landed this place as a filming location. Still close enough to call in favors at least."

"Wow," I said, mouth agape. "Could you imagine if the two of them—"

"Dove says it would never happen," Hannah said with a shake of her head. "Because she doesn't realize how amazing and gorgeous she is."

"Are you going to play matchmaker?" I asked, swiping the remnants of wetness from under my eyes.

"Absolutely not," Hannah said, making an X with her fingers as if warding off a vampire. "Dove is one of my best friends, and if she marries a movie star, I'll never get to see her again. I'm determined to find her a nice wildlife biologist to settle down with so she can live here with me forever."

"So you *are* playing matchmaker. You're just not team movie star," I added with a chuckle.

"Exactly." Hannah gave a confident nod. She eyed me sideways. "Did that help?"

"It did actually," I said with another sniff. "Thank you. It's just been a rough morning."

"I hope things between you two can work themselves out," she offered tenderly. "You seemed so good together."

I shook my head, stroking a hand down Ron's soft, feathered back. "I don't think there's any coming back from this."

Hannah scoffed. "If there is hope for me and Hawk—"

"This is different."

"I literally spied on him and pretended to be someone else to help destroy his family's zoo," she pointed out. "So there really is hope for everyone."

"I appreciate your relentless optimism."

"You know, just because things between you and Finch are different," she hedged, careful to tiptoe around any upsetting words, "doesn't mean that we aren't still friends. I think we should hang out more, grab lunch, go get coffees. If you're socially tapped out, I understand, but if ever you want to hang out, I'd love to, okay?"

"That's really kind of you, thanks."

She looked at me with sympathetic eyes and it made me want to cry all over again. "I really want to hug you right now but I'm holding a flamingo." We both chuckled, and I swiped at my eyes again. "Things Only Zookeepers Say for 500," she added in her best game show host impression.

When I was certain no more eyeliner was running down my face, I said, "I'd really like to hang out some time. Thanks, Hannah."

"Let me take you out to dinner then," she said. "There's a new restaurant on the wharf in town. I really want to go, but Hawk is not a big seafood guy which is seriously criminal considering he lives on a freaking island."

"He should be locked up."

"Agreed."

I thought about how badly I didn't want Finch to see me

feeling like a mess and decided getting dressed up and going out to dinner might help. *Fake it 'til I make it.* "Well, I love seafood, so let's do it."

"Yes!" Hannah cheered. "Okay, I'll get it all set up and—" Her phone buzzed. "That is probably Hawk reprimanding me for not having my radio," she said. "I fled pretty quickly when I heard you crying," she added sheepishly. "I should go before he has to file another incident report." She headed to the door and called over her shoulder, "I'll text you about dinner!"

Daily Specials

kookaburra cucumber

sandwiches

$5.50

Macaw Macarons

6 for $12

Chapter Forty-Four

Frankie

After three margaritas, I confessed everything to Hannah, spilled my whole heart out to her, bribed with drinks and popcorn shrimp.

"You're not even thirty," she said, waving her tipsy hand. "You've got plenty of time to find someone."

I laughed. "I guess Finch did me a favor," I said, swirling my finger around the salt-rimmed glass. "I got to have my quick burn rebound after Jake, and now I can move on." I shrugged, swallowing the lump in my throat. "Yep, I can definitely just move on now. Easy as that."

Hannah placed her hand on my forearm. "My point is you don't *need* to move on. Wallow for a while." She cocked her head at me. "When you're ready, you'll find the right person.

You've got all the time in the world to feel however you're feeling."

I thought Finch was the right person. I *still* thought that. She was just too freaking stubborn to realize it.

"I'm feeling like I stupidly fell in love with Finch Lachlan." I sniffed. "No. Nope." I grabbed my glass and slurped the icy dregs. "We've moved past the crying phase."

"Good. Unless you don't want to—"

"I appreciate the support and validation," I said with a chuckle, rising to stand. "But I'm ready to stop crying. It's my round."

"Last round for me," she said. "Defrosting fish for the penguins tomorrow is going to be brutal."

I grimaced. "I don't even want to think about it."

Thank God I wasn't a zookeeper. I couldn't imagine cleaning up animal poop with a hangover.

I wandered over to the bar, seeing the way the bartender's eyes fell to my hips, tracking every rock and swish. Trailing my gaze over her, I took in her wolf cut, thick, winged eyeliner, and septum piercing. Was she ... checking me out?

I smiled at her, leaning onto the bar with drunken courage. "You are not the last guy," I said, putting on my curious, flirty voice. Oh god, was I flirting with the hot bartender?

You need this, Frankie! I silently shouted at myself. *No more pining for someone who doesn't want you back!*

The bartender grinned. "Very perceptive. Another two margaritas?"

"Yes, please," I said, whipping out my credit card.

The bartender nodded to Hannah. "Is that your girlfriend?"

"Nope," I said with a shake of my head. "Just a friend and co-worker."

"Then the next round is on the house," the bartender said with a wink, and it took everything in me for my jaw to not fall open. I was about to retreat into a giggling fit when the bartender's eyes drifted to my right.

A person leaned their elbows on the bar, and I knew before I even glanced over who it was.

"Sarah."

"Finch," the bartender replied, her eyes darting back and forth between the two of us. "Are you two . . . together?"

"No," I said at the same time Finch said, "Yes."

I turned and gave her a frustrated look before whirling back to the bartender. "We pretended to be together for a hot minute for our mutual benefit, but Finch doesn't do real relationships so—"

"I do now," Finch cut in.

I glared at her. "What?"

"I don't want to pretend anymore, Frankie," she said, talking to me as if we were alone, but there were a dozen people just openly staring at us.

I rubbed my forehead with frustration. She couldn't be serious. Had she seen me flirting and just decided to be protective? She had no right to meddle in my love life when she so obviously didn't want to be a part of it.

"Finch, I really can't do this right now." I turned back to the bartender as if I could just carry on our conversation, but Finch just kept her penetrating gaze fixed on me.

The bartender raised her hands up like a ref calling a foul ball and quickly backed out. "I'm going to leave you two to chat."

Hannah came rushing over, spearing in between us. "You guys okay?"

"I need to talk to you," Finch pushed, not breaking eye contact with me.

"Fine," I said, my heart lodging in my throat. "But people are *staring* at us right now, so let's go outside."

"Is it better if I come or stay here?" Hannah whispered, and Finch huffed.

"I promise not to abduct her, hazard," Finch said. "I just need to share a few revelations I've had, if you don't mind."

"Stay here," I whispered to Hannah. "Enjoy the shrimp. I'll be back in a minute. I'm okay," I added when Hannah looked like she didn't believe me. God, I loved what a bulldog she was for her friends, but thankfully Hannah retreated to our table. I needed to know what these revelations of Finch's meant.

I rushed out of the restaurant, divesting myself of the weighty stares of the other diners. I folded my arms tight across my chest as I stormed down the wharf, Finch hot on my heels, until we came to stand in a golden halo of lamplight. I stared down at the midnight water gently lapping against the wharf beside us as I asked, "What do you mean, you don't want to pretend anymore?"

It felt like my heart was stitching itself back together only to be ripped apart again. The words were so delicate, I could barely ask them. I knew what I wanted Finch to say and I was terrified to hear it at the same time.

"Frankie," Finch said, her voice cracking as she took the last step to me and lifted my chin to meet her eyes just like she had that first night together. "When I met you, I thought I knew myself. I thought I knew what I wanted so completely that it would never change." Her dark eyes welled, reflecting golden lamplight, and fuck it, mine did too, my emotions a mirror to hers. "But from the moment I first saw you, you had me trans-fixed. I thought I could deny it, but being with you, having lunches together, telling inside jokes, and falling asleep wrapped up in your arms . . ." A tear slipped down my cheek, and she wiped it away as she sniffed. "You know how I told you the only thing I could teach you was to ask for what you want?"

"Yes," I choked out.

"Well, I was never very good at taking my own advice," she

rasped. I took a step in closer, holding her watery gaze as she said, "I'm sorry it took me so long to admit it. But I know what I want. Deep down, I've always known. I was just so scared of what it might mean for me, so scared that the truth would hurt us both."

My throat bobbed, fear coiling in me. "What do you want?"

"You," she said, a tear trailing down her cheek and dripping off her chin. "There's nothing I want more than to love you, than to be loved by you. Every other want and desire is so much smaller to me now. I want you, Frankie. I want to be with you. I want us to be real."

I let out a sob, launching forward and wrapping her up in my arms. "I love you, Finch," I said. "I want to be with you too."

Finch's hand wrapped around my neck, and she pulled me into a burning kiss. My stomach fluttered with the intensity of it, tasting the salt on her lips, the brush of her tongue. All of the shattered parts of me started fusing back together. We stayed there kissing each other, promising things only our bodies could. When Finch finally pulled away, she sighed, wiping the last of my tears.

"Let's go home," she said, turning and walking straight off the side of the wharf...

Chapter Forty-Five

Finch

As I fell through the air, my first thought was: *I can't believe I was so love drunk I stepped off the wharf.* And my second louder thought was: *she loves me.*

I didn't care if I was making an ass of myself falling into the ocean like a cartoon animal. She loved me. And I loved her. And I'd been almost too scared to tell her. I'd been so close to losing this feeling, but it was real. *We* could be real.

The summertime water didn't bite with cold as I hit the cresting wave below, barely feeling the smack as I toppled sideways under the churning foam. I kicked upward, and as I was about to breach the surface, I heard the splash of another body hitting the water.

I came up for air, slicking my hair back in disbelief as Frankie popped up beside me, a laugh on her lips. Moonlight streaked her wet hair, glinting off the gently rolling waves that pushed us toward the slick steps that led up to the retaining wall. I beamed at Frankie like an idiot.

"You jumped in after me," I said, grinning ear to ear.

"It was my turn to be the knight in shining armor," she said as she treaded water with a newfound ease. "Maybe we can take turns saving each other."

"Deal." I grabbed her, pulling her into the shallows and spinning her against the steps. I grabbed the rail to anchor myself as I dragged my body into hers.

She'd jumped for me. Something I knew was probably terrifying for her and she did it without a second thought—*for me*. Because to her, I was someone worth jumping for. And I vowed to myself right then that I was never letting her go, that I'd do everything in my power to be the kind of person she deserved. Someone brave. Someone honest. Someone who wanted nothing more than to spend all day getting lost in her softness and falling even deeper in love with her.

I was all over Frankie before we could even climb the first step, kissing her in a way that I hoped would say everything: I'm sorry. I love you. You are everything to me.

She kissed me back, heat and relief flooding my veins in equal measure. I'd thought I'd lost her. I'd thought my foolishness had pushed away the one bright and beautiful thing in my life. But now I knew it wasn't too late. My tongue dipped into her mouth, tasting margarita and rock salt. I hummed against her full mouth, my hands kneading into her ass and pulling her hips flush with mine.

I heard Frankie's phone ringing overhead, her purse discarded on the rickety wharf above us. She pulled away from me with a chuckle, looking up at the beams of light peeking through the splintering wood slats overhead.

"Ignore it," I said with a laugh. I pulled her lips back to mine, my tongue trailing over her bottom lip, and I wondered if we might spend all night in the ocean because I didn't want to be separated from her long enough to get out.

The boards overhead groaned with the creaking of footsteps, and then a familiar voice sounded. "Hey, Frankie, it's Hannah, I'm just checking that you're okay?"

I laughed as I held a finger up to Frankie's swollen lips. She yanked my wrist away and kissed me again.

"Anyway," Hannah continued. "I thought I saw you guys come out to the wharf and—oh god, you're kissing. Oh. Okay. You're, uh, currently making out under the wharf . . . This is going to be a really weird message. I'm glad you two worked things out though! Oh god, okay. I'm going to stop talking now."

Hannah fled back off the wharf, shouting behind her, "Congrats, you two!"

Frankie and I laughed harder as another wave rose and splashed us, rocking us forward. "We should probably get out of the water now," I murmured against her mouth. "But I can't seem to stop kissing you."

"Let's go back to your apartment," she said, looking deep in my eyes as she threaded her fingers in my hair.

"Our apartment?" I suggested, kissing her nose, then I suddenly had that nervous stomach drop as I pulled back. "Unless that's too soon and—"

"Our apartment," she said, cutting off my worried thoughts. "I really don't want to sleep under that fucking tarp at the Salty Dog another night." She pulled me tighter against her, keeping us from toppling over at the next strong wave. "And I can't sleep without you beside me either."

I smiled, barely able to contain it to kiss her one last time before helping her out of the water. We slipped and glided our way up the steps, bear-crawling to the top step and swaying on giddily gelatinous legs. My cheeks hurt from smiling so wide and I didn't care.

I shook my head in disbelief as I grabbed Frankie to kiss her again. Our wet bodies pressed together and water dripped in a circle all around us. I hadn't thought I would ever feel this way, and now I couldn't believe I hadn't felt this way all along. Nothing had felt more right than Frankie's lips on mine.

I threaded my fingers with hers. "Let's go home."

Frankie let out a little, pleased hum and followed. I kissed the top of her wet hair.

"What are you doing tomorrow?" I asked.

"Why?"

"Want to get brunch with me on the mainland? There's this great, little café I want to show you."

The gravel beneath our feet crunched as she paused. "But .. . don't you have to work tomorrow?"

I squeezed her hand and shrugged. "I'm taking the day off."

A smile brushed across her lips. "It's a date."

Daily Specials

kookaburra cucumber

sandwiches

$5.50

Macaw Macarons

6 for $12

Chapter Forty-Six

Frankie

Finch draped her body over mine, pretending to collapse on top of me. Her mosaic of carefully placed seashells that she'd arranged down my torso toppled off as I laughed. The scent of sand and seaweed mixed with the salty breeze as Finch's sun-kissed skin pressed against mine. Her lips trailed across my collarbone and kissed down to the cup of my bikini top.

"We shouldn't be doing this," I said with a chuckle as she dipped her fingers into my top, freeing my breast.

Her warm breath tickled my sensitive skin as she laved her tongue across my nipple.

"Private beach," she said, sucking the budded peak into her mouth. I arched into her touch.

I chuckled, threading my fingers into her hair. "You really liked that lunch I made for us, huh?"

"I really, really did," she murmured. "Now let me thank you properly."

Her hand slid between my legs and cupped my sex. I shuddered, the warm sun baking the sand beneath us. Most people had left at the end of summer, but the September days were still warm. We'd even gone for a swim, jumping through the choppy waves. Swimming in the ocean was still so different than the pool, but I was starting to get more confident with it. A lot of things suddenly felt possible with Finch's hand in mine.

My fingers trailed up Finch's ribs to her newest tattoo, one that peeked right below her racerback top: two flamingos, their necks intertwined to make a heart. I lifted my head to kiss the spot, and Finch playfully pushed me back down on our beach towel.

"My turn," she said, nipping at my bottom lip.

All thoughts of her heartfelt tattoo, a permanent commemoration of the two of us, swiftly left my mind as Finch's hand dipped below my belly and into the waistband of my bikini briefs. I sucked in a breath as her fingers slid down my folds, finding my clit instantly. I moaned, arching as she kept sucking my nipple, working me into a frenzy.

"You have to do your afternoon rounds soon." I moaned. "We should get back."

Finch hummed against my skin. "Tim can handle it," she said, naming the new vet intern. "There's no critical patients right now, and it'll be good practice for him."

The new vet program so far had been a big success. Finch was still pedantic about her level of care of her animals, but I was also impressed by how natural she was as a teacher. She let her interns take the reins, make judgement calls, and practice their skills with the safety net of her expert guidance. I knew she would enjoy having more pairs of hands in the hospital, but her love of mentoring had been a surprise to us both.

It also meant more time for us to have actual days off. Now

that the zoo was open in the off season to private events and school groups, I still had plenty to do too. The job of zoo chef had shifted from a seasonal job to a permanent, full-time one. My favorite was planning the holiday events. With Halloween coming up, we were turning the whole zoo into a haunted adults-only experience. I was having the best time with the spooky menus. But all thoughts of menu planning swiftly left my mind as Finch's fingers started circling me again.

She dropped her mouth to my ear, her breath making my skin prickle. "Maybe we should go into town tonight, rent a hotel room, hm?"

"We both have work in the morning. I haven't put in the leave." My words ended on a moan as she worked me higher.

"Work isn't everything," she taunted.

I laughed, shaking my head. "Who are you and what have you done with Goldfinch Lachlan?"

She propped herself up on an elbow to study my face, my lips parted in lust as she continued to touch me.

"I am the person who is desperately in love with you and would stop the world spinning to have another minute with my lips on yours." Her fingers dipped inside me as she dropped to claim my mouth again.

"I love you," I murmured against her lips.

"I love you too," she said, licking into my mouth. "You are my everything, Francesca Benedetti. The very best part of my life."

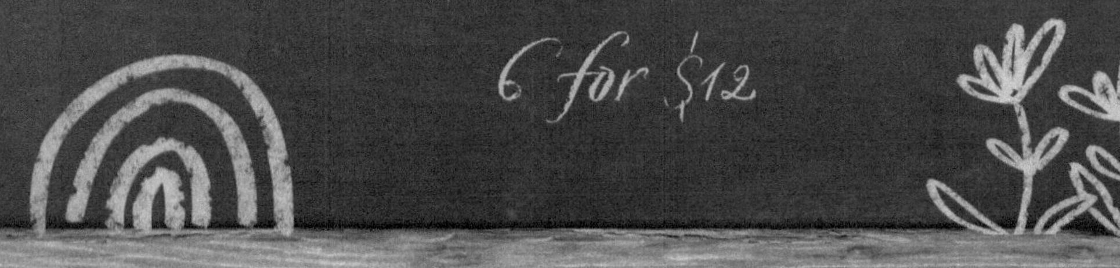

Daily Specials
kookaburra cucumber
sandwiches
$5.50
Macaw Macarons
6 for $12

Chapter Forty-Seven

A few years later . . .

Frankie

I used my keycard to get in the hospital back door. I just needed to sneak up to the apartment before the lunch rush and change out of this shirt that I'd spilled marinara sauce all over. It was truly the most gracious gesture ever that my sous chef pretended not to notice the giant bloodred sauce stain all down my front.

I was halfway to the back stairwell when I heard a string of muttered curses and muffled exclamations. I poked my head into the hallway of the vet hospital. It sounded like Dove. Weird. I didn't think there were any bird exams scheduled on the whiteboard, and I hadn't heard any calls over the radio.

I decided to detour to go check on them. Walking down the

hallway, I found Dove and Finch in the surgery room, arguing in hushed whispers. Dove grumpily held a flamingo under her arm while Finch glared at an X-ray on the light box on the wall. When I opened the door, they both leapt, the flamingo squawking as it was startled, gangly legs flailing. I took in the comedic scene of the sisters frozen, looking like I'd just caught them in the middle of a bank heist.

The flamingo kept squawking until Dove gave it a stern look. "Ron," she snapped.

I guffawed. "Of course it's Ron," I said, walking farther into the room. I had assumed, but I couldn't tell the flamingos apart, unlike Dove. "What did he do this time?"

"N-nothing." Finch tripped over the word, edging farther in front of the X-ray and crossing her arms to make her body wider.

It might have been subtle enough for someone else not to notice, but I knew her well enough to catch the movement. She was standing in front of the light box to obscure something from my line of sight. But why? Was the X-ray truly so heinous she didn't want me to see it? I narrowed my eyes at her sharp gaze, as if she were silently willing me not to look up. But I couldn't help myself. My eyes lifted to the X-ray above Finch's head. Definitely a normal-looking flamingo. Long neck, wings, and round body.

"Why'd you bring in Ron, love?" I asked curiously, darting looks between her and Dove.

Finch kept her arms crossed as her shoulders lifted and fell. "Routine checkup," she said so neutrally I almost believed her.

"You don't bring the flock down here for routine checkups," I countered.

Her mouth tightened. "You pay too close attention, Goldilocks."

"And you don't do X-rays during routine checkups either."

Finch tipped her chin to the marinara stain on my blouse.

"Why don't you go change your shirt? That's why you've come here at this unexpected hour, isn't it?"

I didn't budge, ignoring her as I scrutinized the X-ray further. Judging by the part of the bird that was shown, there was something unexpected in Ron's stomach. He'd probably swallowed another random object thrown into the flamingo pond. Ron really was the trash can of his flock. What had he eaten now? And more importantly, why didn't Finch want me to see it? I looked for any telltale object: keys, balloons, stickers. But when I saw the outline of something round, my mouth fell open and it all suddenly made sense.

"Is that a ring?"

Finch rubbed the back of her neck sheepishly. "Yeah," she said, drawing out the word. "So, um . . ."

"Oh god, you're doing this *now*? In front of me?" Dove groaned, shuffling her way to the door. "Wait until I leave to pop the question at least." She held the door open with her hip. "I'll be in the hallway with Ronald."

Finch shot her younger sister a look. "I was going to say it was a lost visitor's ring that fell in the flamingo pond," she said tightly.

"Oh yeah, go with that. That's better," Dove said as Finch pinched the bridge of her nose.

"I am literally standing right here," I said, my limbs feeling light and fuzzy. "Oh my god. You're going to propose to me, aren't you?"

We'd talked about it for months so I knew it was coming, but I didn't know Finch had actually picked out a ring yet, let alone was planning on whipping it out so soon. Dove disappeared with Ron through the surgery room door, and I wondered how soon it would be before the entire Lachlan clan heard about this. The family group chat—that I was now a member of—was about to blow up. I supposed it was a good thing Dove was holding a flamingo or they'd probably already know.

"Well, this wasn't as romantic as I planned." Finch waved to the X-ray with a laugh. My mouth was still agape so I snapped it shut. "But maybe we can have a redo in a more private location." She eyed the door to the surgery. "One where I can say all the things I wanted to say?"

"What were you going to say?"

Finch grinned wider, walking over to me and taking my hands before dropping to one knee. "I was going to say that you are the most magical, beautiful, loving, incredible person I've ever met in my entire life. I was going to say that I still wake up every morning in disbelief that you are mine. I was going to say that I want to spend the rest of my life with you, feeling the warmth of your love, breathing you in, and glorying in all the wonder that you are." Her throat bobbed as my eyes welled. "I was going to say, Frankie, will you marry me?"

Tears streamed down my face as I pressed my lips tightly together. "And I was going to say yes." I smiled through my tears. "But will you do me a favor? Will you answer a question for me first?"

Finch's brows knit together, but she said, "Anything."

I dropped down to one knee across from her, grabbing out the ring box that had burning a hole in my pocket for three weeks now. Through a flurry of tears, I managed to say, "Goldfinch Lachlan," as I held the box up. Tears started spilling from Finch's eyes, and she cried through the disbelieving laughter. "I never thought soulmates were real until I met you, but these last few years, you've made me believe in seemingly impossible, incredibly beautiful things. I've never felt so loved or cherished, never felt so honored that you let me love and cherish you in return. You are the most incredible person I've ever met, and I would love it if you would do me the honor of being my wife."

Her lips were on mine before I could finish speaking. The taste of our salty tears coalesced as our mouths fused together.

"Is that a yes?" I asked against her lips.

"Yes," she said. "And you?"

"Yes," I cried, holding her to me. I removed the gold band from the ring box, inlaid in small diamonds. Finch admired it as I slid it onto her ring finger.

We both sniffed and wiped our happy tears as Finch said, "I'll have your ring for you just as soon as I sedate the flamingo."

"You better save that X-ray," I said, pointing above her head. "Because we're framing it and putting it on our wall."

We both chuckled as Dove opened the surgery door with her foot and called into the room, "Just waiting for you two to finish kissing and then we can get this surgery on the road." The door began shutting again as she added, "Welcome to the family, Frankie!" Ron squawked in agreement.

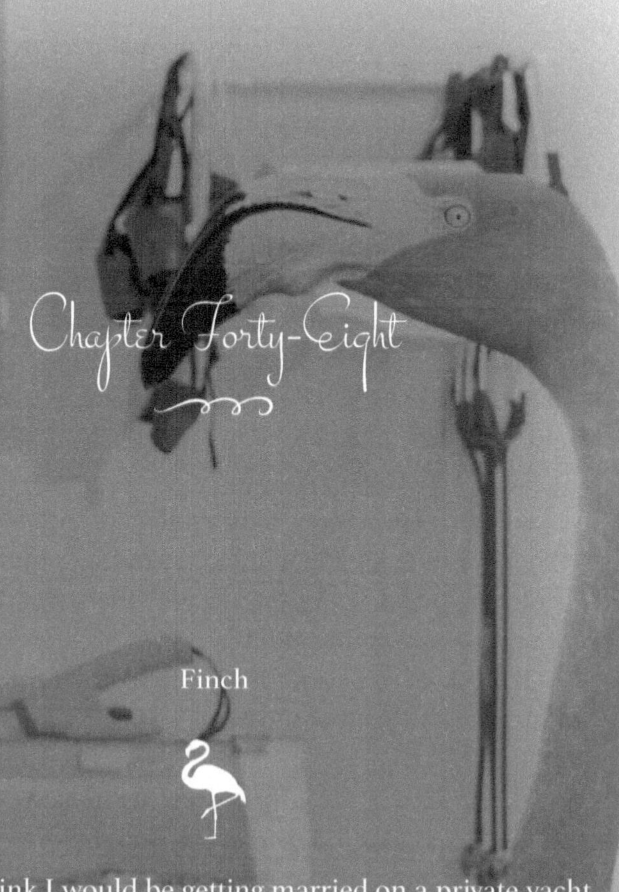

Chapter Forty-Eight

Finch

Never did I think I would be getting married on a private yacht, but turned out Frankie and I had quite a few friends in high places. Hannah had managed to organize the luxury vessel. We set sail through the islands at sunset as Frankie walked down the makeshift aisle adorned in white roses and baby's breath. I was grateful for the even seas as the nerves bubbled up in me, but the sight of her quelled all my fears.

Frankie always looked stunning, but the sight of her in her wedding dress made my heart skip a beat. A flowing mermaid gown hugged her curves, her neck draped in a waterfall of diamonds, her hair curled into flowing golden waves.

There was not a dry eye in the house as she and I exchanged our vows. We kept the ceremony short, the reception located an easy walk to the deck above.

I danced with our nephew, Simon, on my hip, the spitting image of Hawk when he was a kid. I danced a dramatic, goofy tango with him that sent him into a giggly fit.

"Alright, it's my turn," Lark cut in, reaching out and hoisting Simon's little body from my arms. "I think your wife finally has an opening from her adoring circle of well-wishers for you to swoop in."

I glanced over at Frankie as the long line of our friends finally gave her some space to go grab more drinks. "Are you sure you got him? I—"

Lark gave me a stern look as she balanced Simon on her hip, her swollen, pregnant belly protruding prominently in her form-fitting dress. "I live on a farm," she reminded me. "I can pick up a twenty-pound child."

"Of course you can." I leaned in to Simon and added, "You're going to grow up to be as strong as Auntie Lars, aren't you?"

"Alert! Alert! I spy a grandmother making a beeline for Frankie," Lark said. "Get in there now before you miss your chance."

I shot forward, weaving through the crowd and snagging Frankie's hand. I yanked her away from the crowd of well-wishers before our yammering grandmother could reach her.

"I need to ask you a question," I said loudly for the benefit of all the loitering guests.

"Thank you," Frankie mouthed to me as I dragged her down to the bottom deck and out to the front of the boat where guests were technically not supposed to go. But seeing as we were the brides, I thought they'd make an exception for us.

Frankie hugged me, dropping her cheek to the lapel of my slate-gray jacket. Her fingers toyed with my white boutonniere that matched her bouquet. "I thought we'd spend more of the reception for our own wedding together, but god, your family can talk."

"Too late, they're your family now too." I chuckled, kissing the top of her head. "Dance with me?" I asked as she grinned up at me. "What?"

"Last time you asked me to dance with you on a yacht, I fell in love with you."

"And see how well that turned out?" I crooned, waggling the diamond ring on her finger back and forth.

"I still can't believe this was in a flamingo's stomach."

"It gives rite of passage a whole new meaning, huh?"

Frankie chuckled, folding her arms around my neck as we rocked side to side in a slow dance. "I have a confession to make."

"Yeah?"

"The night of that yacht party all those years ago," she said. "I didn't see Jake watching us. I just really wanted you to kiss me."

I laughed and dropped my head to kiss her. "I knew then that I was in love with you," I confessed. "Long before I had the words or the courage, my heart knew. I wanted you to be mine."

"I'm yours," she said softly. "And you're mine. Goldfinch Lachlan Benedetti."

"Francesca Lachlan Benedetti."

"Definitely not a mouthful," Frankie said with a chuckle.

"Definitely not," I echoed as she kissed me again. "Thanks for loving me, Goldilocks."

She grinned up at me. "It was the easiest thing in the world."

"Finch!" Dove called, drunkenly leaning over the railing, her boobs practically toppling out of her dress.

"What?" I barked back.

"It's time to cut the cake!"

"One more song!" I called back, still dancing Frankie around the empty deck.

Dove lifted a hand, squinting at the setting sun, and cursed.

"There's a paparazzi boat following us. So if you don't want the moment splashed all over the tabloids, we better do it now."

"Thanks so much for bringing your fiancé to this intimate ceremony," I grumbled.

"I'm sorry!" she called. "I thought we could keep it under wraps."

"Be nice," Frankie whispered.

I rolled my eyes and kissed my wife on the nose. "You are too sweet, you know that?"

"Come on. I've been wanting you to come taste the wedding cake all evening," she added with a wink. "Not every bride makes her own wedding cake."

"Not every bride is an award-winning chef," I added lovingly. Then I craned my neck up to my sister. "Okay, Dovey, we're coming. Now put your tits away or they'll be in the tabloids tomorrow too."

Dove gasped when she realized the cleavage shot she was giving the open ocean and quickly stood upright, adjusting her chest. "Thank you," she called. "I'm still getting the hang of this."

I gave Frankie one last, deep kiss. "Let's go, wife," I said.

"Okay, wife," she replied with a chuckle. "We're going to be insufferable now, aren't we?"

"Yep, it's our turn," I added and gave her a tight squeeze before leading her by the hand back to the party. As the sun set over the open ocean, I sighed, wandering through the crowds of loved ones, holding the hand of the person who made my heart complete. "If the rest of our siblings are anything to go by, I have a feeling we're going to be insufferably adorable for a really long time."

THE END

I hope you enjoyed Finch and Frankie's Story!
Want more of the Lachlan clan? Read the short story, Winging It, for FREE when you join my newsletter! Scan the QR code on the next page!

If you enjoyed this story, I'd really appreciate you leaving a review, telling a friend, or sharing on social media! Thank you! You're one in a chameleon ;) -Ali xx

SIGN UP
FOR ZOO
NEWS

ALSO BY

Ali K. Mulford Books:

The Prickle Island Zoo Series:

She's a Keeper

Easy Tiger

Party Animal

Maple Hollow Series:

Pumpkin Spice & Poltergeist

A.K. Mulford Series:

The Five Crowns of Okrith

The Okrith Novellas

The Golden Court Trilogy

Acknowledgments

Thank you to all of the real life people and animals who made it into this story! Since I was a kid, I always wanted to either work with animals or write books. I've loved having this opportunity to bridge the world between my two great passions!

Thank you to all of my amazing readers for coming on this new adventure with me. I am so humbled by your support and all the ways you champion my books out in the world!

Thank you so much to all of my Patrons! I love writing new stories, commissioning spicy art, and getting to connect with you on Patreon! A very special thank you to Morgan, JC, Samantha, Abigail, Val, Lindsay, Bri, Kat, Stacy, Lauren, Latham, Leigh, Jaime, Kelly, Hannah, Sarah, Amy, Marissa, Ciara, Linda and Katie! Thank you for being on this bookish adventure with me!

Thank you to Norma from Norma's Nook Editing

Thank you to Enni from Yummy Book Covers for designing the gorgeous covers for this series

Thank you to Holly Dunn for designing the Zoo Map

To my PA, Treece, thank you for helping me launch this new pen name and keeping Team Mulford going! I love working with you!

To my book wifey and publishing bestie, Kate, thank you for formatting this book, designing the gorgeous special edition interiors, and running the Zoo Gift Shop!

About the Author

Ali K. Mulford (also known by their bestselling fantasy pen name A.K. Mulford) is a rom-com author and former wildlife biologist who swapped rehabilitating monkeys for writing novels. A US and NZ citizen, Mulford now lives in Australia rearing two human primates, writing lovable characters, and making ridiculous TikToks (@akmulfordauthor).

www.akmulford.com